WHITE

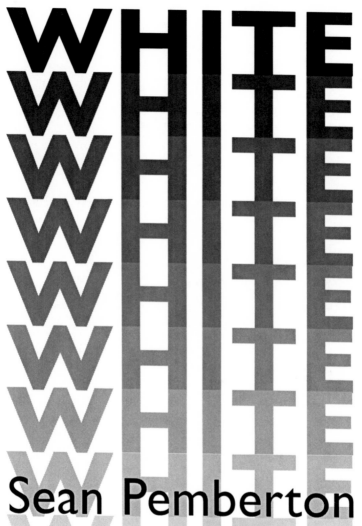

WHITE

Sean Pemberton

REALITY STREET

Published by
REALITY STREET
63 All Saints Street, Hastings, East Sussex TN34 3BN, UK
www.realitystreet.co.uk

First edition 2012
Typesetting & book design by Ken Edwards

Reality Street Narrative Series No 12

A catalogue record for this book is available from the British Library

ISBN: 978-1-874400-59-2

This is for my daughter Emily

May Gardens, 1997 – Lawrence Hill, 2005

white

white

white light

                                    white light

          white light   falling

white

white

light

brightness   split curtains crack white

shine of sun

                              slant beams   white

                  white

white

                                          warm

white

                              white

It is steel. It is a handle. She pulls.

It opens. She steps.

She is in the hall. It is hot. She looks left. She looks the kitchen.

The back door is open. There is the sunlight. He sits on the step. He faces the garden.

She looks at the back. It is white.

There is the sunlight. Smoke moves up.

She walks. She stands in the kitchen. She stands in the doorway. She looks.

It is white.

He turns.

She says.

He says. He lifts the hand. He lifts the hand up. The hand turns. The cigarette is in the fingers. The smoke turns.

He says.

He turns. He faces the garden. He says.

She walks up. She stands behind. She looks.

He points.

He says.

There is the brightness. There is the heat. There is cloudless.

She smells smoke.

There is the blue.

She looks.

He points. She looks.

She looks at the blue.

The white is in the blue. The moon is in the blue. It is half. She looks.

He says.

She looks. The moon is half. She smells sweat. It is half. It is white.

She looks.

She looks the garden. The grass is green.

There is the sweat. There is the smoke. There is the sound of the cars on the motorway.

It is hot.

She turns. She walks.

The door is under the stairs. The lock is steel.

She lifts the hem. She pulls the knickers. It is hot. The windowsill is dusty. She sits.

The curtains are net. The net is white.
She pees.
It is hot.
She sweats.
There is the sound of a bird.
The pee ends. She pulls paper. She wipes. She drops it.
It is hot and she stands. The knickers are white. She pulls them. The hem falls and she pulls the chain.
The door to the garden is shut. The top half of the door to the garden is glass. The glass is under this dust. The sun shines in.

white

white falling

white light

white light falling

warmth

sunlight

heavy

sun

room

white

wake   room

sunlight warm

lick lips

sunlight   beam   curtain crack

edges

stretch warmth

warmth

sunlight

and sun

stretch   stretch

blue pillowcase

blue bedspread

white walls   white ceiling   white light

curtains   orange

light

wipe face   sit

                        wipe face

                                    white

          light beam   fold back cover   over

      floor   carpet brown   light

            light white   white crack

                        stand   to chair

          chair   trousers   trousers black

              step in   button zip

shirt blue   arms   pull

                        buttons

                                              lick lip

                  sunlight   white light

warm   light is gold silver

walk

door white   steel handle   down

corridor   carpet red   walls yellow

left

kitchen   lino red cold   feet

kettle   water   sound

filling falling

kettle   switch   on

cupboard   door   metal rim steel

blue mug to sideboard

down

cupboard   door white

jar glass   coffee

red letters

                                  spoon drawer steel

top off   foil edge torn

            spoon   coffee   mug

    kettle boil

The sun is on the cars. The sun is on the bus.

The light turns green. The bus drives out. The cars drive out.

The bus drives out onto the roundabout. The cars drive out onto the roundabout.

It is blue. It cuts left.

The bus brakes. There is the sound of the brakes.

It is hot. The sun is on the car.

There is the thump. The bus swings. The bus stops.

There are no clouds. There is the sun. There is the heat.

There is the sun on the cars.

There is the sun on the bus.

There is the sun on the roundabout.

There is the sun on the cars and the bus on the roundabout.

He stands.

The bus is red. The bus is behind the car. The car is blue. The car is in front of the bus.

The bus is stopped. The car is stopped.

The bus is in the middle lane. The car is in the middle lane.

It is stopped.

Cars drive past either side.

He looks down the aisle.

The car indicates. The car pulls left.

The car drives to the grass.

He shouts. He shouts down the aisle.

They look at him.

The jacket is plastic. The plastic is blue.

He looks at the faces. They look.

He looks out. She gets out. She stands. She closes the door. She looks at the bus. She stands by the car.

It is bright.

He walks up the stairs. He looks down the aisle. He looks up the aisle. He asks.

They look at him.

He looks at the faces.

Cars drive past.

There is the heat.

He sweats. The jacket is blue.

The handrail shines.

The steps curve. The steps are narrow.

He looks out.

It is bright. The car is blue. She stands by it. She looks at the bus.

He sits. He starts. He looks the mirrors.

The bus indicates. The bus pulls across. He looks the mirrors. The bus drives to the grass. The bus drives to behind the car.

It is hot.

The trousers are black. The jacket is black. She looks at the watch.

The grass is green.

He walks up the aisle. He stops by people. He speaks. He writes.

There is the line of white on the sky.

There is the line of white on the sky.

She opens the door. The door is blue. She leans. She opens the flap. She takes them out.

They queue. They queue off the bus.

It is bright. The sunglasses are black.

They get off.

He sweats. He waits.

Cars pass on the right.

They get off. They walk.

He sweats.

She looks at watch.

He gets off. She looks at phone. He pulls the lever. The doors close. She dials.

The bus is behind the car.
The car is in front of the bus.
The bus is red.
The car is blue.
It is hot. It is bright.
The people walk to the bus-stop.
She talks. She talks into the phone.
He waits.

kettle steam   white click

white light

water pour   white   mug

coffee smell

kettle   door fridge white

carton   green white   white

white milk   coffee browns

carton   green white   fridge shelf   door   shut   white

stir

spoon sink

door

door

white   white light

light switch

white light room   chair

light falling   slants crack

sit

mug   taste   wet

again   taste   wet

again

floor   foil green white shine

green flap packet   open to white

white falling

white paper   white paper open

rectangle white

crease

white   shines yellow on edge

foil   shine green yellow   open

brown   from foil   brown tangle

to paper   paper white

warmth

brown tangle

crease white centre

brown on paper

pull   pull out   pull along

holding

pull   along crease

down foil   packet floor

paper   fold   roll

roll   roll

white roll brown

roll

tuck

tuck in   edge under   roll   and fold

lift   lick yellow shine

light falling

white tube brown ends

lean   brown ends pull out

drop   ashtray   glass grey ash

ends

mug   coffee taste

again

mug floor   lighter blue

    curtain crack beam   ceiling light white

cylinder white

tip to lips   hold

    lighter   press   lights

  orange fire

orange fire to white tip

      catches   catch red

red

suck

    The wall is all windows. The sun shines in.
    He sits. There are eight tables.
    The book is on the table. The book is open. The sheets are white. The sheets are on the table. He writes on the sheet. The coat is blue and he leans over.
    It is hot. The light shines in.
    He writes. He looks at the book.
    There is a shout. He looks up. He looks at the light. He looks behind.

There is a shout. He looks at the door. The door is open. There is the corridor.

The sun is through the window. The sun is on the table. The sun is on the paper. The sun is on the book.

The shout is again. The paint peels above the door. He looks at the book in sun.

They shout. They shout. They laugh and he smiles.

He sweats.

The pen is black. The book is open. He puts the pen in the spine. The letters are black and on the white. The pen is in light on the pages.

He looks back. He stands. The chair scrapes.

The coat is blue. He walks to the door.

The paint peels. The paint is white.

It is hot.

He crosses the corridor. He stands in a doorway.

The chair is plastic and the man is in it. The hair is round him. The chairs are plastic and the men are in them. They watch her cutting.

The hair is on the floor.

suck

    suck in

suck in   hold

    hold   eyes closed

    out

                         suck in

         hold

hold   warmth   heat sweat

out   smoke grey

                smoke turn in light beam

                                sun   crack

        coffee taste   wet   swallow warm

    suck in   warmth

    out

                smoke curl

                                suck in

                                        out

smoke turn in beam of sun

                smoke

    coffee

                            warmth sun

smoke

coffee

smoking

coffee

bend

paper folds   bends in   stub out grey ash glass

ash on fingers   trousers wipe

grey

swallow coffee   coffee end

to stand

unbutton   unzip   down

step out   throw bed

smoke curls light

warmth

white buttons shirt   unbutton   shirt blue

pull down arms   to bed

naked   warmth

chair   back   towel

flowers white big   green patterned orange

wrap   waist

wardrobe

light crack

shelf   soap   toothbrush toothpaste

wardrobe close

door   out

left   into kitchen   lino   red

cross   door   bathroom

blue carpet   white walls

lock steel bolt silver shine   small

brown net

          sink   steel taps stained

     put down soap

          toothpaste left   right thumb open top

     toothbrush right   squeeze

                              cold water

          mint   brush

brush

               sound water   brushing

     spit   brush

     spit

rinse toothbrush

down toothbrush

hands   cup   water   mouth

rinse   spit   again rinse   spit

tap turn stop

left   bath white stained brown   plughole

tap hot   turn

steel shower over jolts

water   water falling   falls shining

sunlight through brown net

noise with water hitting down

water   noise   room

water falling

It hops. The foot is gone.
It hops round feet.

water falling   noise   water

falling hitting bath

undo towel   to sink

bath   touch   water hot

cold   cold tap

wait naked   warm

touch   test   cold tap   touch

step over   step in

to cold splashing   wet water   across naked

wet   warmer

wet   running   running wet

curtain plastic pull   blue stripes white

turn face water   shower   splashing   chest

splashing down

    to curtain   turn   pull back

lean   sink   soap back   curtain pull

turn   back to water water falling warm back

    soap

    soap chest

    bubbles white

soap arms   under arms

    to side   left foot bath edge

soap foot   toes   balancing

leg   thigh   crotch

    down foot

    right foot bath edge

soap foot   toes balancing

soap leg   thigh   crotch

white bubbles   water   falling   sliding

                            heat

            turn   face shower

head tip back   from falling water

   soap shoulders   back   buttocks

          soap arms

water   falling   stains bath white

         bubbles falling

sunlight   warm

window glaze   curtain net brown

                     sun

soap down   take shower

      rinse chest   crotch

shoulders rinse back   falling

legs feet   rinsing bubbles

taps off   replace shower

      right hand wipe left arm

  left hand wipe right arm

  wet drop skin sunlight goose pimples

curtain pull rattle   blue white stripes stained

    step out carpet blue

  sink   towel

         dry

   dry face   goose pimples

dry chest hands   arms

      shoulders

left foot bath edge

dry foot   between toes   pull cloth

leg   thigh   crotch

right foot   bath edge   toes

foot   between pull cloth   leg thigh   crotch

stand

right hand hang towel right shoulder

left hand behind back   towel

dry back

dry buttocks

sunlight

wrap towel

sink   toothbrush   toothpaste

bath   soap

                                                      to door

          steel bolt back slot   out   red lino

  kitchen   cross   out   corridor

      door open right   room

                                              door close

  sun breaking

                              sun breaking curtains crack

      bar of light

dust

          It opens. The dog is looking up.
          He jumps. He jumps up.
          She bends. She calls his name. She smiles and she bends and
      the tail wags. He whimpers. She pushes the door more open.
      The sun opens onto the floor.
          He wags. She steps up. He jumps up. She steps in. She calls his
      name and he jumps. He jumps against the skirt. She calls the name.
          She sweats.
          She puts the bag on the floor. She puts the bag on the floor
      by the wall.
          He wags. He whimpers. She is talking smiling.
          She pushes the door back. She walks in. She walks into the
      hall more.

He jumps up. The paws are on the skirt. She bends.

She strokes. The door swings. She turns. She looks up. She pushes the door. The door shuts.

She turns. She bends again. The dog jumps. The paws are on the skirt.

She kneels. She catches him. He is up on the back legs. He whimpers. The tongue licks the face. The tail wags. She smiles. She calls the name. The tongue is pink.

She ruffles the fur. The fur is white. He licks. She speaks. She speaks to him.

The sun shines through the colours of the glass in the door onto the carpet.

She stands.

She looks back at the letters.

The letters are on the carpet. The paws are on the skirt. The colours are on the carpet. The colours are on the letters. The hairs are on the skirt.

He jumps. She bends. She speaks. She ruffles the fur.

She turns. She looks at the letters.

She bends. He jumps. She picks them up.

The dog jumps against the skirt. He barks.

She looks at the letters.

The phone is on the table. The chair is beside.

He barks. He jumps. The hair is on the skirt.

She turns. She sits. She pulls it open.

The sun comes through in colours.

The two front paws rest on the knees.

She reads.

The eyes watch the face.

through dust in light

soap   tooth brush   toothpaste   dust   table

bar of light   undo towel

naked   warmth

                                                    dry

      towel white rough   green and orange

   dry arms   under arms

                              neck   back

 chest

       foot bed   thigh

             crotch   leg

other foot bed   dry foot toes   rough cloth

  leg   thigh   buttocks

        stand   towel bed

              trousers bed black   down

          right foot   slide in   pull up

left foot slide in   pull up

40

pull up

pull up zip   button

                    wardrobe   door open

                          shirt green   buttons white

                                    hot   sweat

                    left arm in   right arm   pull

round   button buttons white   tuck in

              bed   sit   towel   feet dry

              lean left   drawer   socks black two

              lift foot right   sock   slide in   pull up

left   sock   slide in   pull

              bar light cross carpet

                                                dust   heat

              to stand   to chair

bend   under   shoes black pull out

   right foot shoe bend   pull lace black tight tie

      left foot bend   sock black straighten

                      in shoe   pull lace tie

                   stand

         wipe hands green shirt

                light cracks white   yellow

   to curtains   hands   pull

dust white light   white white   white light bright

                curtain pull

      white light fill   brightness   dust spin

                                          street

   light   sky   sun   shine   cars parked

light white   white falling

                                        blue sky

        light   falls fills

           white light   falling

   turn   bend   mug blue

              to door   light off

left   red lino

  kettle switch

            cupboard   jar

           drawer   spoon

                    unscrew lid

brown   blue mug

  lid cupboard   close cupboard

     spoon in mug   mug blue sideboard

light   from sun   through window

                                                        hot

                        steam

click

    water pour brown   into black

        kettle down   stirring black

            fridge   white door   carton green white

                                            coffee smell

        mug blue   steel spoon in black liquid

spoon   pour milk   black   to brown

        milk   fridge   shelf   shut door

                                    to mug   stir

                    sink   water cold

        rinse spoon   to side

rinse spoon   to side

    drawer   drying cloth   dry hands

          cloth back hang from drawer

      to mug lift   out   right   into room

                  door behind close

                              chair

        sip   sip wet hot

bend   papers

              tobacco

                                roll

    roll   lick

                  stick under

    pull ends brown

to lips

lighter floor

      flick   flick   flame

red catch

     suck in

  suck in

         suck in

    grey smoke out   light bar dust curl

  light   grey curl

     coffee sip hot   coffee

   cigarette suck   suck in

            out

   smoke

light   sunlight from street

smoke

The men are in the front. The women are in the back. The cars are queued.

There is half an hour.

They talk. They look at the traffic. They look ahead. The light shines the cars.

He turns left. The other man holds the map. He tells him and they drive. They turn. They follow the streets.

Then right. They follow the map.

Then right.

It is the dual carriageway clear.

He turns onto it. He drives.

There are fifteen minutes.

There is the front. There are the trolleys.

They sweat. He stops. There is the sun.

They get out. One takes the trolley. He pushes it to the car.

The driver opens. He takes them out. He puts them on the trolley.

The engine is on. He slams.

The men shake. He and the women kiss.

As they kiss he turns. He pushes towards the doors.

The sky is blue. The car is blue.

The women turn.

The door is open. He gets in. He slams. He ducks his head to look and waves. The women wave.

The doors slide back. It is darker. It is cool.

He looks in the mirrors. He turns out looking.

He pushes to the desk. The women are behind. The woman is behind the desk. She smiles.

He speaks.

She takes the tickets. She looks at the tickets. She smiles.

The hat is blue.

The lipstick is red. The nail polish is red.

His hands are wet. He wipes these hands on the trousers. She hands the tickets back. He looks at her.

The women watch.

She smiles at him. She speaks. She points. She smiles.

They turn. He points. He speaks. She smiles. She nods her head.

He smiles. They smile.

The glass is wide. The glass is wide and the glass is tall. The glass is wide and the glass is tall and the sun shines in. The sun shines in on these people.

sun   smoke   light

  smoke   smoke

                                          coffee

fold dead end paper ash glass   heat under finger   crush

    smoke curl sunlight   last coffee

        lick lip   mug blue floor

    up   to drawer   open

paper oblong notes coins round silver gold pocket

        close drawer   to wardrobe

to table   dust   soap toothpaste toothbrush lift

wardrobe   soap toothpaste toothbrush shelf

      bed   wipe hands towel

towel back chair   wardrobe

jacket black   pull off hanger steel

                        wire swings   sweat

left arm into jacket   reach round

right arm into jacket   straighten

                close door wardrobe

                                to chair   kneel

green foil yellow   wrap end closed   papers

        to pocket jacket left   lighter pocket jacket left

                                look round

        door   keys in door   keys from lock

        door open   turn   look round

out   carpet dust hall   close door

        key lock   turn   lock door

keys jacket pocket right   turn

front door

glass red green blue

sunlight through red green blue on yellow wallpaper

dust heat light   sweat

latch twist   open

sun   sunlight   sun bright

out step   door pull behind   shut

sunlight white everywhere

This is the corner. The doors are glass. He pushes them in.
It is cooler. It is quieter.
There is the desk. There is the guard. There is the turnstile.
The guard looks.
He walks to the desk. The guard wears the shirt. The shirt is
white. The symbol is on the pocket. The symbol is blue. The
sleeves are short.
The guard smiles.
The guard says.
He speaks. He moves the hands. He speaks.
The guard smiles. The guard says. The guard smiles.
He looks at the guard. He looks at the turnstile. He looks at

the guard. He speaks.
It is cooler. There is the sound of the cars in the distance.
He smiles. He speaks.
The guard smiles. The guard nods.
He turns.
The street is bright through the glass of the door. He pushes
the glass. He steps out.
The street is bright.

brightness   behind slams shut   bright

        gate   brown wood   ten strips

    bin plastic green   lid black   hedge overgrows

    trees against sky blue   sun   burning

    out gate to pavement   heat   street

left   past car red driveway

    past car blue parked half pavement cracks concrete white

pavement black on grey on white green edges   sun on

                satellite dish

    left   street cross

            to lorry blue   trailer empty

bag plastic green letters black spill paper white concrete

sun

tree lines   right turn   shade under   flicking

leaves are green

past blue lorry empty trailer

trailer

green sack   car bonnet reflects sky   sun

white van

trunks brown grey

from pavement up upward to sky blue leaves green

van red lights

curtains net white   windows

school   fence wire grounds

KEEP DEATH OFF THE ROADS

stick figures run red on white IT COULD BE YOUR CHILD

tarmac parked grey

to alley shade   under trees

trees

sun on

The file is black. The file is on the shelf.

The label is white. The label is on the spine. The label faces out.

The name is at the top of the label. The name is black. The name is printed. The name is the name of the manufacturer.

The name is down the left side of the label. The name is black. The black is print. The name is the name of the type of the file.

The barcode is black. The barcode is at the bottom of the label. The barcode is printed.

The lines are seven. The lines are printed. The lines are black.

There is the handwriting. The handwriting is two sets. The sets are on the label. The sets are between the lines.

The set is between the first line and the second line. The set is on the label. The set is handwriting. The handwriting is cursive. The words are five. The numbers are two. The numbers are years. The numbers are after the words. The handwriting is black. The handwriting is between the first line and the second line. This is the first set. The handwriting is black. The set is crossed out. The lines are across the set. The lines across the set are two. The lines across the set are a different shade of black from the writing in the set.

The set is writing. The set is between the third line and the fourth line on the label. This is the second set. The handwriting is black. The shade of the black of the handwriting of the second set is the same shade as the black of the lines across the black of the first set.

They are capitals. The word is one. The line is under the word. Under the line is the letter.

alley shade under trees   concrete   grey

wire   brick white painted   sun

sack plastic green   left past weeds   weeds

black sacks plastic   heat smell green

plastic cones on side red graffiti concrete wall in red

white smears

shade of trees   quiet   from sun flicking colour of green

shining along length concrete

white sun

heat

playground through metal wire   empty

benches wood

white paint pattern black tarmac

grass green   seesaw

faced by wall   paint scrawl

barbed top wire curls over   against blue

weeds squiggle   twist

paint   lines on wall brick   white paint red brick

to end

buildings tangle alley narrows   weeds overgrown

white concrete white

corrugated iron streaked grey

tangle red metal rust under sun heating

metal

right onto path   tarmac narrow thin

cracked   rough

swells black cracks   names in marker on metal post

long length to end   factory waits   street

alarm on wall

side piled carpet tangle wood bag rubbish black in weeds

sun on all

out   into street   long   empty   sweat

either side open sky under   the factories

car passes   grey van   car white parked

windows white framed peeling

The voice is in the room. This air does not move.
The card is white. The letters are black. She lays it on wood.
The pen is blue.
She draws the line.
She draws the line along the top.
She draws the line along the top of the card.
There is one centimetre of white between the line and the edge of the card.
It is hot. The air is still.
She looks up. She looks at the lecturer.

The lecturer speaks. The voice is in the room.
She looks down. She looks at the card.
She starts to colour in the white.

                          windows paint peeling white

  van parked white

          street wide   workshops   factories

white   white window frames white walls

        van white   tarmac   lines painted white

                          heat   glare sun

  tree   trunk leafless

      rubbish   cans plastic bags   newspaper

jogger opposite   shirt t white black shorts black shoes

            arrows white red letters

        metal paint rusts and peels

past poles   flags flap white dirty against blue cloudless heat and sun   car passes speed

DISTRIBUTORS LTD   stretch tarmac black

to heat   metal manhole cover stamped

black bollards

STUDIOS

windows   red frames blocked with yellow newspaper

heat

SERVICES

and white blue red orange paper stacked forecourt

eleven grey bricks

slabs grey and black stone in wood frames

ice pop wrapper tangles blue red across grey concrete

sun bright across

yellow sign above door   bins big red   blue pipes

LTD   concrete is brown   black car

white arrows in opposite directions

poster white black on wall by green phone box

CARDS red phone box   COINS AND CARDS

left LTD   cardboard box flat in road

yellow line   blue car pass slow   street lamps unlit

sun   total blue sky   heat   walking

sweat

bulge weed tangle wrapper

cellophane by van   white metal white wall black

curls graffiti   ACTION

The sticks are wood. The sticks click. The sticks click four.

The noise is then in the room. The people look up. The people look at the stage. The people look at them.

There is this noise. They do not look up. They look at the hands. The hands move.

The bassist looks at the bass. The guitarist looks at the guitar.
The drummer looks at the drums.
The man walks past to the toilet.

wall white   ACTION black

red sign black letterbox RECEPTION

red phone box   no people

tarmac patchwork   concrete black grey brown white

painted yellow

crisp bag   sun

heat   light

drain black in gutter   red brick bridge over

white on red TRACY I LOVE YA above

under   into dark   dark tunnel   cooler

posters   torn strips colours   hanging

out   out of cool   into sun   bright

sunlight where cars pass

green white yellow beacon   black white crossing

heat sun face   sweating

sun   cars red blue pass

cross   opposite pavement   houses

dog shit

cream paving slabs cracked

gardens   small red flowers

roundabout middle   painted circle white

yellow cones plastic   white arrows on blue

signposts   black letters   arrows

white building massing high cool shining

green frames of windows in sun

white high   in sun

cars queue out red white blue   left turning   and out to

accelerate

out to lights   at end

cross

boarded up   NEW LEASE   ALL ENQUIRIES

BOOKMAKERS   red strips

sound of television

round black bin to blue poster

TWO GREAT REASONS FOR LIVING

on bank   right corner

sunlight on pavement   signs

signs four on pavement outside shop

newspaper advertisements

NEWS   TOBACCO

right   handle

bell ring   into cool of dark

It is the morning. He is at the desk. He types.

He types the numbers. He looks at the sheet and he looks at the screen. He types the numbers.

The fan turns. The windows are open.

They come in. They talk. They talk to each other.   They look round the room. They look round the room as they talk. They talk. They leave.

He looks at the sheet. He looks at the numbers. He looks at the screen. He types the numbers.

The sun is bright on floor.

He sweats.

It is the afternoon. He types. He types to the end. He turns over the page. He looks at the watch.

The window is open. The fan turns.

From outside there are the voices of people walking past along the road.

He looks at the sheet. He looks at the numbers. He types.

He types down the page. He types the numbers in.

There is the heat.

He looks at the watch. He looks at screen. He saves.

He stands.

He leaves the machine on. He takes the jacket from the back of the chair.

Outside there is sun. Outside it is bright. Three girls lie on the grass. The girls wear sunglasses. He looks at them. He looks at the skin. The girls look at him.

He walks past. The girl turns over.

He looks left. He looks right. Cars pass.

He crosses. He walks to the door.

There is the smell of the smoke.

There is the smell of the beer.

There is the smell of the sweat.

It is darker.

There are the people.

There are men. There are women.

The screens are big. He walks through the people. He walks to the bar.

The second half starts. The talking stops.

They watch the screens. He watches the screen.

He watches the screen. He stands side on to the bar. From time to time he looks round. The barmaid is not there.

He watches the screen.

The players move on the screens. The players are the colours. The players are the colours on the green.

The ball moves on the screens. The ball is white. The ball is the white that moves between the colours on the green.

They watch the screens.

The air is smoke.

She comes. He leans. He orders. She nods.

The colours move. The white moves. The white moves between.

She puts down the glass. He gives her the note.

He lifts the glass. He drinks.

She pushes the buttons. The numbers are on the screen. She looks at the numbers.

It is hot.

The sun outside white.

They watch. She comes back. She gives him the change. He nods. He puts the change in the pocket.

He drinks.

They look at the screens.

shade shop   magazines colours shelves to right

product colours shelves to left

product colours shelves centre   past

up aisle   to back

wood counter   colour wrappers sweets piled

woman glasses sits behind counter

cigarettes packets colours cabinet behind

left bottles whiskey wine

right doorway to dark

packet green tobacco foil yellow

packet papers green

zone of travel card day

she lays tobacco papers on wood

card from beneath

presses buttons machine   slides card in

machine buzz   card out   lays card wood

smiles   price   money hand   change

thanks

card pocket inside jacket

tobacco papers pocket outside jacket left

thanks   smiling

back   down shade aisle to

sunlight through glass at end

black headlines newspapers left

door   open   rings

brightness   heat

out   sun street

It is red. The wall behind is white. The front left door is open. The gravel is dry. The wheels are black. The sun is on it. The sun shines. The trims are silver. The trims reflect the light. The handles are black. The red heats. The sun is on the back left window. It is red. The mirror on the front left door reflects in the window on the front left door. The front left door is open. There is the smell of the metal heating. The wall is white. The shadow of the door is on the gravel. The gravel is brown. The shadow is black on the brown. It is red.

sun bright street   heat

left over paving   cracks   stained

    bank   TWO GREAT REASONS FOR

      man is red   wait

    silver car out then blue car

over white lines swinging left   onto carriageway

    behind lights

              as cars pass

    white building mass

  in green garden

flags seven against blue   sky   sun blaze

    heat   sweat

        sign red on front

man greens   cross tarmac black to grey pavement in sun

under road signs   40

on other side of railings grass is green   watered

            round corner   along

white building left   green window frames

                           silver plane in hot sky

                           white line stretching

       lampposts tall hang over carriageway

            loudness   traffic

   three lanes one way packed

            three lanes other way   packed

noise of traffic always

                              building left white in sun

       flags fly against blue

    sun

cars lorries coaches vans carriageway right

red car   red road sign

              red letters on front of building

    white concrete

                              window frames green

    walking white pavement in heat   hot

        sun eyes   hot

                    white paint lines pavement

cracks between slabs zigzag

          feet man blue jeans   t-shirt black

        with plastic bag of white right hand

    sideburns   middle-aged   passes

      sound of traffic in heat

    long building of white and seven flags

  fly

        blue flap   white benches on green grass

                                red letters on white

        cars buses lorries   the sun

white around green windows   paths of white gravel

        beds red yellow blue green bushes   flowers

        white blinds   green frames   no faces

                        the grass green

        three lanes full blue cars red lorries green coaches noise

hands sweating

        three lanes full silver cars   red buses white vans

        black taxis other way speed   sound overtaking

speeding constant   noise   white lines between   noise sun on all

and woman   sitting

dress of red   black tights   on white bench

He is naked. The dress is blue.
He is on the bed. She looks at the body.
He looks at the face. The body is white.
The curtains are closed.
She speaks.
He looks at the face.
He speaks.
She looks at him. She looks at the face.
The dress is blue.
She walks to the bed. She sits on the bed.
She looks at the body.

tights black   dress of red   on white bench

                        beside white building

white building   black-haired ponytail

feet on tiptoes   up   mid-twenties

shoes of black   reading

                        behind black railings

white flowers in sun heat beside her

further back guard brown uniform walks gravel path

past   grey brown white paving slabs

chewing gum circles

black railings left   six lanes traffic noise right

sun ahead

cars under sun and blue sky

white paint on black tarmac

white line on blue sky

end of grounds of white building

three benches white wood

one back kicked out   gap empty

green trees background

orange purple flowers on grass scatter

under sprinklers turning

houses left terrace

driveways concrete   cars parked

six lanes buses cars   noise

green grass weeds in paving cracks dirt edges

strip of green centres road

T lampposts overhanging lanes painted white

yellow white number plates   dirt with black letters

dust   heat   red brake lights

sound of traffic always

sweating

The pavement here is wide. These railings separate the pavement from the road.

They stand against the railings. They face the station.

The sky is blue and there are no clouds.

The afternoon is late and the people are many. The people walk into the station. The people walk out of the station.

There are five. One starts to fasten the poster to the railing. The poster faces the station.

The papers are in bundles. The bundles are five. They each hold a bundle.

The cars pass. People walk in.

The cars pass. People walk out.

One speaks. They listen.

One walks in one direction. One walks in the other direction. They carry bundles.

Three face the station.

They spread out. They face the station. The papers hang from the left arms. Copies of the paper hang from the right hands. The papers in the right hands hang down facing the station. The front pages hang down facing the station.

He walks pavement. The people walk. He carries a bundle. The sun is in eyes. The people look. He looks at people.

The doorway is boarded up.

The doorway is between two shops.

He stops.

People walk past. People walk past fast. People walk past fast in both directions.

He turns his back to the doorway. He faces pavement. He looks at people.

He hangs the papers over arm.

The right hand takes paper on top. The fingers of the right hand hold the top edge of paper. The paper hangs down.

The paper faces the pavement. The front page of the paper faces the pavement.

The paper faces people. The front page of the paper faces people.

He looks along the pavement. He looks at the people walking. He looks at the faces.

traffic noise in light

brake lights unlit   pass   red dull

on right along carriageway under T lights

74

constant white red green blue in sun

engines   exhaust fumes

house on left rubble of slates on driveway

powder white cement   sand

gravel brown piled garden

blue plastic sheeting

white paint house   wooden fence

no curtains   bare walls

past van parked in heat shine reflecting

houses sun sky in blue metal side panel

sun on weeds at verge crack

black split bag spills rubbish   paper cans wrappers

six white slabs

patches of weeds of green

the sun

carriageway stretch black out

lined white

under Ts of lights six lanes passing

pine green high into blue from garden shadows over

steel white glass of car

pink flowers in bed   red roses door

heat

then grey pavement greys

then three lanes cars and three lanes cars with bus

grey back of street metal sign

white arrows on road

sky blue over

sweat

reflections in windows of sun and street

a white line   towards the sun

SOLD   past

sign for stop ahead

woman old short hair grey picks nails waiting glasses

man middle-age hair black cardigan brown waiting

coach opposite direction red white and glass

T of lights   cars   cars

trees of park opposite side

cars

REQUEST STOP   white on red

grey pole yellow sticker QM15 in black letters

against blue of sky

and cars

sun

heat   heat

He looks at lights. The glass shines. The metal shines.
He looks at people. The people are big. The people are fast.
The people walk fast.
He looks at the lights. He looks at the colours.

cars   shine heat

QM15

sun on windscreens   white sun

BUS STOP   yellow paint on edge of road lay-by

three lanes both ways

trees green other side park   above them blue

sweat   cough

pocket   packet of green   flap open

paper white centre fold

green packet to pocket

noise of traffic   sun   heat on face

                                    white

green yellow foil shine   open edges

                        white paper open

        hold open between first second fingers left

                first finger along centre fold

        cars pass   windscreen light

                        green yellow foil palm

                coach red white   faces

                green yellow foil   pull out brown tangle

tangle between left forefinger white paper

                                                                        hold

        sun white on paving slabs   sun heat on hand

up road   traffic   no bus

                   woman old looking   looks away

    cough

                          woman grey hair

pull tangle   pull tangle brown out

     unpack tangle onto paper white

              edges

                              roll

   edge in   and under   roll

roll

     edge lick   yellow   stick

    stick paper

    white tube forefinger thumb

ends   strings of brown pinch out

        cars pass   heat   still

dry

                pocket   lighter

    white tube mouth

        flick lighter   light white

    into red   heat on car noise

                        and suck in

                suck in

lighter to pocket

        foil fold   to pocket

                cough   coughing

            wipe mouth   swallow

suck in   out smoke

                              smoke

                  smoke

            up road   cars cars car lorry

   cars of white   cars blue   sun length

   lorry   green canvas on sides

                                    white sun

                              smoke

The unit is steel. The parts are two.

The left is sink. The bubbles are in sink. The sink is steel.

The taps are two. The taps are steel. The taps hang over the sink. The cloth hangs between the taps and is stripes. The stripes are white and the stripes are green.

The plug is plastic and this plastic is black. This plug is chained and the chain is steel. The chain is fixed to the edge of the sink below the taps.

There is the hose. The hose is plastic. The plastic is grey. The hose end points into the sink.

The threads are wet. The threads are grey. The threads hang from the end of the hose into the sink.

The drainer is right. The drainer is steel. The stains are on steel. The stains are white.

The hose is grey and runs from the sink across the back of the drainer. The hose is grey and at the right edge of the drainer the hose curves down behind the washing machine.

The sponge is on the drainer. The sponge is green.

The drying tray is on the drainer and the yellow is plastic.

These plates are on the drying tray. The cups are on the drying tray. The knives are on the drying tray. The forks are on the drying tray. The glass is on the drying tray. The mugs are on the drying tray. The spoons are the drying.

The hose moves. The hose jerks. The hose moves and the hose jerks and the water comes out. The water is coming out and is soapy. The water is grey.

lorry   green canvas

   trees over opposite

            cars   noise   sunlight

         black glasses woman looks   grey hair

   weeds green verge   yellow flower tangles in sun

            suck in   out

         smoke

         flick

                  Ts of lights   green centre strip

            sun and heat   white

      traffic slower   faces

83

SOLD dirty red on dirt white

opposite direction two buses red   faces looking forward

sky blue   white line thickening   fading

constant noise traffic

smoke   flick

bin overflowing black plastic

cardigan brown man walking slow up grey pavement

watching road

red cans   yellow polystyrene   white paper

turns slow walking back

newspaper headlines spill

to mouth   suck in

sweat forehead   out

smoke

wipe forehead back hand

flick   heat

sweat   smoke   heat

wet trickle left arm down side of torso

cough   coughing

sky blue   second white line

silver plane glinting glinting sun

up road   nothing

suck in   out

drop end   stand scrape foot

scrape of dirt brown white

heat on slabs   traffic noise constant

movement   man and woman up pavement

up road   red bus speed   single deck   jolting

man and woman edge pavement

driver behind screen bent   sun   light on windscreen

woman hand out

driver watching   watching driver

indicator flick   woman drops hand

wipe hands trousers   watch

woman man step back from green weeds tangle kerb

bus slowing   indicating in   red light

flash in white sun

bus pulls in red long

slows to stop   indicating

doors glass fold open slow

driver looking down steps

black glasses duck   in   up steps

          raises head to look driver

     man follows to steps   onto handrail

          woman shows pass   on into bus

     man holding steel rail   up steps three

step up black step behind man

          sweating   passengers looking

     man counts money tray

                    blue handrails down aisle

          card inside pocket jacket

man tearing paper white off machine

                    lorries buses speed past behind driver

     man looks ticket   walks down aisle

     up last step   show pass driver

thick eyebrows nods   looks mirror indicating

down aisle

bus pulls out   away into road

stagger with swing down aisle

handrails blue

They push trolleys. The shelves are stacked.
She looks along. She chooses cash only.
The man takes out the cheque book. The shirt is white. He looks at the check-out girl. The check-out girl gives him the pen.
There is the noise of the people pushing trolleys. There is the noise of the people talking.
He signs it. He tears it out. He gives it to the girl. He gives the pen to check-out girl.
The button at the neck is undone. The sleeves are short.
The next is a woman. This dress is yellow.
The items are on the belt. The belt is black.
The woman walks to the end. The bags are plastic.
The check-out girl passes the items through. The till beeps each. The items slide to the woman and the woman puts in bags.
The check-out girl turns. The check-out girl says.
The woman opens the purse. There is the sound of the child crying. There is the sound of the child crying. The woman looks in. It is bright. The woman takes them out. The woman gives them.
The lights are bright. The magazines are in racks. The chewing-gum is racks.
He has three items. The check-out girl passes them. There are the beeps. He puts them in the bag. The t-shirt is blue.
The check-out girl turns. The check-out girl speaks.

He says. He holds his hand up. He smiles.

He walks back the aisle. There is the smell of sweat. He smiles. He walks back into the shop.

They wait.

She looks at the front of the magazines. The check-out girl looks at the nails. There is the sound of the child crying.

She repositions the sunglasses on her head. The sweat under her arm goes cold as she raises her hand.

He returns. He walks up the aisle. He hands it.

The till beeps.

The bags are plastic.

The check-out girl turns. The check-out girl says.

He puts the hand in the pocket. He takes out. He looks the note. He hands it.

The check-out girl types in numbers. There are the dark patches on the blue t-shirt under the arms. She tears off this receipt. The change is coins. The check-out girl places the coins on the receipt. The checkout girl places the change and the receipt in the hand of the man.

She is next. The belt moves. The items stagger.

He takes the coins. He puts the coins in the pocket. He puts the receipt on the counter beside the bags and he lifts.

She walks the end. The check-out girl lifts. There is beep. The item slides down.

The bag is plastic. Plastic white. She bags.

Announcement.

Till beeps eight. She opens another bag.

The till beeps seven. She places in bag.

The check-out girl turns. The check-out girl opens a bag. The check-out girl puts items into the bag.

The suit is blue talks into the walkie-talkie. He walks past.

The check-out girl looks at the till. The check-out girl speaks the price.

She puts in the toothpaste. She opens the handbag. She looks in the handbag.

blue rails   out into road pulls away

hold   to seat   central doors right

89

seat right empty   sit

jolting   cars pass right

man woman middle-aged seat right ahead

woman black hair braid red jacket

bald man hairs combed over

herring bone jacket black and red

sun rectangles on floor

trees left   five lanes cars buses   two lorries right

heat

jacket   off shoulders   arms out   to lap

rattle of bus   jiggle

slow to red lights out front window

pull behind stopped cars

hot   cars inch in shine

                                              wait

orange   and green   cars pull out

gears change   up   out

    left   onto roundabout

  traffic swings lanes   round in sunshine

        indicating   indicating in

left   pull into bus stop

    old woman stands   up aisle slow   grey hair

  doors hissing open   driver watching mirror

    she speaks

    steps down

doors slow shut hiss   driver already looking mirror

        indicating out

wait   for traffic

       office block concrete glass in sun under blue

   waiting   edges

  sun on high windows   sweat

          edges lane indicating

   gap   and pulls out   away swinging

   round roundabout jolting

  through green lights   heat and sun

  brightness   white   slow

slow   stop at red behind cars lorry

          traffic left right behind

man rucksack walking pavement tree shade distance

jolt out at green

   swing into left lane indicating left   driver looking

left   left out off roundabout

onto tree road

It is a restaurant.

People are in. There are tables. People sit at tables. People eat.

They walk in.

They look round.

The candles are on tables.

The friends are at table. The table is at the back. They see the friends. They wave the friends. The friends wave back.

The waiter is beside them. They speak. They smile. They point.

The jacket is white. The waiter sweats. The waiter smiles. The waiter nods. The waiter stands back.

They walk to the table. They walk to the friends. They smile. They speak. The friends smile. The friends speak.

The menus are red. The candles are on.

The chairs are at table. They sit on the chairs. They sit down on the chairs at the table at the back.

They smile. They look at the table. They look at the table. The cloth is white. The candles are lit.

They smile. They talk. They laugh.

The waiter is there. The jacket is white. The waiter smiles. The carpet is red.

They look up.

The waiter smiles. The waiter speaks.

They look at each other. They ask each other. They speak. They turn to the waiter. The eyes look up at the waiter. The waiter looks at the eyes and faces. The faces speak.

The waiter smiles. The waiter writes on the pad. The pad is white. The waiter stands back.

They turn. They look at each other. They talk. They smile. They move hands. They laugh. The hands move cutlery. The eyes look clothes.

There is the sound of the people talking. There is the sound of the knives and there is the sound of the forks and there is the sound of the plates.

The waiter smiles. The waiter holds the tray. The drinks are on the tray.

The waiter smiles. The waiter speaks. The waiter puts the drinks on the table. The waiter smiles. The waiter stands back.

They lift the glasses. They look at each other. They smile. They drink. They sip the drinks. They smile. They talk. They laugh. They smile and they talk and they laugh and they drink.

It is hot.

They are landscapes. They are on the wall. They are lit from above. The frames are wood.

The jacket is white. The waiter smiles. The waiter speaks.

They look at each other. They look at the menus. The menus are red. They lift the menus. They look at the menus.

The waiter smiles. The waiter speaks. The waiter stands back.

They look at the menus. They look at each other. They speak. They bend forward. They point to the menus.

The waiter smiles. The waiter speaks.

The faces look up. The faces look up at the waiter. The faces look at the menus. The faces look up at the waiter. The faces speak.

The waiter smiles. The waiter writes.

The waiter smiles. The waiter speaks.

The faces look at the menus. The hands turn the pages. The faces look at each other. The faces speak.

The faces turn up to the waiter. The faces speak up to the waiter.

The pencil is red. The pad is white.

The menus are red. The jacket is white.

The carpet is red. The walls are white.

The candles are lit.

The waiter smiles. The waiter takes the menus. The waiter stands back.

They turn to each other. They lift the glasses. They smile across the tablecloth which is white. They talk.

The arms of the women are bare. The candles flick.

They lift glasses. They sip the drinks. They talk. They laugh.

They look round. The dark is outside the window and the window is big at the front. The curtains cross the lower half of the window.

94

They look at the people. They look at the food on the plates on the tables in front of the people and the food on the dishes on the tables in front of the people.

The waiters smile. The plates are white. The waiters put the plates on the table.

The tablecloth is white. The jackets are white.

The waiters smile. The waiters bring the dishes. The waiters put the dishes on the table.

The waiters smile. The waiters nod. The waiters stand back.

The tablecloth is white. The plates are white. The dishes are white.

The food is colours. The colours are on the dishes. The colours are on the plates.

They look at the plates. They look at the dishes. They look at the other plates. They look at the other dishes.

They shake out the napkins. They talk. They look at the colours.

They lift the dishes. They lift the spoons. They lift the colours from the dishes onto the plates.

They lift the knives and they lift the forks.

They eat.

left off roundabout   left lane blue cars   red lorry

left lane of six lanes

past rucksack blue red piping

sudden left pull stop judder at bus sign shelter

doors hissing   driver looking down

girl up steps

multicoloured top   eyeliner green   twenties

shows pass   on into bus

young girl   voice asking cost ticket   pays

multicolour girl sitting

girl seat at front

doors hissing   driver mirror

indicating out

sun on roofs   white light in mirrors

out into lane   up gear up hill

past rucksack

cars   five lanes on right

rattling   over hill   towards sun

pass bus   two white vans

dirt   sun

even speed   stretch carriageway   cars

   police car opposite direction

no siren no lights

       jiggles   rattles   windows dirt

    a green garage

   above showroom for cars three flags fly against blue

billboard   car and water girl shower   naked back

    cars outside flats parked line   sun shining windows

      houses terraced stretching both sides

         rattling

     bell rings   red lights   BUS STOPPING

rings again

     man rises striped blue white shirt

   slowing indicating in   slow

                    to stop   hissing

shirt striped man down centre steps

                              looks up to window

    up front steps man white haired

   blue trousers blue jacket

                  pays   shirt cream

to seat   turns looking down bus

        indicating out   gap   pulls out

    forward

                                      rattling

                  sunlight

    across lights turning orange

    rattle   up hill   to stop at reds

blue bus   pulls alongside   faces

young girl young man arm in arm pavement left

orange   changing gears sound

green   up   and out

forward again rattling

and on   in sun

flats left   trees surround

flats out of trees   up tall to blue of sky

wipe forehead sweat

slows   slower   cyclists two in red white

woman billboard showers

bell rings   BUS STOPPING in red

slows   indicating behind cyclists

middle-aged man woman rise

black braid   hair   combed over bald

       to stop   hissing

               they go down steps

    hissing again and out into left lane

                     gears change sound up

          up to cyclists   out into middle

   passing   indicating

cyclists left heads down in helmets black pushing

            pushing   buttocks

       shops on right

    building boarded up left

  press button   bell rings   BUS STOPPING

           left round bend curving

  slowing   slowing

into stop between parked cars

up   hissing

                    follow cardigan brown man down aisle

wait man go down

                                        thank driver

        down steps

                        into sun

He waits. They wait
The walls are orange. The carpet is blue.
The seats are plastic. The plastic is brown.
The queue is three. The first spells the name and the radio
plays. It is tinny.
The leaves shine and the man walks in. It is tall. The man
looks at them. The man calls. They are green. The woman
stands and the woman follows the man out.
The DJ speaks. The voice of the DJ cannot be made out.
There is heat.
He stands. The carpet is blue he crosses. He touches them.
He touches them with the fingertips. It is tall. They are plastic
and the plastic is green.
He walks back. He sits. The plastic is brown.
The wall is orange. The poster is colours. The music is tinny.
There is blue and there is green and there is red and there is yel-
low. He sweats. He reads the poster.
The man sits.

The magazines are on the table. The table is wood. The wood is brown. The woman lifts.

The legs cross. They are brown.

It is tinny.

white

black two steps down to sun grey paving cracks

cardigan brown sits red seat under shelter shaded

brightness   white

in heat   round shelter   shop fronts

TRAVEL AGENT

HIRE AND SALE

glass windows dust   VIDEO

along pavement in white of sun

red sign white metal pavement outside newsagents

ICE CREAM   cartoon children dancing

sticks

red white on right cyclists

metal shutters   dirt

HOUSEHOLD GOODS

INDIAN CUISINE

telephone box   glass panels   black frame

TELEPHONE in white

COINS in red

traffic passing continuous sound

car parked yellow line

blind sun

blazing

black white arrow   straight ahead

sweating

arrow to left   two arrows right

hang jacket left shoulder

traffic lines queues in lanes   constant

side street left

I KNOW WHAT MY FIRST CHOICE WOULD BE

yellow sign under

GROUND FLOOR TO RENT under awning

shop   boarded up   postered over red yellow blue pink

OF THE SUMMER   graffiti

hand middle finger up on shutter metal

OPEN SEVEN DAYS

no breeze   white light

shop fronts metal grilles

grey dirt metal shutters thick

white sun on white pavement cracks and chewing gum

to corner

traffic lights   intersection

blue railings between

pavement grey and tarmac road black

red green blue blue white cars grey lorries dirt red buses

at lights

black boxes buttons white yellow WAIT

heat   light   WORLDWIDE EXPORT

round corner left

The plastic is white. The cap is blue. The milk is in.

heat   corner to wide pavement grey stretch shops left

lampposts over road

bread plastic trays piled at wall

COPIES 10p

stand metal red   magazines   bright   sun

    OFF LICENCE red on white

FOOD

£1.99

  bin rubbish green   heat

     sun on windscreens shop windows   sweating

man bench t-shirt blue jeans blue   sun blue sky

   traffic noise   butchers awning green

    white striped dirt

     dust   sun

   right to steps   down   to road

    cones yellow white   island concrete small

     cars parked red green white

EXTRA in red orange

bins black five

        sweating   white light

NEWSPAPERS AND MAGAZINES ONLY

slow pass car   BROWN GLASS ONLY

        GREEN GLASS ONLY

        red car   van speeds

CANS ONLY

        queue traffic lights

CLEAR GLASS ONLY

        liquid dark spill across pavement grey

red top woman bends trolley   buttocks

bags plastic white

CARPETS AND FURNITURE

light white

phone boxes two   COINS AND CARDS

OFF LICENCE

doors supermarket automatic slide

man out t-shirt round waist   shaved head

CHINESE FOOD TO TAKE AWAY

van white   man beard distance by rusted railings

DISCOUNT STORE

cross

trays red plastic against shutters metal grey

right   past railings

bars white black on road painted   cross

car stops   face man glasses looks

grey pavement   sun   chewing gum

                            red paint spill

     plastic cones red white   planks red white striped

    round hole edge pavement

                     HAIRDRESSERS

          under green trees

     houses terrace left

   van white car silver car blue parked sun heating

           to shelter sign blue white BUS

They sit. They sit in the groups. They sit alone. They sit on the benches. They sit on the grass. The sun is on them. It is hot.

The sun is hot. The shadows are under the trees. The path is between the trees. She walks down. She looks at them sitting. The path is concrete.

The bag is over the shoulder. The jeans are blue and the bag is leather. The bag is leather is brown. The hair is red. The hair is long. The cardigan is a blue pale.

The sun is high. Some eat sandwiches. There is the line of white across the sky.

The gates are open. She walks out. The stickiness is under the arms. The pavement is black.

The sun is hot. It is high.

She stops. She looks left. She looks right. The car stops. She nods. She crosses.

The light is on her.

The light is on the car.

She stops on the pavement. She looks at the watch. She looks at the numbers. She walks.

She opens.

It is darker. It is cooler. She looks.

The girl is at the desk. The girl looks. The girl smiles. She walks to the girl.

She smiles. She speaks. The girl smiles. The girl looks down at the book.

She looks round. She looks at the women. She looks at the hands cutting the hair. She looks at the hair dyed. She looks at the hair.

She looks at the women. The women look in the mirrors. The women look in the magazines. The hair is on the floor.

The girl smiles. The girl speaks. The girl points.

She smiles. She speaks.

The sweat is cold under the arms.

She turns. She walks. She sits.

The bag is leather. The can is cold. The hand takes the can from the bag. The fingers pull the tab. The can is cold in the hand. She pulls and it is open.

The fingers push the hair back over the right ear. It fizzes in her mouth. It is cold.

She sips. She looks. She looks at the reflections. She looks at the reflections in the mirrors. There are the reflections and there are the reflections of the reflections.

She sips. It is cold. It is cold in the hand. It is cold in the mouth.

The magazines are on the table.

to shelter   empty

sides back glass   black roof   seats plastic red sloped

sun heat

white paint splash over grey slabs

car passes blue   sun glint

weeds green base pole sign

jacket over knees

packet green   white paper out

down street sun   nothing

sweating   packet back in pocket

packet foil yellow green   unfold

brown tangle   to paper

tangle tobacco strings brown on white

edges foil fold back   pocket

edges paper white   hold   roll   roll

tuck in

under roll   lick   stick down

face terrace   flowers

white light street

shred brown end pull

lighter   light

suck   suck in   suck in

tip reds

in sun   heat   burn

out   suck in

opposite pavement girl twenties

jeans   t-shirt white   hair blonde long

two children   one crying pram

man twenties t-shirt jeans black moustache

stops leans shelter side looks up road

smoke   sweat   trickling

   cough

van blue pulls in opposite side

                  smoke turning heat air

       man sunglasses   slams door van

 walks direction shops

  suck in   out

newspaper pavement blows

     photograph woman black white smiling

moustache man moves   spits pavement

    There is the queue for the information. They are told the information. There is the queue for the payment. They pay. There is the queue for the enrolment. They enrol. There is the queue for the information. They are told the information. They walk looking for the room. They find the room.

     photograph smiling turns pavement

suck in out   sun on face

newspaper moves   smoke   heat

green of trees

sky high   blue   cloudless

                        sun bright

suck in   smoke   street

ash flick   drop end   stand   crush

        hands wipe shirt   heat

                                sweat wet under arms

up street   nothing

car horn distance   still

heat

                        car horn   again

        bus round corner   red double-decked

driver   behind black glass

red   pulls in indicating   to stop

        stand

moustache up past conductor steps into deck lower

step up   past conductor

up steps narrow turning

top deck empty

no-one   to front

bus pulls out   hold rail   swaying

sweat trickle under arm

front seat   right front corner   windows dirt

bus swaying sunlight down street

heat

dust smell

The windows are open. The fans are on. The fans turn.
He smiles.
The shirt is white. The trousers are black. The tie is yellow.
He smiles.
The sun shines the wall. The wall is white.
They are hot. There is the noise of the traffic through the open windows. They look at him.
He smiles. He speaks.
He smiles as he speaks. He smiles at them all in turn as he speaks and he looks at them all in turn as he speaks. He smiles.
They look at him.

sun dust

    heat   dust smell

sun heat through window dirt

               out   into road   accelerate

jolts   change

    up under bridge green   rust brown

               trees avenue   shuddering up

old houses windows boarded brown

gates prison left   men uniforms   laughing

metal shines

swing   past cars   parked red green yellow

metal corrugated grey silver   building site

crane tower over metal to blue stretch

heat

pull in   judder   to stop hospital

treetops over road   green leaves sun   white

light

The book is on the table. The book is shut.
The book is paperback.
The face is up. The face is white.
The name of the book is blue. The name of the writer is
black.
The blue is on the white and the black is on the white.
The blue is above the black.

sun   light on green   blue car passes

pull away hospital stop

green leaves in heat

flats right   curtains lace placard window letters

parked cars behind spiked rails metal gleam

pavement man child pram woman child pram child

bin green

low building long left

building site yellow huts prefab

pitches rugby football left

pads striped white blue on white posts

two boys at stop   bus pulls in

woman and girl hand in hand opposite pavement

out   juddering

school playground

running children painted purple on white walls

FREE WEEKEND AND EVENING CALLS

at traffic lights to stop   and wait

old houses   scaffolding   workmen whistling

waiting

GOOD FOOD   LOUNGE

ENTRANCE

waiting lights

TRADITIONAL HOT AND COLD FOOD AVAILABLE

to green   out right from light

men four

round red white striped wooden paling

looking into hole

slow   to let car blue car silver pass

heat in bus   windows open

under dirt bridge railway blue dirt and purple yellow

shops   windows flashing white sun

sweat wet under arms

waistcoat plastic yellow brushing road

LAUNDERETTE beside   CHINESE TAKEAWAY

trees over parked cars   leaves shining sun

bus swing right

There are stairs and she walks down. There is kitchen and she walks in.

She pushes down the switch. The cup is on the side. There is a little in the bottom. She tips it.

She puts it on the side. The teaspoon is on the side. She unscrews it. She puts the lid on the side. Coffee is on the spoon. She lifts it and she puts it in. She lifts it up and she lifts it out and she puts it in. She puts it into the cup.

She puts the coffee in. She lifts the packet. The boiling starts. She lights it. The kettle clicks. She tips. It goes in. It is black.

She opens the fridge.

She takes the milk.

She takes the milk out.

She pours it.

She pours the milk in.

She pours it in and brown.

The pouring stops.

She puts it in.

She closes.

She sits. She sits down. She sits down at the table.

She sits down at the table in the sunlight. She sits down at the table in the sunlight and she smokes. She sits down at the table in the sunlight and she drinks.

She stubs it. She swallows the last. There is the sunlight outside and on the table. She stands.

There are stairs and she walks up. There is the room and she walks in.

There is the desk.

The desk is at the window. The sunlight comes in the window. The sunlight comes in the window and on the desk. The sunlight comes in the window and on the papers on the desk.

She sits.

The paper is white and the writing is blue.

She looks at it.

She looks at it.

She reads. She reads the writing.

The sunlight is on her face.

She lifts the next. She reads.

She lifts the next. She reads.

swing out right   old lined with tree trunks grey

dress short black

blonde hair roots black

black shoes   legs white in sun

slow   single decker opposite direction

roundabout green lawn circle

flowers blue red purple

yellow sun   flowers

    sweat under arm   smell dry dust

          left   tree-lined   old houses tall

cars parked sides   narrow

slow   wait intersection

    left to right red double-decker crosses

     rattle out   in sun

through traffic lights   left

    both sides lined trees

           cars line parked both sides

    men two stripped waist scaffolding up house front

slow   crossroads   wait

    ladder man high up posts hoarding poster

to right

stop   wait

pedestrians cross pedestrian crossing

sun through tree leaves sweating

yellow balls flick

and off   on   forwards

under railway bridge

heat   white

It is the street. It is hot. They walk it. Sun comes down.
It is the roundabout. They are at it and they turn right at it.
The milk van is there.
They walk it. They talk. They walk past the milk van. The
milk van is in street. The street is long and they walk it. The heat
comes down. They talk.
The path is off to the right. There is creosote smell. They
walk down it.
It is the canal. They stop. They look at it.
They sweat. The path is along the edge of the canal. They talk.
They walk it. The ducks are in the canal. The ducks look at
them. They walk it. The ducks bob.
The path turns. They turn left. They walk along it.
They look at it. Ducks bob. The ducks look at them. The sun
is in the water and the ducks are in sun.

There is the bridge. The path is under the bridge. They walk under the bridge. They walk into the shadow. The shadow is cool. The shadow is dark. They walk out of the shadow.

In the sun it is hot. The water is in the sun. The water reflects.

The canal is there. The canal is on the right. The ducks are in the canal.

Flats are on the left.

They walk it. They talk.

They walk it. They walk. There are boats. There are boats and the boats are on the other side. They walk. They talk. They look at the boats as they walk. The boats bob. The boats are tied to the bank. The boats are tied to the other bank. It is hot and the ground is dry.

They walk. They walk and talk. The ground is hard in the sun. It is hot.

The canal is on the right.

The boat is on it.

The boat comes. The boat comes down. They walk. They walk towards the boat and the boat comes towards them.

The man stands. The man stands in the sun. He is at the back. It is green. He looks along the canal. He looks down along the canal in the sun. He looks at them. The letters are red. The letters are on the green. They look at him. They talk. He looks at the canal. He steers.

There is the green of the boat. There is the red of the letters.

There is the blue of the sky. There is the brown of ground.

The ground is hard. It is hot.

They sweat. They walk. They draw level.

They draw level with the boat. The boat draws level. They look at it. It is green. They look at red. They look at the man. The man looks at the canal.

It is quiet.

It is hot.

They sweat.

It passes.

They pass.

The ripples hit the side.

The ripples hit the side of the bank and the flock is over. It is low. It is V. It is slow. There is the honking.

Sun falls down.

They walk it. The canal is on the right. The trees are on the right. The trees are on the left. The light is in the trees. The light is in the trees.

The flats are on the left. The flats behind trees.

The golf-course is on the right. The golf-course behind trees. The trees are by the canal.

They walk the path. The path is hard. They sweat.

They walk. They talk.

The man wears the cap. The man pulls the golf trolley. The man walks the golf-course.

The flock is again. It is in the sky. It is bright. They are on the blue. They look at the sky. They look at V. It is hot. It is bright in the sky. They walk. They talk.

It is hot.

They are sweating. The flats end and the houses begin.

There is the sound of the traffic on the motorway on the other side of the golf-course.

They walk. They walk the path. Heat comes down.

The bridge is the second. The ground is hard. The bridge is over the canal. The cars are over the bridge over the canal.

The path splits. The paths are hard. The right is under it. The left is up to it. They walk up to it through the trees. They walk up to it in the light flicking through the trees.

Cars pass. It is narrow. Cars beep before crossing.

They wait for the cars to pass. When there are no cars they cross.

They cross.

They talk in sun.

Pavement is black.

They talk. They walk.

Cars pass. Cars pass them. They walk. Behind them cars beep at the bridge. They walk.

The path is to the right. The path is gravel and the gravel is red. They walk the gravel. They walk away from the road.

They walk up the path. They walk up the path into trees towards sky.

The path is up the hill. The path is into trees.

It is hot. The light is in leaves. The birds are in trees. There is the movement on the branches.

They talk and sweat.

Out comes the path. The path is out into opening. The trees surround it. The grass is green and is yellow and is brown.

The birds move in the trees. There is the heat. They walk across it and then the path is climbing again up into trees.

They talk. There are the shadows of the leaves. The path is the gravel. The gravel is red. The shadows of the leaves quiver on the red.

They walk up.

Between trees.

Birds move.

They walk up between leaves in shadow.

They walk out into sun.

The sun is bright. The sky is blue and high. There are no clouds.

They are on the hill.

dark under bridge railway   then out into

                                             blind light second

smell burning   pavements of people

stall of flowers   people in out station

                          cars parked sides

          crowd crosses lights

        railings chaining bike left

three girls teenage arm in arm laughing sun left

coffee shop right   white light length street

cross crossroads   bus shudders   sway

                blue material of seat dust

sunlight on street

man woman young jeans

ESTATE AGENTS   woman first man holding door

                to stop

people on   up to top deck   seats fill

opposite seats talking foreign twenties three girls one boy

                pull out to wait at lights and wait

The line is white. He stands at the edge.

There is the shouting. There is the movement.

The ball comes over. He looks at it. The sun blinds. He drops the head. He turns.

The ball rebounds. He sees the ball.

He hits it.

The light is bright. The light is bright on the green. The green is pale. The sky is high.

The ball rises. The ball is in the air. The ball is up. The ball moves up into the air.

The light is bright. There is movement. They watch the ball.

The ball moves. The goalkeeper moves. The goalkeeper moves into the air.

The goalkeeper stretches. The goalkeeper is stretched. The gloves stretch out.

The ball is in the air.

The goalkeeper is in the air.

They look at the ball.

wait at lights   then out

in foreign words

out left into road cars stretched parked either side

bus rattle

talking fills bus   chats   murmurs

sun shines on windscreens   cars parked

flower boxes colours outside flats

satellite dishes three on blue

over intersection

TO BE OR NOT TO BE

tall houses   three stories   basement

trees   dry   sun

cars and white van pass

                              green pub

     grey hair man holds hand boy roller-skates

swing right   pull in to edge

               single red decker passes

     and pull out judder

     tall houses under blue sky and sun

dust   sweat   she laughs

fat woman hair short purple top

   teenage girl watching holding football

   ticket machine whirrs behind

   look up   show ticket   on

        crossroads   full voices   wait

black taxis three behind each other

brown girl skin between top tight and jeans tight

on bike past cycling

swing rattling left   sun

The sunlight is in the garden.
The cat is fat. The cat is black.
The cat is tensed.

left into sun to stop sudden behind taxi waiting

pile fruit piled pavement red yellow boxes of green purple

shops line

scaffolding hangs white sheets plastic

sun white on street   people walk

bus jumps   dust

lorry piled rubbish white bags bags bin black

to lights to wait

girl perfume for second

dust   heat   sweating

baskets colours flowers above orange pub windows

purple white green

                                                            sun

        sudden accelerate   wide road carless

    tall flats tall behind green railings

            white bricks edge brown walls

    woman reading magazine at stop   looks up

        gold letters on black bin behind

            girl breasts bounce round white t-shirt jogging

red top woman posts letter bundle pillar-box red

    swing left   to stop   two taxis black at lights sweating wet

to green   out

in heat

                                        to more lights red

                    behind one taxi

          sun on tall houses either side stretch up to blue

          people at stop opposite side watch waiting

heat   faces

lights to green

          out   into road wide   sun bright full

                              stop ahead

          man waves   slow

                              pulling in to stop

          bright light white   sweating

The ceiling is white.

The plastic is white. The plastic opens the mouth.

The dentist pulls the light. The light shines in. The light shines into the mouth.

She looks at the light. The knobs are black.

The dentist bends. The dentist looks.

The assistant bends. The assistant looks.

The assistant puts it in. The end is under the tongue. The sucking starts.

She looks at the light. The light is white. She sweats. She is hot.

The dentist is on the right. The assistant is on the left.

The dentist looks in. The assistant looks in.

The dentist holds it.

There is the sound.

The dentist bends. The dentist puts it in.

There is the smell.

sweating

      bus to stop

   white out on street

                 bell rings

        voices   laughter

bell rings   pull out into road

   black taxis line outside station

                              sun length of street

                out   right   into wide

accelerate   to lights

                                            green

    skyscraper grey concrete sectioned blue talls left

crowding out of station in

                                    white sun on faces

coach double decked multicoloured letters sides

        left past crane slow lifting girder high to blue

    CHINESE RESTAURANT on right

                                        PHARMACY

CAN'T billboard

            high flats of glass reflect blue cloudless

        floors jut out   glass and white stone

The stage is black.
The light appears.
The light is red.
The light is on the middle of the stage.
The light brightens.
The light spreads.
The light spreads across the stage.
The light covers the stage.
The stage is red.
She walks on. She walks on from the left.
The dress is white. The dress is long.
The light is on the dress. The red is on her skin. The red is on the stage. The hair is long.
The light is on the dress. The light is red. The dress is white.
The girl waits.
The light turns green.
The music starts.
The music starts slow.
The music starts quiet.
She waits.
She waits.
The girl starts to turn.
She turns slow.
She turns to the right.
She turns. The music is louder.
She turns. The music is faster.
She turns.
The light turns slow from green to red.
The music slow gets louder. The music slow gets faster.
The girl turns slow.
The dress is white. The dress turns. The dress is long. The light is on it.
The light is red. The light is on the dress. The red is on the dress. The red is on the white.
The music gets louder. The violins start faster.
The dress turns. The dress turns in the light.
The note is high. The violins hold the note. The note is held.

The light is red. The light is brighter. The light brightens.
The girl turns slow.
The music is loud. The dress turns.
The music gets louder. The dress turns.
The light is redder. The dress turns.
The light is brighter. The dress turns.
The music is faster. She is turning.
She turns slow. The hair long down at the back. The dress turning in light, the hair long down it back.
She turns. The music loudens. She turns it in the dress and the dress turns with her. She turns slow and the light is red. The music loudens and the music fasts.
She turns.
The girls walk in. The girls walk in from the right.
The girls stand in the line behind her.
The dresses are black.
She turns slow.
The music is loud. The music is fast. The light is red. The light is bright on the dresses and the faces.
She turns slow. They stand in the line. The dress turns. She turns. They face the audience.
The music stops.
She stops.
The light turns white.
She stands. She faces the audience.
She breathes. She sweats.
The light is white.

      right sudden   shops line either side

                      on left blue taxi

     to behind queue of cars

shop   SECOND HAND   cameras

DENTAL CARE

newsagent   poster   newspaper stand outside

heat   noise of traffic

bus rattle   chatter

girl twenties ahead with child pram   bends

to stop at red lights

FRUIT AND VEGETABLES

BANK   sun on

lights green   sweating

accelerate

man cashpoint black t-shirt black sunglasses

two lorries pulled in   men loading unloading

FAST FOOD   flowers pub windows

CHEMIST   RESTAURANT

taxis queue cars

                              slow

                                             heat

CLOTHES   BUREAU DE CHANGE

          BANK

                         RESTAURANT

     ESTATE AGENTS   CAFE

sun on signs names colours posters

                              sun on

          clothes people pavement cafe looking

up at bus through sunglasses black

          the light on the pavement

                    bald man

     to stop at red

                                  ahead green trees

          green   to right

     sudden into road wide of

          people traffic rushing moving waiting moving crossing

                              and sun heat

     He sprays. He sprays it. He sprays it on.
     He sprays it on the bath and he sprays it on the sink. He
places it down. There is the smell.
     The pad is green. He lifts it.
     He rubs. He rubs it. He rubs the bath.
     He rubs the pad on the bath. He rubs the pad on the liquid
on the bath. He rubs the bath.
     He stands. He rubs the sink. He rubs the pad on the sink.
The sink is white and the pad is green. He rubs the pad on the
liquid on the sink. There is the smell.
     There is the sun outside the window and there is the pattern
on the glass.
     He stops. He stops the rubbing.
     He puts it down. He lifts the cloth. It is orange. The cloth is
orange.
     He turns the tap. The water falls. The water falls into the
sink. The tap is steel. The water is cold.
     The plug is round. The plug is black. He puts it in.
     He puts in the cloth. It is orange. It is cold. The water fills
the cloth. He lifts.
     He twists. The water falls. The water falls out into water. The
water falls out into water in sink.
     He turns the tap. The water stops.
     He turns. He bends.

                              139

He wipes. He wipes it. He wipes the bath. He wipes the bath with the cloth. The cloth is wet and the bath is white.

He wipes the liquid off the bath.

There is the smell.

He sweats.

He stands. He turns.

He pulls the plug. The water falls out. He turns the tap. The water falls in. He puts the cloth in. He puts the cloth in the water. The water is cold. He holds the cloth in the water falling. He rinses the cloth. It is cold. The cloth is orange. He lifts. He squeezes. The water falls out.

He twists. The water falls in.

The sun is a white on the window.

He turns the tap.

He wipes the sink. He wipes the taps.

The taps shine the light.

He wipes the liquid off the sink. He wipes.

He turns the tap. He rinses it.

He puts it on the floor beside the pad.

It is orange and he turns it off.

There is the smell.

He turns. He reaches. He reaches up. He reaches up above the bath.

The showerhead is white. He takes it out of the slot and points. He points it into the bath.

He holds it with the left. He looks up. He reaches up with the right.

The knob is plastic. It turns.

The water comes out. The water comes out strong. The water is cold. The water comes out strong out of the head.

He points. He rinses.

He rinses the bath.

He rinses the side. The liquid rinses away.

He rinses the bath.

He turns. He looks at the sink.

He pulls. The water sprays the floor. The water sprays the sink.

He rinses. He rinses the sink. He rinses the sink with the spray. The spray is cold. He rinses it.

He looks up. The right hand points it at the sink. The left hand stretches. The left hand turns the knob. He is stretched out and he stretches. He is stretched and the water stops.

He shakes it. The drops fall in.

He turns. He lifts it up. He slots it in.

The hands are wet.

He bends. He lifts the bottle. He puts the bottle against the wall. He puts the bottle against the wall under the sink.

The bin is metal. The painting is on the bin. The painting is the flower on the bin. The plastic bag is white in the bin.

He lifts the cloth. The cloth is orange.

He lifts the pad. The pad is green.

There is the smell. The hands are wet. The flower is on the bin.

He puts the pad into the bag in the bin and he puts the cloth into the bag in the bin.

The pad is in the bag. The cloth is in the bag. The bag is in the bin. The painting is on the bin. The painting is a flower.

He sweats.

There is the smell.

Sun is on the window.

He stands. He turns. He turns the tap.

The soap is on the dish. The dish is on the windowsill.

He lifts the dish. The ledge is on the sink. He puts the dish on the ledge on the sink.

The dish is white. The ledge is white. The soap is white.

The sun is white. The window is white with sun.

He lifts the soap.

The water is cold.

He rubs the soap. The soap he rubs between the hands. The soap he rubs between the hands is white. He rubs the soap between the hands under water.

The water is cold.

He lifts the hands. He puts the soap on the dish. The dish is white. He rubs the hands.

He rubs the hands. He rubs the hands together. The bubbles are white.

He puts the hands into the water. The water falls onto the hands. The water falls into the sink.

He rubs the hands. He rubs the hands under the water.

He rinses the hands.

The water is cold.

He turns the tap. The water stops.

people in heat

street wide packed

waiting

walking   looking shops

people line either side   clothes shops

sun white on length of street

traffic queues waits   on   slow queue

sun on cars taxis buses people

people cross between cars buses   looking sunglasses

pavements of people looking walking watching

talking sweat

in sun

traffic edging both lanes

girl teenage   holds child's hand

walking bare stomach blue tattoo

   gold in belly button turning to clothes in window

              pigeons on eaves

        queue at lights

in all directions   looking   walking talking sun

  windows   talking   other people

 crossing looking   recrossing

        bare skin

   walking   looking   talking

recrossing

    shops

      bare skin different colours

   in sun

overtake two buses red at stop

dust and chatter

white bare arms bare legs black bare stomachs brown

pull behind third bus   waiting

man runs door third bus

looks in up   doors open   he gets in

sweat

white cleavage   walking

man slow with stick

to stop

two women in black get off bus ahead

t-shirts

straps over shoulders

sunglasses

girl holds flower

man young watching from bench wooden

holdall blue on ground

bench painted green

families   prams   babies

placards

women   posters   clothes

shop fronts   sun   girls

sunglasses

glass sun   windows

yellow lines on road

covered

uncovered   by traffic inching

in sun

woman buttocks

man blonde black roots

to traffic lights stop   trailer green white red

child looks up to woman from pram

sunglasses turned windows

to green

The wall is pebble-dashed.
The door is on the bottom right.
The door is on the bottom right of the wall.
The door is painted. The paint is red. The paint peels.
The number is steel. The number is fixed to the door.
The letterbox is steel. The letterbox is fixed to the door.
The sun shines on the steel.
The button is the bell. The button is plastic. The plastic is white. The button is set into the rectangle. The rectangle is plastic. The plastic is black.
The window is on the first floor above the door. The window is single.
The window is on the first floor to the left of the single window. The window is double.
The window is on the ground floor below the double window. The window is to the left of the door. The window is triple.
The windows reflect the sun.

lights green

young man young woman hand hand look window CDs

young women   bare skin

bus rattling forward slow   heat

siren distance

people step off pavement into road

looking

SALE!   SALE!   SALE!

accelerate   sun

football shirt white blue

man red hair beard

man t-shirt black and moustache

bell rings

man green shirt woman red t-shirt opposite seat stand

and down aisle

people standing

people walking   shops   sunlight

on and off buses

sun   OPTICIANS   woman long hair black   GAMES

man in shorts

CHEMISTS   colours ALL ELECTRICAL GOODS sun

sunglasses   NEWS   MAGAZINES

girl fixes strap bra

ICE CREAM   children sun sweets

through green lights

long hair swings in sun   girl's breasts

swing in to left

The tongue is in the mouth. The mouth is open. She kisses.

Her tongue is in the mouth. The tongue is in her mouth. She kisses it.

They kiss.

The mouths push. The mouths push against. Her mouth pushes against him. There is wetness. She kisses him. He licks the tongue.

His mouth is wet. She wipes the hand. He wipes the hand across. She leans in.

The wetness is in the mouths. The tongues move in. The tongues move in the wetness. The tongues move in the wetness and the mouths. The lips wet slip.

The hand is on the thigh. They kiss. They kiss. The hand is on the thigh. The hand moves. The thigh moves. The kissing is on.

The mouths are in the mouths.

The hand moves. The thighs move. The skirt moves up. The knees open.

The tongues lip. The tongues are wet in.

The skirt moves. The skirt moves up. The skirt moves up the legs. There are the kisses. The hem moves above the knee.

The knee is bared. The knee is bare. The hand is on the knee.

Lips slip. The tongues lick.

She holds him. They are the kissing. There is the kissing. There is the wetness. Tongues slip in.

He holds her. It is hot. The curtains are closed. The sun outside.

The kiss it is wet. The eyes are closed. They lean. They lean in. They lean sideways. They fall back onto the bed.

The tongues lick lips. Her tongue licks against him. The fingers are unbuttoning. The buttons are white. The blouse is white. The fingers unbutton the buttons.

The bra is white. The skin is white.

They kiss. They are lying on the bed and they kiss.

The blouse opens white. The blouse opens wide.

The fingers open the blouse wide. The blouse is white. The skin is white.

It is hot. They sweat. There is the wetness. There are the tongues wet in the mouths. The bra is white. The tongue moves over his teeth. The fingers touch the cup. Her mouth is in.

She kisses. The eyes are closed. He kisses. The kissing is in. She holds him. The fingers lift the cup down. The breast bares.

Her lips are wet. Her face is red. She kisses. The breast is white. The tongues slide. The lips are wet. The lips are wet in. The fingers touch. The fingers touch it. He touches it. He touches the white. He strokes the white. The kissing is in.

He touches the red. He pulls.

The sun is outside. Her tongue moves in. The fingers move.

The tongue is in the wetness. The tongue is in the mouth. It is hot. The curtains are pulled. The tongue touches the tongue. The sun is bright outside.

The tongue is in. He pulls. The curtains are pulled. The hand moves to the knee.

It is wet. She kisses. She kisses him. Her face is red. She pushes it against him. She holds. The hand moves. The hand moves up the thigh. The thighs open. It is the afternoon. She kisses him. The skirt is around the waist.

She kisses. She is kissing him. She kisses the mouth. His tongue is in. The hand moves up. The hand moves up the thigh. She puts her fingers in the hair. She puts her fingers in the hair. She holds the hair tight. She holds the head.

The hand is up the thigh. The fingers are in the hair.

The thighs open. The mouths are in each other. The mouths are in each other's mouths. She holds the hair.

She kisses the mouth. The fingers are inside the thighs. She pushes the mouth against her. The fingers stroke. The knickers are white.

The tongues are wet. The tongues are inside. There is the wetness. She holds the hair. The fingers touch.

She sits up.

swing left to stop red

UNDERGROUND

THEATRE with lights flash red white

lights green   right sharp to side street

BAR   YMCA   HOTEL

                         past parked lorry

sun white   dirt in heat

          people   sunglasses

RESTAURANT   ANTIQUES

     BOOKSELLERS

                              accelerate in sun

     MUSEUM on left

  slower

  pillars cream brown   steps down behind railings

to stop

  people standing   down aisle   down steps

                    ICECREAMS

talking   sunglasses on

people up and down museum steps

top deck empties

sun   heat   dust

portacabins

men yellow waistcoats plastic behind railings smoke

It is dark. It is morning. It is early.

It is stacked in piles.

It is morning. They drive vans. They drive vans through the gates. It is stacked in piles. It is early. They load it. The lights are on. They load the piles in. It is dark.

They drive. They drive the vans.

They drive west. They drive north. They drive south. They drive east.

They drive. They drive in the dark.

The lights are on and it is dark. They drive.

They drive. They drive the vans through the dark.

They drive the vans west through the dark. They drive the vans through the dark north. They drive the vans down through the dark southwards. They drive the vans east through the dark towards the dawn.

It is dawn. The dawn rises. It is the morning. It is early.

The vans stop. They open the doors. They take it out.

They put it outside the supermarkets.

They put it outside the newsagents.

They put it outside the petrol stations.

They put it outside the corner shops.

It is early morning and the piles are strapped. The piles are on the pavements. The piles are on the pavements outside the corner shops. The piles are on the pavements outside the newsagents. The piles are on the pavements outside the supermarkets. The piles are on the forecourts outside the petrol stations.

It is early and morning. The straps are plastic.

It is morning. There is the light in the sky. There is the light whitening in the sky. The lights in the streets go out.

It is the morning.

They pull up the shutters. They unlock the doors. They turn off the alarms. They carry in the piles.

They turn on the lights. The lights flick on.

They take scissors. They cut straps. They open piles.

They stack it.

They stack it on shelves. They stack it on counters.

They stack it in the corner shops. They stack it in the supermarkets.

They stack it in the petrol stations. They stack it in the newsagents.

They stack it in the east of the city; they stack it in the west of the city; they stack it in the north of the city; they stack it in the south of the city.

The sun rises. The light falls into the streets and it gets hotter.

It is morning. The doors are open. They come.

They walk to the shelves. They walk to the counters. They look at it. They look at the front. They read the headline. They pick it up.

They give money. The tills open and the tills close. They take the change.

They leave the shops. They leave the newsagents. They leave the supermarkets. They leave the petrol stations.

It is day. The sun is high. The light falls down.

They read it.

They read it in parks. They read it at desks. They read it on buses.

They read it in pubs. They read it in beds. They read it walking.

They read it on benches. They read it in baths. They read it on trains.

They read it eating. They read it smoking. They read it drinking.

They read it in cars. They read it on planes. They read it in gardens.

There are no clouds.

They read the columns. They read the national news. They read the financial news.

They read the editorials. They read the television. They read the cartoons.

They read the results. They read the reviews. They read the letters.

They leave it on tables.

They throw it in wastepaper baskets under desks.

They put it on dashboards.

They push it into rubbish bins on emptying streets.

It is evening. It is cooler.

out   into road

            past portacabins behind railings

                left   up street

sun on flowers behind railings   rattling

                railings left   window boxes right

            to stop behind taxi at entrance to square

        cars pass right to left   green trees ahead

                out   accelerate into square

                    dust smell   people walking in sun

sun on square

        park of trees in centre

   green leaves in light   ring bell

         sweating heat

  swaying to right

      up from dust seat as bus slows

into stop on left   stopping

        down aisle   empty seats

     down curve narrow stairs

  past conductor   thanks

step   then step   then

into white sun pavement   heat blazing bright heat

   It is black.
   It is black.
   He waits.
   The button is on the front. He looks at the button. He
presses it. He waits.

It is black.

There are no lights.

He listens. There is the sound of the traffic on the street outside.

He presses the button. He holds the button in. He listens.

He lets the button out. He listens.

It is black.

He looks at it.

He stands. He leans forward. He pulls it forward. He looks behind.

There are leads. There is dust. There are black leads. There are grey leads. He looks at them. The dust is grey. He looks at it.

He leans. The leads lead into it. He sweats. He pushes each lead. He pushes each lead in. He pushes each lead into it.

He stands. He wipes the forehead. He looks at it.

He presses the button. He listens.

It is silent.

He looks at it.

It is black.

He sweats.

He takes off the jacket. He hangs the jacket on the back of the chair.

He leans. He looks behind. He looks at the dust. He looks at the leads.

He reaches around. There is dust. He pulls out the power lead. He drops it. He drops it behind the desk.

He stands. He bends. He looks under the desk.

The lead leads to the plugs. The plugs are in the wall. He crawls under. He looks at the switches. The switches are down.

It is the morning.

He crawls out. He stands. There is dust. He wipes the hands on the trousers.

He sweats and there is dust.

He looks at the next desk. He walks to the next desk. He leans forward. He looks behind.

There are leads. There is the paper clip. There is dust.

He pulls it forward. There is dust. He pulls out the power lead. He drops it behind.

He stands. He sweats. He bends. He looks under.

The plug is in wall. He crawls. He pushes the switch up. He pulls. He pulls the plug out.

The dust is on the floor.

He crawls out. He stands. He holds the lead.

He turns to the first desk. He places the lead on the desk. He rolls up the left sleeve. He rolls up the right sleeve.

The sun is window. There is sound of traffic outside.

He lifts the lead. He leans. He leans forward. He pulls it forward.

The window is to the left. The sun is in the window.

He reaches behind. He looks. There is the dust.

He reaches. He plugs the lead in. He sweats. He drops the plug behind.

He stands. The sweat is in the armpits. The sweat is on the forehead. The sweat is on the face.

The left arm wipes sweat across the forehead. He sweats.

He kneels. He crawls.

He reaches. He reaches to the wall. He is wet under the arms.

He pushes the switch up. He pulls the plug out. He puts the old lead behind him.

The second plug hangs down. He takes it. He reaches. He pushes the plug in. He pushes it to check. He pushes it to check. He pushes the switch down.

The dust is in the carpet.

He crawls out. The hands are wet. He stands. The hands wipe on the trousers.

He looks at it. The left arm wipes across the mouth and the right forefinger pushes the button in.

He stands. The hands are on the hips.

He looks at it.

It is black.

sun white pavement   heat

red bus   lane marked yellow

white lines on tarmac black

black bin pavement

red bus stopped   engine turns off

jacket hang left shoulder

passing bus open-top tourists sunglasses sun looking

trees across road park

black t-shirt man twenties plastic bag white hand passes

boy teenage jeans blue looks timetable shelter shade

old buildings white   railed black

blue sky over

past woman looking traffic

hair brown shoulder watching

sunshine on windows

heat   sweat

white

The newspaper is on the table. The tin is on the newspaper.

The screwdriver prises off the lid. The handle is red.
The paint is white. The stick stirs the paint.
The hair is black. The brush is on the table.

sun shining length of street

sweating

stop lights   LOOK RIGHT

dirt on plastic yellow white cones

sun on face   car passes blue

bright

white car blue car at lights waiting flash

indicators orange

white top woman   old shorts black

bag plastic   white trainers

other side waiting

waiting shade of building for lights

                    green   cross

        past woman

                        to pavement   in heat

    old buildings   railings black

                                    HOTEL 100M

    cars parked either side

                                        arrows white on blue

        girl skirt blue denim t-shirt green tight

                        heat   sweating

                    BUREAU DE CHANGE

    She finds it. It is cooler in the shop. It is long. It is red.
    The cotton is thin. The buttons are white. The buttons are
up the front.
    She looks at it. She looks for the tag. She looks at the tag.
    She looks at it. She takes it off the rail. She holds the hanger.
She holds it up. She looks at it.
    She turns. She looks. She looks the mirror. She walks to the
mirror.
    She holds it. She holds it up. She holds it up against her. She
looks at it. The head tips. She looks.

She looks.

She looks.

She turns. She walks to the cubicles.

The assistant stands. She shows the assistant. The assistant gives her the token. The token is plastic.

She steps in. She turns. She pulls the curtain.

There is the hook. She hangs it on the hook.

The seat is plastic. She takes off the jacket. The plastic is grey. She puts the jacket on it. The jacket is red.

She pulls the t-shirt. She pulls the t-shirt up. She pulls the t-shirt over the head. The plastic is grey. The t-shirt is blue.

The bra is black. She bends. She pulls off the trainers. The t-shirt is on the jacket.

She stands and unbuttons and unzips. The feet are bare. She pulls them down. The knickers are black.

She puts the jeans on top of the t-shirt on top of the jacket on the chair. The t-shirt is blue. The jacket is red. The plastic is grey and the jeans are blue.

It is red. She unbuttons. She takes it off the hanger. She pulls it over the head. The arms slide in.

She buttons.

She pulls the curtain. She steps out.

She turns. She stands. There is the mirror. She looks. She looks in it. She looks at it. She turns. She turns. She looks. She smooths. She looks.

She stands on the toes. She looks.

She sweats under the arms.

She looks at it. She pulls it out to the side against her.

She looks at it. She stands on the toes. She looks at the hips.

She turns. She looks over the shoulder. She looks at it.

She turns. She looks at it.

She looks at it.

She turns. She walks back in. She pulls the curtain.

She unbuttons. She pulls. The hanger is black.

She pulls on the jeans. She zips. She buttons. The jeans are blue.

She pulls on the t-shirt. She pulls on the trainers. The trainers are white.

She turns. She lifts the jacket. She lifts the hanger.

She pulls the curtain. She looks in the mirror.

She gives the token. The token is plastic.

She gives the dress. The dress is cotton.
She steps back into the shop.

BUREAU DE CHANGE white on red

man twenties   glasses   black hair

yellow black rucksack   walks ahead

heat   railings black

JACKETS £60

girl ponytail twenties   blue trainers

red top black trousers sitting pavement hand out

SKIRTS £25

sunlight

cars parked black silver green shine

noise of traffic

blue sky white light

TRAVEL

signs   grey lampposts

blue of sky reflects in windows

tall building TO LET

chewing gum pavement   cracks   splits

sun

cooler shade of buildings

man pulls black canvas trolley

sunglasses

There are the people playing the tennis. There is the sun on the people playing the tennis. There are the voices of the people playing the tennis. There is the sound of the rackets hitting the balls.

They walk slow. The hand holds the hand. They walk past the tennis courts.

The path goes down. The path goes between trees. It is cooler. They wear the t-shirts.

The hand holds the hand. They walk. They are between trees. They walk down the path. The leaves of the trees are above them. The sky is above. The sky is the blue. The sky is the blue above the leaves of the trees. The leaves are the green. There is the sound of the rackets hitting the balls.

They stop. There is the bench. They sit.

They talk. They look.

It is hot and there are people in the sun. The people in the sun wear the sunglasses. There are the people in the sun who are lying sunbathing. There are the people in the sun lying sunbathing looking through the sunglasses at the people in the sun lying sunbathing looking through the sunglasses.

The sun down on them.

They sit in the shade. They sit in the shade on this bench. The bench is in the shade. They look at the people. The people sunbathe.

There is the sound of the voices of the people playing the tennis on the tennis courts. There is the sound of the rackets hitting the balls on tennis courts. There is the sound of the traffic on the road in the distance.

They talk.

There is the path. The path is black. There are the two women walking along the path. There are the two women walking along the path past the bench. There are the two women walking along the path towards the gate at the end. The gate is black. They look at the two women.

There are the dogs. The dogs are two. The dogs are big. The dogs are black.

There is the man walking the dogs up the path. The dogs sniff. The dogs strain.

The man walking the dogs passes the women walking. The sun is hot. The shade is under trees. The dogs walk past the bench. The slobber is white. It is cooler under the trees. The man walks. The man walks past.

There is the sunlight above the leaves of the trees and there is the gate at the end of the path. There is the sound of the voices of the people playing the tennis on the tennis courts and there are the two women walking down the path towards the gate at the end of the path. There is the sound of the traffic in the distance and there is the heat and the sweat and the smell. There are the people lying on the grass sunbathing in the sun looking through the sunglasses at the people lying sunbathing in the sun looking and there is the man walking up the path and there are the two dogs pulling the man up the path and there is the sound of the rackets hitting the balls on the courts.

cooler building shade

man trolley black canvas into crowd

yellow lines double on street

CAR COOLERS

pigeon pavement hopping newsagents

SAME DAY DEVELOPING AND PRINTING

girl tall blonde jeans upturned ankles bare

yellow cardigan woman

LET BY

stands   postcards   colours

RISTORANTE ITALIANO right

The wardrobe is white. The wall is white. The desk is white. The paper is white.

There are four holes. The margin is blue. The lines are grey.

There is the stack. It is stacked. He lifts it. He stacks it. He places it on the white.

The ruler is white and the pen is orange.

He lifts the ruler. He puts the ruler on the page. He puts the ruler on the right of the page. The holes are on the left of the page. The holes are on the left of the page and the ruler is on the right of the page. The margin is blue.

He lifts the pen. The pen is orange. He puts the tip of the pen on the paper. He puts the tip of the pen on the paper against the edge of the ruler.

The pen is orange. The ruler is white. The markings on the ruler are black.

He pushes the tip of the pen along the edge of the ruler. The tip of the pen makes line along. The line makes the margin down the right. The line is black and the paper is white.

The paper is white. The margin on the left side of the paper is blue. The lines are grey. The margin on the right side of the paper is black. The holes are through the paper. The holes are inside the margin on the left side of the paper.

He lifts the page. He turns the page. He puts the page face down. He puts the page face down on the white. He puts the page face down by the stack.

The pages are seventy-four. The pages are white. He lifts the ruler. The margin is blue. He places the ruler. The lines are grey. He takes the pen. The holes show the white of the desk. He places the pen. The desk is white. He draws the line down.

He lifts the page. The window is open. He turns the page.

He places the page face down on the page.

The stacks are two. There are more pages in the first stack.

The stacks are two. There are more pages in the second stack.

There is one stack.

He puts down the pen. He puts down the ruler.

He lifts the stack. He turns the stack. He squares the stack.

He places the stack on the desk. He places the stack in the centre of the desk. He places the pen to the right of the desk. He places the ruler to the right of the desk.

The desk is white. The ruler is white. The pen is orange.

He wipes the hands on the trousers.

push door   RISTORANTE

                              open to dark

no queue

cool   tiles dark red floor tables right counter left glass

cake   salads   sandwiches

man fat hair black apron white

cooler

order

man yells foreign to back room

pay   change

wipe sweat

end of counter   wait   counter smeared

fat man   cup white   coffee

plate white   danish

thanks

lift cup plate

turn

walk to back to steps down

through double door brown back pushed

cool

The front is glass. The sides are glass. The back is glass.
The glass reflects the buildings. The glass reflects the sky.
The glass reflects the light.
The glass reflects the glass. The glass reflects the glass
reflecting glass. The glass reflects the glass reflecting glass
reflecting glass.

door double brown back pushed

four steps down

tiles yellow cream   black tangle pattern worn

brown wood dark table worn white

ashtray brown glass

crushed ash grey   cigarette bent brown ends

cellars glass two   white half full brown empty

black powder   black lids   white grains

bubbles white froth milk coffee brown hot milked

brown rim stained white cup

                                                            cooler

white saucer white circled red thin narrower stripe

sweat

plate white circle

crumbs round danish   light brown

bite   sweet

                              sweat heat

sweet in   chew   sweet sugar

crumbs   fall

crumb finger lick

ashtray glass brown transparent

bite

chew sweet   swallow

sweet

The cars are on the street and the shoppers are on the pave-ment. The light is in the street and the light is on the buildings. The windows reflect the light and the tourists are behind the guide. The cars are in the side street and queue.

She stands on the pavement and looks at the street. The sun-glasses are on her. The man talks to himself as he walks past and it is hot and horns sound.

The tourist points to the bus. The bus in the street. The tourist points speaking and does not see her. The bus is turning red. She is looking up at the signs and she does not see him. The bus is in the street. They bump. The book drops.

She bends. She bends to it. The tourist is speaking and he is in the sun behind him. The tourist speaks and his hands move to her. She is picking up the book and looking up to him in the sun. She squints up. She smiles. She nods. She speaks.

She looks at the street.

The cars are in the street and they pass. The vans pass. The buses pass. The lorries pass. The taxis pass.

The sun reflects on the cars. The tourists follow the guide. The people walk past. She looks at the street.

She looks at the book. She opens the book. The book is maps. She opens the pages. She opens the page.

There is the noise of the traffic on the street. There is the noise of the people on the pavement. The light is on them.

She looks up. She looks up the street. She looks down. She looks down the street. She looks at the buildings in the street. She looks at the walls of the buildings in the street.

There is the line of white on the blue.

She looks at the book.

ashtray transparent   crumbs   heat

shine geese fly left right bronze three on cream paint dirty

bumped wall lines

tobacco   roll   light   curve smoke white

white stick paper brown head specked yellow tipped

under black grey white ash

flick ash ashtray glass brown

square chair cooler

dark wood

brown cream reeds weave seats

through wood door man man woman talk fast

foreign words   English words

sort cutlery metal plastic drawers

spinning coin spinning tabletop plastic

machine whirr

talk tables quiet

red black red cylinder curved hose

sip   smoke

The rows are three. The rows are three of ten seats. The three rows are of ten seats. There are three rows of ten seats facing forwards.

The seats are red.

There is the whiteboard. There is the whiteboard and there is the chair. There is the whiteboard and there is the chair and there is the table.

There is the whiteboard and there is the chair and there is the table and the whiteboard faces the seats and the chair faces the seats and the table is in front of the chair.

The whiteboard is behind the chair to the right. The table is in front of the chair. The table is between the chair and the seats.

There is the second table. There is the second table in the corner.

There are the three jugs. There are the three jugs on the table in the corner.

There are the twenty cups and there are the twenty saucers. There are the twenty cups and there are the twenty saucers on the table in the corner.

There are the twenty plates.

There are three jugs and there are twenty cups and there are twenty saucers and there are twenty plates and there is the table and the three jugs and the twenty cups and the twenty saucers and the twenty plates are on the table.

The jugs are plastic. The plastic is black. The coffee is in the jugs. The coffee is black.

The windows are high on the walls.

The man walks in and the woman walks in.

The man carries the jug in the right hand. The jug is plastic. The plastic is black. The water is in the jug. The water is hot.

The woman carries the basket in the left hand. The cartons are in the basket. The cartons are plastic. The covers of the cartons are foil. The cartons are small. The milk is in the cartons. The milk is white. The cartons are thirty-eight.

The man carries the basket in the left hand. The biscuits are brown. The biscuits are thirty-two in the basket.

The woman carries the basket in the right hand. There are twenty-three tea-bags.

The man walks to the table. The woman walks to the table. The table is in the corner.

The man puts the jug in the right hand onto the table.

The woman puts the basket in the right hand onto the table.

The man puts the basket in the left hand onto the table.

The woman puts the basket in the left hand onto the table.

The woman leaves the room.

The man leaves the room.

extinguisher red black at door

plastic black hem edge from flip-top plastic orange bin

                      heat

onions

stands man young

       down back black hair tangled

cigarette   top purple blue jeans

white magazine

table corner   man rucksack purple

with girl rucksack small white red

ponytail brown wide scrunchy black

man purple top young leaving steps

brown ponytail from plastic white green bag on table

takes orange bottle   unscrews   sips

man bald fleece red jacket sitting

sip   smoke

People walk out. He walks to the side. People walk out. People walk out into sun. He watches people walk out.

People walk out of dark. People walk into sun.

He puts hand in pocket. The tin is metal. The lid is green. The lid is on.

The hand pulls off the lid. The rust is in the lid. The rust is orange. The lid fits on the bottom.

He squats. The back is against the wall.

The tin is on the ground. The tin is in the sun. He takes the packet of papers. The packet is green. He takes the paper. He places the packet in the tin.

The paper is white. The paper is a v. The v is open. The paper is white.

The paper is in the left hand. The right hand picks up tobacco.

The v is open. The fingers hold open the v. The fingers place tobacco in the v. He looks up at people.

It is bright. The v is white. Tobacco is brown.

The fingers pull tobacco. The fingers pull tobacco along. The fingers pull tobacco along v.

The left thumb is in v. The left thumb is on tobacco in v. Left thumb holds tobacco in v. V is white. The tip is white. Tobacco is brown.

The tip is in the tin. The tip is white. The fingers take the tip. The tip is round. The fingers take the tip and the fingers put the tip in v. Tip is small. Tip is in v. Tip is white. V is white. V is paper. Tobacco is brown in v.

The tip of the finger slides the tip against tobacco.

The sun is bright hot. He looks up at people. People walk out. People walk into light.

V is white. Edges of v fold over. The edges of v fold over tobacco and the edges fold over tip. Edges are together. The tips of the fingers of the hand rub the edges of v together.

He rubs.

He folds.

He folds it in.

He folds it in under.

Under the other.

It is in.

He rolls.

It is o.

V is o.

He licks. He licks the strip. The strip is sticky. He sticks it.

He looks up. He looks at people. People walk into sun.

He puts the end in the mouth. The roll is white.

The lid is green. The green is on the bottom. He takes the green off. He puts the green on. The green is on the top.

He puts the tin in the pocket. He stands. He looks. He looks at people. Light is white. He is standing. He takes it out. It is blue. He takes it out of pocket. It is blue.

The lighter is blue. The roll is white. He lights. Flame oranges. Light is white. He lights it. The paper is white and the paper is red and the paper is ash and he sucks in and the tobacco catches.

He sucks in. He sucks into the lungs. He sucks it into the lungs.

He holds it.

The smoke is in.

He holds it.

He breathes out.

People walk out. People walk out into sun. Sun is white. People blink.

red man fleece jacket   polo black neck

hair thin blonde bald point forward combed over bald

she grey bottoms jogging

jumper blue rides up

as she leans forward vest black   mid thirties

jeans girl baggy blue down steps

down sits   suede shoes brown socks

one hand sandwich   A4 typed sheet other hand

hiss frying   bacon

knife scratches

man eggs cutting fork on bacon plate white

The sun is on the mantelpiece and it is face down on the mantelpiece. It is on the mantelpiece. The strap is black. The clasp is steel.

The face is round. The face is down. The face is face down. The face is face down on the mantelpiece. The sun is on it face down on the mantelpiece.

It is in sun. The back is steel.

The strap is black. Holes are in one length. The clasp is at the end of one length. The clasp is steel.

The length with the holes lies out. The length with the clasp curls. The length with the clasp curls over. It curls over the back of the face.

The back of the face is steel. The sun is on it. The clasp is steel. The clasp touches the length with holes. The sun is on it.

scratching   cutlery silver meat red white egg yellow

one hand girl sandwich notes turns over

blouse white   jacket leather black

shouts baby

one girl sandwich hand   red dye hair brown short neat

earring rings ear left gold circle plain

handbag black plain

crimson rucksack small

two corner women

one holds baby bald jumpsuit blue

she pale lips thin wide open for

other hand sandwich big green red colours

colours   fall   blouse white

cream yellow mayonnaise

She fills it. She plugs it in. She turns it on.

The pot is heavy. The pot is green. The green is outside. The outside is green.

White is inside. White is on the inside. The pot is white on the inside.

She puts it on the ring. The ring is on the cooker. She puts the pot on the ring on the cooker. The pot is on the ring on the cooker.

She opens the oil. She pours it. She closes it.

She lifts the salt. She shakes it. She shakes it out. She shakes it out onto oil. She shakes it out onto oil in the pot. She shakes it out onto the oil in the pot on the ring. She shakes it out onto the oil in the pot on the ring on the cooker.

The oil is yellow and the salt is white.

She sweats.

She waits.

She waits.

The sunlight window.

The kettle boils.

She turns on the cooker. She turns on the ring.

The steam is in the air.

The ring is under the pot.

The steam rises and it clicks off. She lifts. The water boils in it. She lifts it. She lifts it across.

She tips. She tips it. She tips it up. She tips it up and she tips it in.

The water pours out and pours in. The water boils out of it. She pours the water in. She pours the water out boiling onto the salt on the oil in the pot on the ring on the cooker.

The ring heating.

She fills it. She plugs it in. She switches it on.

She waits.

The ring heats the pot.

The water heats the pot.

The pot heats.

She waits. She looks out of the window. The sun is outside and bright.

She opens the door. The sun is on flowers. The sun is on grass.

The heat is on flowers. She looks. She looks at them. The sun is on them.

The pot heats. The water cools. The pot heats. The ring is hot. The ring heats the pot. The room is hot. The pot heats. The pot is hot. The ring heats the pot. The pot heats the water. The water heats.

She looks at the flowers.

She looks.

The water starts to boil. The water in the pot starts to boil. The water in the kettle starts to boil .

The kettle boils. The kettle is boiling. The water is in the kettle. The water boils. The water is in the kettle boiling. The kettle boils the water. It clicks.

She lifts it. She lifts it across. The kettle is across.

The kettle is in the air. The kettle tips. The kettle tips and the water boiling tips and the water boiling tips into the water boiling and boils.

She puts it down.

The packet is on the side. She lifts the packet. She looks at the packet. She opens the packet. She looks at the boiling.

She lifts a handful. She takes a handful out. She lifts a handful out into the air. She lifts a handful out and across the air.

She drops it. She drops the handful into it. She drops it into the boiling. The boiling lessens.

She takes a handful. She takes a handful out.

The water boils. The handful crosses. She drops it. She drops it in.

She looks at the boiling. The water boils.

She looks at the boiling. She takes a handful.

She drops it. She drops it into it.

She drops it into it. She drops it into it boiling. It boils. She drops the handful into the water.

She takes a handful and she drops the handful into the water in the pot.

The water is in the pot.

The pot is on the ring on the cooker.

The sun is outside white.

The pot is boiling.

The steam goes up. The steam goes out the door.

She looks. She stirs. She stirs it. She stirs it boiling.

She looks at the clock.

The spoon is wood and the wood is brown. The water boils. She stirs it.

She puts the spoon on the side.

She opens the fridge.

She takes out the bread.

She puts the bread on the side.

She takes out the margarine.

She puts the margarine on the side.

She closes the fridge.

The plastic wraps the margarine. The cellophane wraps the bread. She puts down the plate and she takes out the knife.

She unwraps the cellophane. She cuts a slice. The handle is black. She puts the slice on the plate.

She cuts a slice. She puts the slice on the slice on the plate.

She wraps the cellophane.

She takes out the knife. The handle is white.

She lifts off the plastic. The lid is plastic. She puts it in. The handle is white. She pulls. She pulls it along. The yellow goes on. The blade is steel. She takes it out. It is the yellow and the white and the steel. The sun is bright in the window. The steam rises. The hand on the clock clicks once. She looks at the clock. She pushes it over. She pushes it over the slice. She pushes the blade over the slice. She pushes the yellow over the slice. She pushes the yellow on the blade over the slice on the slice on the plate. The plate is white.

She lifts the slice. She places the slice on the worktop. It boils.

She places it in. She pulls. She pulls along the yellow. The yellow slides up. The yellow sticks. The yellow slides up and sticks on. She pulls it.

She sweats. The margarine is on the knife. She pulls it. She pulls the knife. She pulls it. She pulls it along the slice. She pulls the blade along the slice.

The yellow sticks the slice.

She closes the yellow. She opens the fridge.

She puts the yellow in.

She puts the bread in.

It is sun outside. It boils. The bread is beside the margarine. She closes it.

She takes the handle black. She puts the handle black into the sink. She looks at the clock.

She takes the handle white. She cuts the slice on the plate. She takes the slice on the worktop. She puts the slice on the plate. She cuts the slice on the plate. The slices are on the plate. She looks at the clock.

The steam goes out of the door. She puts the knife on the plate. She lifts the wood and she stirs.

She lifts the kettle. She puts the wood on the side.

There is the crumb. There is the crumb beside the plate. The fingertip touches the crumb. The fingertip lifts the crumb. The fingertip goes between the lips. The fingertip goes into the mouth. She fills it.

She plugs it in. She switches it on.

The yellow is in the fridge. The plastic is in the fridge. The bread is brown. The yellow is on the slices. The bread is in the fridge.

The slices are on the plate.

The knife is on the plate.

The knife is in the sink.

The circles on the plate are blue.

She lifts the knife. She puts the colander in. The colander is in. The colander is in the sink. She puts the knife on the side.

She looks at the clock.

The spoon is in. The spoon is out. The pasta is in the spoon. The pasta is on the plate.

She opens the drawer and she takes out the fork.

The kettle boils.

She puts the fork beside the plate. The knife is on the plate.

She lifts the knife. The steam goes out the door. The sun is bright. She places the knife beside the fork.

The piece of pasta is in the mouth. The kettle clicks off.

She eats it.

She lifts the second piece.

She eats it.

She looks at the cooker. She turns off the ring. She lifts the tea-towel. The ring is on the cooker. The pot is on the ring. She lifts the pot.

She lifts the pot. She lifts the pot across. The water boils. She lifts across with the tea-towel. It boils.

She pours. The water pours out. She pours it out. The water boils out into air. She pours water out boiling into air. The water boils out into the colander. The colander in the sink. She tips it in.

The water splashes out. The water splashes into the colander. The water and the pasta splash out boiling into colander in sink. The water and the pasta splash out into sink. The pasta yellow and green. The water spills through holes boiling. The pasta is in.

She puts the pot on the ring. The ring is cooling.

The sun is in the garden. The bees are in the flowers.

She lifts the kettle. She tips the kettle. The water outs.

She tips the water out over the pasta in the colander in the sink. She puts the kettle on the side.

The pasta drains.

She turns. She lifts. She pours.

She pours the oil out in. She pours the oil out into the pot.

The oil is in the bottle.

The oil is in the pot.

She puts the oil down. The oil heats.

She turns. She lifts. She shakes. Water spills out.

Water spills out into sink. It splashes. Water spills out of holes into sink. The pasta is white and the pasta is green and the pasta is in the colander.

She turns. She tips the pasta into the pot.

The pot is white and green.

She turns. She puts the colander in the sink.

She turns. She turns on the ring. She lifts the wood.

The wood is the spoon. The spoon is wood. She turns it.

The wood is the spoon. The wood is the brown. The spoon is wood. She turns it.

She turns brown wood in the pot. She turns the pasta into the oil in the pot on the ring on the cooker and the oil heats.

She lifts pepper. She lifts and shakes it. She lifts it and she shakes it in. She shakes pepper into the pot.

She lifts the spoon. She stirs again. She stirs it in.

It heats.

She reaches. She opens the cupboard.

She takes the jar. She twists it.

It is red inside.

The spoon is wood. The spoon is too big.

She opens the drawer.

She takes metal. She takes it. The metal is spoon. She puts the metal into the red. She pulls it out. She pulls out red. She pulls out red and she puts it in pot.

She spoons two spoons.

She spoons two spoons in.

She puts down the metal.

She twists it. She puts it down.

She lifts the metal. She lifts the metal and stirs the red in. The red stirs into the green and the red stirs into the white. She stirs it in.

She stirs it. She stirs it into the pasta. The pasta white and the pasta green.

She stirs. She stirs it in. The ring heats the pot and she stirs it in. The pot heats the pasta and she stirs it in. The pot heats the red and she stirs it in.

The heat is in the room. The bee is against the pane.

She stirs.

She turns off the ring.

She stirs.

She lifts it. She tastes.

She lifts the tea-towel. She lifts the handle. She lifts the pot.

The spoon pulls the sauce onto the plate. The spoon pulls the pasta onto the plate. The spoon pulls the sauce and the pasta onto the plate. The sauce and the pasta are on the plate.

The sun is outside.

The sun is inside.

The sun is on her back.

The sun is on the floor.

The line is on the sky.
The pasta is on the plate.
The bread is on the plate.
She puts the pot into the colander.
She puts the tea-towel on the side.
She turns on the tap. She turns on the hot tap.
The water is cold.
She bends and she opens. The water falls. The water falls into the pot.
She squirts it in. It is green. She squirts it in green. The bubbles start.
She stands. She rinses the hands.
The bubbles are in the pot.
She lifts the tea-towel.
The bubbles spill into the colander.
She dries the hands and she turns off the tap.
The pasta is on the plate.
The bread is on the plate.
She puts down the tea-towel.
She lifts the plate.
She lifts the knife and fork.
She turns.

green red bits sandwich fall blouse white cardigan brown

hair curls long to breasts

down sandwich lifts can red silver drinks metal

lips licking   thirties

back woman other t-shirt grey

neck hair brown   bra bumps

forehead big eyes stare baby blue wide fat and looking

shirts blue two

to each stretching arms

screaming

photo wall glass footballers

jeans faded grey   hairs grey black   chin doubles

tartan red blue dull shirt

dull apron orange   glasses thick black

black eyebrows thick enters

tidies table   leaves   whistling

The table is in the bar. They sit in the bar. They sit at the table. They talk at the table.

The bar is dim. The door is open. The sun comes in.

They talk.

They talk.

The bar is cooler. They are at the table. They talk.

They are at the table. They lift the drinks. They sip the drinks. They talk.

She looks round the bar.

She looks at the walls. She looks at the pictures on the walls.
He talks. The song plays.

He takes off the jacket. He puts the jacket over the back of the chair.

It is cooler in the bar. The sun is outside. He talks. It is darker in the bar. The music is on. She looks at him. She talks.

The door is open. She talks. She looks at the men come in. He looks at the men come in. She talks. The song plays.

The ice melts in the drinks. The men walk to the bar. The men stand at the bar. She looks at the men.

The song ends and the next song starts.

She sips the sip of the drink. The drink is cold and she talks. She looks at his eyes. He looks at her eyes. He talks. The lips move. She looks at the lips move. She looks at the eyes. She listens to the words. She listens to the song.

The men are at the bar. The men order beers and they drink. She looks at the men. The song is on. He listens to the song. It is cooler in the bar. He listens to the words. She sips the sip. He looks at her sip. She looks at him. The sun is through the door. She sips the drink. The ice is in the bottom. They sit at the table.

whistling tune bits

last coffee   pocket tobacco   up

around table corner   under footballers blue white

up four steps

door double brown back pushed

dull tiles red   past counter   glass

thanks   glass door

                         CLOSED

pull   step out   down steps

                              to pavement white sun

He pushes. He sweats. The light is hot. He pushes across.

The grass is lines. The lines are grass. The grass is cut. The grass is lines.

He pushes it. He sweats.

The lines are straight. He cuts the lines. He pushes across the grass and cuts the lines straight and sweats. The sun is brightness.

There is a knock. He stops. He looks round. He blinks.

There is at the window the woman.

He lifts the hand off the handle. He raises it. He blinks. The mouth of the woman moves. He blinks.

The hand wipes the sweat. He walks to the window.

She is opening the window. He walks to it.

There are the lines which are straight. The car passes. The blue is the sky and the white light is the sun.

He walks.

The hands wipe the trousers.

The window opens out. The woman leans out.

The woman speaks.

He nods.

She holds the tube in the hand.

He takes the tube in the hand.

He looks at the tube. The window is closing. He looks at the woman. The woman nods.

The hand wipes the trousers.

He looks the tube. He looks the tube. He looks the letters on the tube. He looks the words on the tube. He sweats. The sun is wet.

He flicks the top and squeezes. The right hand squeezes. The right hand squeezes out. The right hand squeezes it out into the left hand white. It is white. He looks at it white.

Sun is hot.

There is this whiteness. He rubs it on the right shoulder. The whiteness is cold.

He rubs it on the neck.

He squeezes it. It comes out. He rubs it on the arm.

He squeezes it. There is this white and he puts the tube on the window sill.

He rubs it on the hands. The hands rub on the shoulders. The hands rub on the arms. The hands rub on the neck.

He rubs it in. The hands try to rub on the back. He tries to rub it in. He rubs it in. It is cold.

The sun is high on lines. The lines are straight.

It is white. It rubs in.

The sun is white.

He rubs it in. Lines are green.

There is the smell of the cream. There is the smell of the grass. There is the sun. There is the t-shirt on the window-sill.

He puts the tube on the window-sill. He lifts the t-shirt from the window-sill. He wipes the hands on the t-shirt. He puts the t-shirt on the window-sill

He walks across green. The green is in lines. He walks to the mower. The lead is orange and the cars pass. He flicks the lead out of the way. The faces in cars look. He presses the handle and it starts.

The noise starts. He pushes. He holds the handle in and he pushes. He pushes it over the grass.

The grass cuts. The grass cuts into lines. The lines cut down onto the grass and the grass lies in lines.

There is the smell of cream. There is the smell of grass.

It is white and hot. He pushes.

Cars pass. The faces look the windows.

He pushes.

The sun is white. The sun is hot.

He lets go of the handle. He stops pushing.

The engine whirrs.

The engine whirrs down.

The handle is orange. The lead is orange. The mower is green and the grass is green and the sun is white.

The hand wipes the trousers. He sweats.

He walks off the grass. He walks on the concrete. He walks to the door.

Inside it is cooler. He walks up the corridor. He walks into the room.

The plug is black. The lead is orange. He turns it off. He unplugs it. He takes the plug to the window.

He pushes the window open. He places the plug on the window sill. The lead is orange and he closes the window.

The plug slides. The plug slides off the window-sill.   T h e plug falls. The plug falls to the concrete.

The faces look out of the cars.

The hands wipe the trousers. The back of the hand wipes the forehead.

He walks down the corridor. It is cooler. It is darker. He walks out of the door.

The brightness is a white.

He walks to the door. The door is the garage. He opens it.

It is dark. It is cold. He steps in.

He takes the spanner.

He walks out. He walks to the mower.

It is hot. It is bright.

The sun is hot. The sun is bright.

The metal of the spanner is cold.

There is the smell of the cream.

The bright is white.

He is kneeling.

There is the smell of the grass.

He kneels. The grass sticks. The grass sticks to the skin. The grass sticks to the hands. The grass sticks to the back.

Cars pass and faces look.

He tips the mower onto the side.

The grass sticks to the skin. The grass sticks to the sweat. The grass sticks to the cream.

The grass sticks to the blades. The grass sticks inside. There is the smell of it.

He scrapes it out.

    white sun blaze   steps down

    white pavement cracked black lines

left   shop   postcards   signs

cars parked blue blue white in heat

yellow lines road

man twenties combed hair blonde   rucksack green

old buildings   black railings

BUREAU DE CHANGE white on red

jeans white woman forties runs boots black

lights   wait

white cars   blue cars   black taxi   red man wait

four red phone boxes

green leaves of trees of park

behind railings black across road

shining heat

green man   cross

black railings

phone boxes shade of trees   sweating

left through railings to park

green bin

off pavement

under green

cream path

sweating

The print is rolled. The print is rolled up.
The print is a woman. The woman is naked.
The band is elastic.

heat   shine

green   cream path

heat on trees   pigeons   flap   fly

path diagonal cross park wide between

beds of red and yellow and green

sunlight leaves

to centre   cream slabs jigsaw circle in leaf shade

revs cars trucks vans as bus beeping reverses in distance

traffic

heat

slats brown bench wood metal frame black

sit   jacket lap

sun on bench   sun trees

dapple   footsteps   wing flap

cars distant   tarmac holes cracks grey

bag plastic turns white red white red breeze

wheels bike whirr

smell of heat

keys pocket jangle walks by

slabs cream slot circle

upturned cream concrete cups hold trees

concrete cream   brown wood   grass green

leaves green   wood brown   metal black

branches surround cream jigsaw centre

rubbish bins brown wood metal black

lined with bags plastic black

sunlight through leaves   birds swing flap

birds around jigsaw cream centre

three circles black raise concrete cup cream

cupping plants green brown thin

sniffing   people benches

sun

trunk thick brown

breaks one side of cream centre

tall   overhang

branches

breeze moves leaves   sun glitters

heat

running sniffing ground dog black small follows

jeans denim jacket glancing back

green collar jingling silver

The chairs are plastic orange. The posters are paper on the wall. The leaflets are colours on the table.

She sits on the chair. The chair is between the table and the wall. She looks at the table. The leaflets are on the table.

She looks at the leaflets. The leaflets are on the table. The piles of leaflets are three. The types of leaflet are three.

She lifts the leaflet. She looks at the leaflet. She puts the leaflet down.

She lifts the leaflet. She looks at the leaflet. She puts the leaflet down.

She lifts the leaflet. She looks at the leaflet. She puts the leaflet down.

She looks at the piles. She looks at the table. She looks at the wall. She looks at the posters. She looks at the colours. She looks at the floor. The carpet is blue.

She looks up.

She looks across the office.

She looks at the windows.

There are the windows of the buildings across the street. In one window there is the woman cutting the hair of the man in the chair. There are the hands of the woman moving and there is the mouth of the woman moving.

She looks at the office.

There are desks. There are people sitting at the desks. There are the posters on the walls. There are the papers on the desks. There are the computers on the desks. There are the people looking at the computers.

She looks at the table.

She bends forward. She bends down.

She lifts the bag.

She sits up. She opens it and looks inside.

She takes out the book.

She closes the bag is black. She puts the bag black back on the floor. The carpet is blue.

She opens. The corner is folded down.

She unfolds the corner is folded down.

She looks at the page. She looks at the words.

She reads.

There is the man in the suit. The man is in the suit. The man speaks again. The man is looking. She looks at the man.

She opens the mouth. She speaks. The man smiles. There is the clicking of the people typing on the keyboards.

She is folding the corner. She is standing. She is lifting the bag.

The bag opens. The book is in the bag. The bag closes.

heat   shadow flick sun

turn

195

black dog collar jingling silver

people crisscross cream centre walking   avoiding

jeans flared blue   crimson jacket   black rucksack girl

balding blue nose picks jeans man thirties

left of cream centre bench   bald ponytail

glasses large round   grey jacket

grey trousers   talks hand mobile phone black

far bench   suit dark blue   shoes black   shirt light blue

socks light blue   hair black   glasses   sandwich   book

left bench silver black bike propped

yellow hard hat beside him

yellow waistcoat plastic   trousers black

sandwich   beard black

plane hum

bench right   hat wool blue

blue jacket jeans   red rucksack   eating nuts

siren distance

car

black railings

brown trunks green leaves high

sun dapple

section of street in distance   people

shop awning

glass glints   lights   glitter   sign

red lorry   blue green truck   police car

red bus   yellow car

distant light   red

amber

green

above shops grey blocks in sun

against blue

grey blocks

grey black pigeons strut green necks on black tarmac

sudden panicked   all panic   flapping whirr away

flock whirring wings

heat   sky blue

click girl's heels

    There are the seats. The seats are in lines. The seats face forward.

    The seats are four hundred. The seats face the curtain. The seats face forward.

    The seats are blue. The curtain is black. The curtain is shut.

    The seats face forward. The seats tip up.

    The labels are on the backs of the seats. The labels are metal. The numbers are stamped on the metal.

The seats are in rows. There are the rows and there are the rows. The rows curve. The rows curve forward.

Now the people walk in. The people walk in and the people look at the curtain. The curtain is black. The people look at the seats. The seats are blue.

The people walk the aisles and look the seats. The numbers are on the metal. The metal is on the seats.

The seats are rows. The rows are seats. The people walk the rows. The people talk. The people point the rows. The people talk. The rows are blue. The metal is stamped. The people walk the rows.

The people walk and talk. The people bend. They bend forward. They look the numbers. The rows face forward. The people bend forward to look the numbers.

They talk. They push the seats. They sit.

The people sit on the seats. The people look at the curtain. The curtain is black.

The people look round. The people look at the people. The people look at the people. The people look at the programmes. The people look at the words. The people look at the photographs. The people point. The people talk.

The people walk the rows look the numbers.

The people stand to let the people pass.

The people look the numbers. The people sit. The people talk.

The people sit in the seats. The people fill the seats.

There is the talk. There are the programmes. There are the photographs.

The people turn. The people look behind. The thumbs touch the metal. The people look the people. The people look the people look the people.

The lights dim. The talk dims. The people look at the watches. The people look at the curtain.

The lights dim. The talk whispers. The people whisper to the people. The heads nod.

There is dark.

There are whispers.

There is a cough.

The curtain opens.

                              up from bench

        heat   girl's clicks

    cream path   bench asleep man

                        colours litter bin

      brown trunks thick   leaves green dark

  sun   flowerbeds   pink feet pigeon

        to black railings   out

    out of shade leaves into   bright

                        sun blaze

                  cracked pavement white

    man tall bald pointing map to woman

    three girls pointing out

          light   green man

      LOOK LEFT

                    cross   in sun

        blue car red van wait lights

                              red bus distance dust

to island

          girl teenage rucksack green mother short hair red

                              both in black

        white van round corner

                    wait   red

              bright light   sweat

              green   cross

                              to pavement

    The finger-tip presses the button. The television stops.
    He stands up. He looks at the room.
    The curtain is net. The net is white. He lifts it.
    There are no clouds. The cars are along the street. There is
no person in the street. There is the line is white on the sky.
    He looks.
    He lets it go.

He looks at the room. He walks to the sofa. He sits.

There is silence.

The remote control is black. He lifts the remote control. He looks at the remote control. The remote control is black. The finger-tip presses the button.

The television starts. The colours start. The colours move into the room. The sounds start. The sounds move into the room.

He looks at the colours and he listens to the sounds.

The finger-tip presses the button.

The colours change. The sounds change.

He sees the colours move. He hears the sounds move.

He presses the button.

There are the colours changing and there are the sounds changing.

He looks at the colours. He looks the colours move.

The finger-tip presses.

The colours change. The sounds change.

The finger-tip presses.

The television stops.

The television is black.

He looks at the room. He wipes the hands on the trousers.

He stands.

The doorway is out of the living room. The doorway is into the hall.

The stairs are out of the hall. The stairs are onto the landing.

The doorway is out of the landing. The doorway is into the bedroom.

There is the bed. There is the chest of drawers. There is the wardrobe.

The carpet is blue. The blue is dark.

The duvet is blue. The blue is pale.

The sky is blue. The blue is outside and pale and high and the line on it is white.

He looks at the room.

The pillowcases are blue.

The sunlight is in the glass.

The shoes are leather and the leather is brown.

The fingers untie the laces. The fingers pull open the laces. The fingers pull off the shoes.

The shoes are beside the wardrobe.

The shoes are on the carpet.

The shoes are brown.

The carpet is blue.

He takes off the jacket.

He opens the wardrobe.

He takes out the hanger.

He hangs the jacket on the hanger.

The hands go into the wardrobe.

He hangs the hanger in the wardrobe.

The fingers touch the top button. The top button is buttoned.

He pulls off the tie. The shirt is white. The wire is inside the wardrobe door. He hangs the tie over the wire.

It is hot.

The fingers unbutton the button. The button is at the top. The shirt is white.

The line is white.

He walks to the bed. He sits on the bed. He lies on the bed.

The hands are behind the head. The sweat is under the arms. The sweat is on the shirt. He looks at the ceiling.

He sits.

The right hand unbuttons the left cuff.

The left hand unbuttons the right cuff.

The sunlight is across the bed.

The foot lifts up. The foot is on the knee.

He takes off the sock.

The foot lifts up. The foot is on the knee.

He takes off the sock.

He stands.

He walks to the basket.

He lifts the lid.

He puts the socks in the basket.

He drops the lid.

He looks at the room.

He walks to the window. He looks out.

The sun is a white on the street. The line is a white on the sky.

The sky is blue. The line is white on blue.

There are no clouds. There are no birds.

The car starts. The car in the street starts. The car starts in the street.

The lights flash. The lights flash red. The lights turn off.

The car drives down the street.

The car turns the corner.

The sound fades.

There is silence.

The street is empty.

The line is white.

The window is white.

He turns.

He walks to the door. He presses the switch. The light turns on.

He walks to the windows. The curtains are green. The curtains are green and heavy. He pulls them. The curtains are thick.

There is dust.

The light is in the room. The blue is duvet. The blue is light. The blue is dark. The blue is carpet.

He walks to the wardrobe. The fingers unbutton the button. The fingers unzip the zip.

There is the crack between the curtains.

He takes off the trousers. He turns the trousers upside down. He straightens the seams of the trousers.

The trousers hang over the arm.

The hand is in the wardrobe.

The hanger is in the hand.

The trousers are on the hanger.

The hanger is in the wardrobe.

The boxer shorts are blue.

The boxer shorts are in the basket.

He looks up. He lifts the hand.

The hand moves to the top of the wardrobe. The hand moves. The fingers touch magazines. The fingers take magazines.

He walks to the bed.

He lies on the bed.

The head is against the headboard and the magazine is in the hands.

The words are on the front. The photographs are on the front. The photographs are colours.

The words are inside. The photographs are inside. The photographs are colours.

He looks at the words. He looks at the photographs. He looks at the colours.

The pages turn.

The pillow-cases are blue.

The blue is pale.

The duvet is blue.
The blue is pale.
He looks at the photographs.
The photographs are colours.
The colours are photographs.
There is the sound of a car passing.
There is the line of sunlight between the curtains.

right along white pavement

CAR PARK

black top trousers flared girl teenage green rucksack

mother black top black jeans hair red short

scaffolding up

COMMISSION FREE

blue car yellow car white car red van

grey van brown bus open-topped white car

white car white van red bus black taxi

clock above overhang   in sun

hands metal   wrong time

      manhole cover shining

NOW SERVING

         bald man blue jeans

      window boxes   pink green

           HOT MEALS FROM £6.95

moped buzz

                   orange taxi

          light

             heat

        BAR SNACKS

         TO LET

   TAKE AWAY

                HOTEL

to crossing at green light

There is the spinning. It spins. It spins in the loft.

It spins. It spins in the loft. It spins in the dark. The loft is dark. It spins in the dust. The dust is in the loft.

There is the spinning.

There is the knock. The knock is sudden.

It spins.

There is the knock.

It spins.

There are two knocks.

The spinning stops.

It listens. The chest goes up and down. It listens. There is the dark. It listens. It listens in the dark. There is the heat. There is the silence.

It listens. It listens. The chest goes up and down.

It spins. It spins again in the dark.

There is the bang. The bang is sudden. The bang is loud. The bang is underneath.

It stops. It listens. The chest goes up and down.

It listens.

There are the voices. The voices are below.

The chest goes up and down.

It listens.

There are sounds.

There is the knock. The knock is sudden. The crack of light is sudden. There is the crack of light opening into the dark.

It spins. The chest goes up and down.

There are steps. It hears the steps. The steps are on the ladder. The steps get closer.

It spins and spins.

It spins faster.

past green light   crossing

    white concrete cuts grey pavement length

                    herring bone jacket talks beret

sun high white circle

blaze

spires and cranes in blue above trees bus

CONTROLLED ZONE

cones red across nearest lane

white arrow on blue sign

portaloo green plastic

tar smell

machine laying black thick wet black shining

hammering

PEDESTRIANS white arrow on red

man lights green

blue car

                              cross to bikes padlocked

under trees green   to red stands metal by railings black

              traffic noise

heat   sun

                    leaves reflected in big glass

                                              right

        phone boxes red two

      poster two girls teenage

green hair spiked with white yellow daisies in

                    fifties bald black glasses

              red bus   white car

                    left around corner

        green on blue   BE HIPPER

white car

MAJOR ROADWORKS

NEW APARTMENTS FOR SALE

She opens the fridge. She takes out the bottle. She closes the fridge.

She opens the cupboard. She takes out the glass. She closes the cupboard.

She turns off the light.

She walks into the hall.

She puts the bottle on the table. She puts the glass on the table.

She locks the door.

She opens the drawer. She takes out the box of matches. She closes the drawer.

She puts the box of matches into the pocket. The pocket is on the front of the dress.

She lifts the bottle. She lifts the glass. She turns off the light.

She turns.

She walks to the stairs. She walks up the stairs to the light.

She walks into the bathroom. She puts the bottle on the floor. She puts the glass on the floor.

She takes out the box of matches. She opens the box of matches. She takes out the match.

She closes the box of matches.

She walks to the windowsill.

She lights the match.

She lights the first candle on the windowsill.

She lights the second candle on the windowsill.

She shakes the match.

She puts the match on the edge of the sink.

She opens the box of matches. She takes out the match. She closes the box of matches.

She holds the box of matches in the left hand. She holds the match in the right hand. She holds the match in the right hand against the box in the left hand and she scrapes. She scrapes the match alight.

She lights the third candle on the windowsill. She walks to the bath. The match blows out.

She puts the match on the edge of the bath.

She opens the box. She takes out the match. She lights the match.

She lights the first candle on the edge of the bath. She lights the second candle on the edge of the bath. She lights the third candle on the edge of the bath.

She blows out the match.

She puts the box of matches into the pocket.

She lifts the second match. She walks to the sink. She lifts the first match.

She bends. She puts three matches into the bin under the sink. She stands.

She lifts the fourth candle on the windowsill. She lifts the third candle on the windowsill.

She lights the fourth candle from the third candle.

She puts the fourth candle on the windowsill. She puts the third candle on the windowsill.

She turns. She looks. She walks to the door.

She turns. She turns off the light. She looks.

She turns. She walks onto the landing.

She stops. She turns. She walks into the bathroom.

She walks to the bath. She bends. She puts the plug into the plughole.

She stands. She turns the hot tap. She turns the hot tap on.

The water falls into the bath.

There is the sound of the water falling into the bath.

She turns. She walks to the windowsill. She takes the jar off the windowsill.

She turns. She walks to the bath. She opens the jar as she walks.

She tips. She tips the jar. She tips the powder out. She tips the powder out of the jar. She tips the powder in. She tips the powder into the bath. She tips the powder out of the jar into the hot water falling into the bath.

She stops tipping. She screws the lid on the jar.

She turns. She walks to the windowsill. She puts the jar on the windowsill.

She turns. She walks to the bath. She bends. She turns the cold water tap on.

She straightens.

She turns.

She walks out of the bathroom.

She walks into the landing.
She walks out of the landing.
She walks into the bedroom.
She turns on the light.
She walks to the dressing table. She lifts the bottle.
She walks to the door.
She turns off the light.
She walks into the landing.
She walks out of the landing.
She walks into the bathroom.
She walks to the windowsill.

She unscrews the bottle. She tips the bottle. She tips the oil. She pours the oil. She pours the oil into the burner.

She screws the top back on the bottle. She puts the bottle on the windowsill.

She takes the candle out of the burner. She turns the candle on its side. She lights the candle from the second candle on the windowsill. She turns the candle upright. She puts the candle in the burner.

She turns. She walks out of the bathroom.

She turns. She walks out of the landing.

She turns on the light.

She turns. She walks across the bedroom.

She looks the street. The lights are on the street. The cars are on the street.

She looks the lights.

She looks the cars.

She pulls the curtains.

She walks to the bed.

She unbuttons the buttons on the dress.

She takes off the dress.

She walks to the wardrobe. She opens the wardrobe. She takes down the hanger. She hangs the dress on the hanger. She hangs the hanger in the wardrobe.

She reaches behind. Her fingers touch the clasp, her fingers push the clasp, and the clasp undoes.

She holds the cups against the breasts. She takes the straps down the shoulders. She slides the feet from the sandals.

She takes the cups from the breasts and then the breasts are naked.

She turns. She puts the bra on the bed.

She places the thumbs in the knickers. She places the thumbs in the elastic of the knickers. She bends. As she bends she pulls them down. She steps. She steps out twice. She steps out of the knickers twice.

She puts them on the bed beside the bra.

She turns. She walks to the door.

She pushes the door to. The dressing-gown hangs behind the door. She takes down the dressing-gown.

She places the right arm into the dressing-gown. She reaches behind. She places the left arm in the dressing-gown.

She pulls the dressing-gown. She pulls the dressing-gown around her. She ties the dressing-gown.

She turns. She walks to the chair. She lifts the towels.

She turns. She walks to the door. She pulls open the door. She turns off the light.

She walks onto the landing. She turns. She turns off the light.

She walks into the bathroom. She turns.

She closes the door.

She turns. She walks to the bath.

She bends. She puts the towels on the floor beside the wine. She puts the fingers in the water.

She stands. She turns. She walks to the door.

She undoes the dressing-gown. She takes off the dressing gown. She hangs up the dressing-gown.

She turns. She walks to the bath.

She bends. She touches the water.

She touches the water.

She stands. She turns off the cold tap.

She turns.

She walks to the window-sill.

The flames flick.

She lifts the clip.

The left hand holds the hair up.

The right hand clips the clip on the hair.

She turns.

She walks to the bath.

She bends.

She touches the water.

She kneels.

She lifts the bottle.

213

She holds the bottle in the left hand. She holds the cork in the right hand.
She pulls.
She places the cork on the floor.
She takes the bottle in the right hand.
She lifts the glass in the left hand.
She pours.
She sips.
She places the bottle on the floor.
She takes the glass with the right hand.
She sips.
She stands.
She sips.
She bends.
She touches. She stirs.
She turns the tap.
She stands.
She lifts the right foot.

sweating

NEW APARTMENTS

coach red blue green white double deckered

crossroad   lines yellow crisscross

red bus turns after coach

BE HIPPER green on blue

green trees centre street

shaded buildings tall old grey red

HAVE YOUR CREDIT CARDS JUST EXPIRED?

man ponytail

patch black tarmac

sun   heat   bright

lights turn red

left to crossing

red man wait

BOX OFFICE

green lights to orange

RESTAURANT

cars   dust

man twenties

two girls twenties   teddy bear rucksack

red car blue car   taxi

silver long coach

WORDS AND MUSIC

man round stomach out green t-shirt

looks books window

edge pavement   black bag brown boxes cardboard

against railings rust and black

TO LET

heat sweat

black taxi

hotel awning

flowerboxes red white purple

queued buses red

pedestrian crossing right

blue white striped t-shirt jeans blue trainers white

man   twenties   looks left

woman brown red fast food bag looks left

skirt stretch

LOOK RIGHT

LOOK LEFT

The office is the new one. They sit at the front. They are two. They wait. They face the room.

The sun is outside. The windows are open.

People come.

Men come in.

Women come in.

They sit.

They talk.

The two at the front sit. The two at the front wait. The two at the front watch the people come in.

The sunlight comes in. The sunlight comes in the windows. The sunlight is bright. The windows are wide. The sunlight is outside. The sunlight comes in.

The people come in. The people sit in the sunlight. They sit. They talk.

People come in. There are not enough seats. People stand.

They sweat. They talk.

The secretary turns. The secretary speaks to the treasurer. The treasurer nods.

The secretary stands. The people look at the secretary.

217

The secretary speaks.

The secretary speaks. The secretary looks at the treasurer.

The treasurer stands. The treasurer speaks. The treasurer sits.

The secretary speaks. The secretary asks the people watching. The secretary waits. The people look at the secretary. The secretary looks at the treasurer.

The secretary looks at the people. The secretary speaks.

People raise their hands. People look round. People look at people. People whisper.

The secretary speaks again. The hands go down. There are no hands.

People look round.

The secretary sweats. The secretary speaks.

The secretary looks at the treasurer. The treasurer writes.

The secretary turns. The secretary asks the people watching.

A hand lifts. People look round.

The secretary speaks.

The man stands.

The man speaks.

The man asks.

The people look at the secretary.

The man sits.

The secretary looks at the treasurer. The treasurer stands.

There is the sunlight. There is the sunlight in oblongs on the floor.

The treasurer looks at the man. The treasurer speaks.

A hand lifts. The treasurer looks at the woman. Everyone looks at the woman. The woman speaks.

The treasurer nods. The people look at the treasurer. The treasurer speaks.

The treasurer stops speaking.

The treasurer looks at the secretary. The treasurer sits.

The secretary asks. The secretary looks at the faces.

The secretary speaks.

Hands rise. People look round. People look at people. People whisper.

The secretary looks at them. The treasurer looks at them.

The secretary speaks. The hands fall.

The secretary speaks.

Three hands rise.

The people look.

The people look at the hands. The people look at the three.
The people look at the secretary.
The treasurer writes.
The secretary looks at the faces. The secretary speaks.

LOOK LEFT

round corner   long street in sun

TO LET red on white

SHOES

street white light

paper white bits stuck ripped lamppost

scaffolding opposite covered white yellow plastic

girl twenties   cardigan blue   dress blue

hair shoulder brown

bag patterns red black looking window

takes arm man trousers black

t-shirt black   shoes black   brown hair short window reflects blue cardigan crossing road

small feet   white arrows road

white paving stones

TO LET red on white

grey boxes metal phones electrical

traffic lights   yellow black boxes

button white   lit light

cross green

BUSES ON DIVERSION

red arrow on yellow

cars parked on pavement between trees

sun on white wood

boarding windows

above windows reflect railings buildings opposite

GB

green car   blue car blue car   white car

dust   light

bag plastic white moves

branches flapping white green leaves blue sky

sweating

sun heating red car pavement

back bumper hangs

back tyre left flat

front light left broken

red door buckled panel reflects sun

graffiti

cardboard boxes rubbish pile steps

white van windows painted white

into sun   white

looking   cross

The sun is on the pavement. The sun is on the window. He walks in.

There are seven people in. It is cooler. He sweats.

The girl stands. The girl is behind the counter. The girl looks up. The girl smiles.

He sweats. The piece of paper is in the pocket. The jacket is blue.

The fingers take out the piece of paper. He sweats. The letters are on the paper. The letters are black. The paper is white.

The fingers unfold. The fingers pass. The girl looks.

He speaks.

The girl looks at the piece of paper. She speaks.

The girl walks to the computer. The girl looks at the piece of paper. The girl looks at the keyboard. The fingers press the keys. She looks at the screen.

The girl walks to him. The girl smiles. The fingers pass the piece of paper. She speaks.

The piece of paper is white. The letters are black.

He nods. The fingers fold the paper. The fingers put the piece of paper into the pocket. The pocket is inside. The jacket is blue.

He takes off the jacket. He sweats. It is cooler. The sweat under the arms is cold.

The girl walks out from behind the counter. The skirt is black and the blouse is blue.

The girl walks. The girl walks to the back. He walks. He walks to the back.

The girl walks. The girl walks to the right. He walks. He walks to the right.

She looks at the shelves. He looks at the shelves. She speaks. She looks.

She looks along. He steps closer. He looks at the spines. She kneels on one knee. The tights are black. She looks along.

She reaches. She takes it out. She looks at it. She looks at the front cover. She stands.

She smiles. The fingers hold the book. The fingers hold the book out. She speaks. The nails are bitten.

He smiles. He speaks. He takes the book. He speaks.

She looks over his shoulder. There is the woman at the counter.

sun

cross into shade building overhang

trees bent from pavement to light

red car   blue cars   black taxi   white car

concrete bollards blunt cream

van white on pavement

plants   traffic noise

white short dress girl

twenties heels bare knees legs bare blonde long hair

suit black shirt white man unbuttoned neck eats crisps

hair greys

children boys two blonde look up at woman

building glass reflects

skyscraper   church tower

aerial spikes   trees   sky blue

                                              sun

cars parked white blue red silver yellow

        sun street

    pedestrian crossing   red lights

    black cars pass shine sun

blonde hair man forties   jumper blue reads bench

                pink flowers bed behind

        LOOK RIGHT

                cross black tarmac to grey pavement

    poster green red on bin beside telephone boxes two red

left   pedestrian crossing   lights red

white car passes sun white on windows

lights back red yellow

        building scaffolding yellow opposite

              LOOK LEFT

cross green lights behind

curly hair green sweatshirt man young jeans black

          cardboard under green trees

             brown bench wood

     CAFE   sunlight   heat

   green bin   white paint on lamppost

telephone box   red   over cobblestones

   fifties woman

white jacket black skirt black shoes stockings white hat

searches handbag black lifted on leg up

black rubbish bag plastic

The people walk in. The doors swing closed.

There is the sound of people talking. There is the sound of knives and forks on plates.

The people join the queue. People are in the queue. They lean forward. They look at the food. They lift the trays.

The people behind the counter are two. There is the man behind the counter and there is the woman behind the counter. The man behind the counter and the woman behind the counter wear white. The cap of the man is white. The cap of the woman is blue.

The man and the woman hold the plates in the left hands. The man and the woman speak to the people in the queue. The people in the queue look. The people in the queue point. The people in the queue speak.

The man and the woman lift the spoons. The man and the woman lift the spoons of food. The man and the woman lift the spoons of food onto the plates.

The plates are white.

The spoons are steel.

The people look. The people speak. The people point to the meat. The people point to the potatoes. The people point to the vegetables.

The man and the woman pour the gravy from the ladle. The man and the woman hand the plates to the people.

The people take the plates. The plates are warm. The people put the plates on the trays. The trays are brown. The people slide the trays along the rails. The rails are steel.

They slide to the tea machine and they slide to the coffee machine. They put the cups on the machines. They press the buttons. The coffee comes out. The tea comes out.

The cups are paper.

People open the fridge. The bottles are plastic.

People stand at the salad. People lift colours in spoons. They put colours in containers. The spoons are steel. The containers are plastic.

People queue with trays. People lift forks. People lift knives. People lift spoons.

The woman sits behind the till. The woman looks at the trays. The woman presses the buttons.

The sun comes through the windows and falls on the tables.

The woman speaks. The people hand the money. The till opens. The woman hands the change.

People look across the room. People holding trays look across the room. People holding trays look across the room at people sitting at tables looking.

People walk. People walk across the room. People walk across the room between tables.

People sit.

People take the plates off the trays. People take the cutlery off the trays. People take the packets of salt and the packets of pepper and the packets of sugar off the trays.

People lean the trays against the legs of the seats.

under tree bag black plastic

SPECIALIST DECORATOR'S MERCHANT

on pavement under sign JAZZ SHOP red on white

female legs long black tights   black flat shoes

from step one leg stretches on grey pavement

one knee lifted up

edge skirt   legs shoes

face body arms hands hidden by wall

smoke puffed out

hand flicks out ash in sun

under trees

green

past girl teenage shop step smoking sitting

skirt black black top   blue eyes looking

white lines tarmac zigzag

CINEMA red on white

FILMS in blue on white

NOW BOOKING

poster colours in sun

wall carving stone above men lions horses shields

IMPERIAL ROME

green bin

blue sky

green leaves of trees

woman bare legs short skirt

holds hand man   collar hair brown

black jeans   denim jacket

two white cars pass

blaze

LET BY

into square   traffic at lights   queue at theatre

AIR QUALITY IMPROVEMENT

black metal grey boxes

black red motor bike accelerates corner

newspaper flapping on

yellow lines painted on

road tarmac middle of square

       traffic accelerates   green lights

           into sun square down

sun down on red bus white cars yellow car van cars

siren distance

         heat   white

   tall blonde woman in grey   waits to cross

red double decked bus   red car

black taxi   red car

    yellow white plastic cones   arrows white on blue

         accelerating

The brick is red. The brick is small. The brick is in the tub.
The tub is blue. The bricks are in the tub. The tub is on the sofa.

She takes the brick. The brick is red. She takes the brick out of the tub. The tub is blue.

She looks at the brick. She sways.

The left hand holds the brick. The right hand holds the sofa.

She holds the brick. She looks at the brick. The brick is in the hand. She sings. She sways.

She turns. The hand leaves the sofa. She babbles.

She kneels. The floor is wood. She sways. The wood is pale. The hand places the brick on the wood.

She sings. She babbles. She stands.

The left hand holds the arm of the sofa. The sofa is leather. The leather is yellow. She sways.

She stands. She stands on tiptoes. She looks over the edge of the tub. She looks into the tub. She looks at the bricks. She babbles. The bricks are in the tub.

The hand reaches in. The hand takes the brick. The hand takes the brick out.

She looks at the brick. The brick is yellow. The right hand passes the brick to the left hand.

She stands. She sways. She sings. She looks at the brick.

She stands. She sways. She stands on tiptoes. She looks in the tub.

The hand reaches in. The hand takes the brick. The hand takes the brick out.

The brick is red.

She looks at the brick. The brick is red. She babbles.

She looks at the brick. She sings.

She looks at the brick in the right hand. The brick in the right hand is red. She sings.

She looks to the left. She looks at the brick in the left hand. The brick in the left hand is yellow.

She sings.

She sings. She looks at the yellow brick. She looks at the red brick. She looks at the yellow brick. She looks at the red brick.

She sings.

sun on white arrows on blue

pedestrians cross green lights

cars wait lights

couple old stop   join queue cashpoint

corner

traffic queue into distance between buildings high

sky blue sun blaze

cars silver red blue   taxis black   red bus

queue

heat and sweating

white trailer pavement piled green bags plastic

brown jacket man pulls holdall black on wheels

cracked paving

passes blue jumper woman thirties

jacket blue over left arm   hair curl red

TELEPHONE   red box

blue jacket

street crowd people   cars   traffic slow queue

ESTABLISHED 1914 back coach

buildings

blue sky

high   sun   down   white

ONE HOUR PHOTO

fat man   plastic bags   sweat

WATCH REPAIR

girl twenties black jeans t-shirt

books colours under arm

crossing between cars looking

BUREAU DE CHANGE

Men are on the pavement. Boxes on the pavement. Women the pavement. Children are on the pavement. Bags are the pavement.

The men walk. The women walk. The children walk. The men walk and the women walk and the children walk up and down the pavement in sun. They walk in both directions. They walk around the bags. They walk around the boxes.

The sun shines into the street. The sun shines on the cars. The sun shines on the men and the women and the children. The people walk. The cars drive. The people walk the pavement and the cars drive the street. The sun shines into the street.

It is the morning.

The man drives the lorry. The man stops the lorry. The men get out. The men are three.

The men walk onto the pavement. The men walk the pavement. The men walk to the bags. The bags are plastic. The plastic is blue. The blue is pale. The sky is blue. The line across is white.

The hands are in the gloves and the rubbish is in the bags. The gloves lift the bags. The gloves carry the bags. The bags are blue. The hands are in the gloves. The gloves throw the bags into the back.

Two walk back. They walk to the bags. They lift the bags.

They sweat in the street.

One stands at the back. There are the buttons. The finger is in the glove. The glove pushes the button. The machine starts. There is the noise of it.

The jaw opens. The jaw moves up. The jaw moves out. He looks in the lorry. There is the smell. The jaw moves down. It closes down. The jaw closes down on the bags. It pulls them in.

The people walk past. The cars drive past.

The men carry the bags. The men throw the bags in. The jaw drags back. The plastic is blue.

The man stands at the back. The men walk to the bags. The finger is over the button.

The cardboard is brown. The boxes are cardboard. They lift the bags. They carry. They throw in the bags.

They walk to the boxes. They walk to the boxes sweating. They lift the boxes. The gloves are yellow. They carry. They throw in.

There is the sun down on them. There is the shop that sells the clothes. There is the girl running out. There are the jeans that are blue. There is the box that she gives him.

He throws it in.

short hair woman wipes nose

BUREAU DE CHANGE

traffic queues to lights

pedestrians cross

INDIAN CUISINE

man forties   long hair pony-tail black   skinny

sunglasses black t-shirt white

brown pattern shirt open neck loose over jeans black

walks yellow lines edge road looking

sun on blue   cars white dust

girls two twenties tight t-shirts

one points side street

man tall

short hair   army trousers   white vest

white long lorry   black car red car

white coach tourists

black motorbike helmet   green car dark

three red buses

theatres   signs   colours

sweating

people queue sun

FIRST FLOOR

man   fat shaved head   t-shirt black   ring lip

touches belt white of woman jeans blue   white bra top

big blue tattoo at bottom tanned back

into jeans under white belt

sunlight falls down street

boy young plastic bag yellow over shoulder

CASINO

red bus red car   white car

red car   black car   noise revving bike

black blue striped t-shirt

blonde child white shorts looking up

couple forties hold hands walking

top down red sports car at lights man sunglasses black

taps wheel music

blue vest top   black skirt short

opening   street opening out

scaffolding over pavement up wall

                                    road widen

    into square people cars moving

    sunlight old buildings   tall   white

     moving   sun

                    heat

It is blue. It is carpet. The envelope is against the wall. He takes it. The carpet is blue. He turns. He kneels on the blue.

The dust is in the carpet

The envelope is brown. It is big. It is padded. He tips.

The coins fall out. They fall onto the blue.

There is the pile. The pile is silver and brown. The pile is on the blue.

He puts the envelope behind him.

He looks. He takes the handful. He puts the handful on the blue. He puts the handful on the blue between him and the pile. There is the silver and there is the brown.

He sorts. He sorts brown on the right. He sorts silver in the middle. He sorts brown on the left. The silver is in the middle. The brown is on the left and the brown is on the right and the silver is in the middle.

The sun is through the windows. The windows are open. There is the noise of the traffic in the street outside. He sweats.

The one pences are the brown on the left. The two pences are the brown on the right. The five pences are the silver in the middle.

He sorts.

He sorts the handful.

He lifts. He lifts a handful. He places the handful. He places the handful on the blue. He sorts the handful.

He lifts. There is silver and there is brown. He places the handful. He sorts.

238

He lifts. He places on the blue. He sorts them.

He lifts. He sorts.

It is five pence. The five pence is bigger than the five pences.

He turns. He lifts the envelope. He puts the five pence in it. He puts down the envelope.

He turns. He sorts.

He lifts the handful. He sorts the handful.

He lifts the handful. He sorts the handful.

He sweats.

It is foreign. It is silver.

He turns. He lifts the envelope. He puts the coin in. He puts it down. He turns.

The carpet is blue. The horn of the car is outside. He wipes the hands on the trousers. He looks at the window. The sun is through the window. The dust is in the light.

He lifts the handful. He sorts.

He lifts the handful. He sorts.

The carpet is blue. He stops. The pile is not there. There are three piles.

The pile on the left is brown. The pile in the centre is silver. The pile on the right is brown.

The pile on the left is brown and the pile on the right is brown and the pile in the centre is silver.

The carpet is blue and it is under him. The envelope is brown and on the blue.

He stands. He sits on the chair. The can is still cold. He opens the can. There is the hiss. He looks at the piles. The piles are three. He sips. The hands smell of metal.

He stands. He kneels. He puts the can on the blue.

The centre is silver. He takes the handful.

He counts ten.

He counts ten.

He counts ten. He counts ten.

He counts ten piles of ten.

He sips. He stands. He walks to the chest of drawers. He opens the drawer. The plastic bags are in the drawer. The plastic is transparent. The letters are black on them.

He walks. He kneels. He sips. As he sips he reads. He looks at it. He reads the words.

The bag is small. The bag holds one hundred five pences. The bag holds five pounds of five pences.

He puts the can on the blue.

He holds it open. He counts. He counts one by one. He counts them in one by one.

Sweat trickles into the eye. The back of the hand wipes the eye. The cars pass outside.

He counts them in. He counts five pences in. He counts ten piles of ten five pences in.

He folds the top. He places it on the blue to the right.

He sips.

He takes the handful. He counts. He counts into piles.

He counts ten piles of ten coins.

He holds it open and he counts them in. There are ten. He counts them in. There are ten. He counts the coins in.

He folds the top.

He sips.

He folds five.

There is the silver. The silver is the pile. He counts it. There are eighteen. There are not enough to fill.

He takes the bag. He holds the bag. He holds the bag open. He puts them in. He puts eighteen in.

He folds. He turns. He puts it on the envelope. He puts it on the brown. The brown is on the blue.

The sun is a diamond.

He turns. He lifts. He reads.

The bag is small. The plastic is transparent. The letters are black. He reads.

The two pences are brown. The bag holds fifty. The bag holds one pound.

He sips.

He lifts. He counts. He counts them in.

He folds.

He lifts. He counts. He counts them in.

He folds.

He lifts eight bags. He counts. He counts into eight bags.

He folds eight bags.

There are eight bags.

There are twenty-eight two pences left. There are not enough to fill.

He lifts the bag. He puts the two pences in the bag. He folds the bag. He turns and he puts it on the envelope.

There are thirteen bags. The bags are on the blue.

There are two bags. The bags are on the brown.

The sun is on the back. He sips. He sweats.

It holds one pound. It holds one hundred one pences.

He lifts it. He counts them. He folds.

He lifts it and he counts them. He folds.

He lifts it and he counts them and he folds.

He sips.

He lifts. He counts. He folds.

He lifts. He counts and folds.

He lifts and counts and folds.

The hands are wet.

He lifts and counts and folds.

He lifts, counts, folds.

There are eight bags.

There is one penny. There is not enough to fill.

He lifts the penny. He lifts the bag. He puts it in. He folds.

He turns and places it on the envelope.

There is nothing. There are bags.

He stands. He sits. He tips the head. He tips the can. He swallows.

The sun is across the knees.

There are twenty-four bags. The hands smell of metal.

There are twenty-four bags.

There are twenty-one bags on the blue in the sun.

There are three bags on the brown in the sun.

The dust is on the window. The carpet is blue and the envelope is brown and the envelope is on the carpet.

He stands. He walks. He opens the drawer.

The plastic is white. The letters are red.

He walks. He opens it. He kneels. It is big.

There are twenty one bags. He lifts the handful. He puts the handful into the bag.

There are fifteen bags. He lifts. He puts the handful into the bag.

There are eleven bags. He lifts the handful. He puts it in.

There are seven bags. He lifts the handful. He puts the bags into the bag.

There is one bag. He lifts it. He puts it in it.

There is one bag. He lifts it. He puts the bag beside the chair.

He wipes the mouth. The can is empty. He smells the metal.

There is the bag of bags. There are twenty one bags in one bag. The bags are in the bag. The coins are in the bags.

The coins are in the bags and the bags are in the bag.
There are three bags on the envelope. He lifts the bags.
There is the envelope. He lifts it.
He puts the bags in the envelope. He puts the envelope against the wall.
There is one bag. There is one bag beside the chair. He lifts the bag. He walks. He opens the drawer. He puts the bag in the drawer. He closes the drawer.
The back of the left hand wipes the forehead.
He walks out. He walks up. He walks in.
He turns the tap.
He wets the hands. He soaps the hands.
He rinses the hands. He soaps the hands.
He rubs the hands. He rinses the hands.
He soaps the hands. He rinses the hands.
The water is hot. He soaps.
He rubs. He rinses them.
He turns it off. The pattern is on the glass. He dries.
He walks out. He walks down. He walks in.
He makes tea.
He walks out. He walks in. He sits.
He sips.
He looks.
The sun is a diamond on the carpet.
The envelope is against the wall.
He sips.
The hands smell of metal.

                                    white buildings

sun

cars buses taxis accelerate cross square

                        tall white buildings

heat

people walking walking looking walking waiting looking

under blue high

red cars white cars red buses

blue t-shirts   black trousers   long hair

blue jeans   red tops   spiked hair

woman looking at child points up

two teenagers waiting looking

man woman sixties cross between cars at lights in heat

lights changing   orange   green

flag red on white against blue top building waving

yellow lines

left

UNDERGROUND

down steps

darker

white lights blur reflect white tiles

circle area   UNDERGROUND   white tiles

people moving walking talking

heat

glass lights   white roof

people

TO TRAINS

black arrows on white

PLATFORMS 3 & 4

boys girls teenage shouting blue jeans queue barriers

waiting laughing tickets hands

PLATFORMS 1 & 2

voices calling talking   trains distance

                    laughing shouting   feet

        turnstiles rattle

            ticket machines queues waiting watching

                                                    heat

                                    noise

                grey concrete

The dress is red. The dress is on the chair.

            queues   ticket machines gleam

        walk round circle   to opposite end

tunnel cream grey yellow

        lights ceiling reflect cream grey yellow tiles walls

                colours posters   people walking

yellow tiles to steps   sunlight up at end

up steps toward light

hems legs jeans red heels coming down

handrail black up

to blue sky high   heat   sun   heat

bright   light

people   crowds

people looking   walking   shops

LOOK RIGHT

fat man twenties short hair   shirt checked green white

girl fat twenties   hair short   hooded top green

railings   traffic   taxis

RESTAURANT

street long   tall buildings distant in sun under blue

bus brown yellow open top   tourists sunglasses

                                   two men camcorders

                        blue taxi   green car

          blue jeans carries plastic bag blue

                        PASTA

                        BUS LANE white on red

          red lights under red flags over pavement

          red double-deckers two

lorry white   men unloading boxes brown

                        people walking looking talking

          people traffic moving sun

                                   sweating

                        flower boxes red green

   sunglasses   pavement bag paper brown turns   heat glass left   glass windows books colours

SCAFFOLDING green on white

blue lorry dust parked

down left   pavement grey

left   glass doors reflect sunlight

bald man suit pushes glass revolving   follow

walk in

push glass door   revolving sun   around

out   to glass steel shining white stone

The telephone is on the table. The table is at the bottom of the stairs. The telephone is ringing.

She lies on the bed. She looks at the television colours. She listens to the television sounds. She listens to the telephone ring.

The telephone rings. She listens to the telephone ring. She listens to the door downstairs open.

The telephone stops ringing.

She listens. She looks at the door.

She listens. The man calls.

She gets off the bed. She walks to the door. She opens the door. She walks onto the landing. She looks down the stairs.

The man is looking up. The man holds the phone. The man holds the telephone out. The man speaks.

She walks down the stairs. She smiles at the man. She speaks. She takes the telephone.

The man turns.

The man walks into the room. She lifts the phone to the mouth. The door closes. She speaks.

She speaks. She listens.

She speaks. She listens.

She speaks. She listens. She laughs.

She speaks. She listens.

She speaks. She listens.

She speaks. She listens. She laughs.

She speaks. She listens.

She speaks. She listens.

She speaks. She listens. She nods.

She speaks. She listens. She speaks. She puts the phone down.

She turns. She walks up the stairs.

The door is open. She walks into the room. The television is on. She closes the door.

She lies on the bed.

She looks at the television.

entrance   shining glass wide steel   light on stone

metal   sun   down

steps

white shine tiles   cooler

glass   metal

tables black   books piles

TOP 20

covers colours facing outwards

paperbacks   hardbacks   men women looking

GIVE A BOOK

posters   banners   colours

HERE AND NOW

white light

up steps

HUMOUR

PEOPLE

books fill   black shelves

people looking   couples   singles

cooler   LIFTS

up stairs   shine

metal handrail

light shine down on stairs through wide windows

GENTLEMEN

Cars go. Cars go under. Lorries go under. Vans go under. Cars go under. Coaches go under and buses go under. Cars go under.

In light.

Cars go under. People cross. There are the women. The women cross. Cars go under. The women push the prams. The light is bright. People cross. There are plastic bags.

The cars go under. Boys lean over. The boys watch. The boys watch cars. The cars go under. The boys lean. The boys watch cars go under. Cars go under.

Buses go under. Boys watch lorries go under. The boy is short. The boy leans over. The cars go under. The boy stands on the tips of the toes. Cars go under. He holds the top rail. Buses go underneath. The boy watches the cars go under. The boy watches cars go under in sun.

Cars go under in sun. They sit in the cars. They sit at the wheels. The windows are down and they go under. The radios play the music. The glasses are on black. They look at the cars ahead. The cars ahead go under. They go under. They look ahead up the road.

Six lanes. Three lanes and three lanes. Cars go under.

The lines are white.

Sun.

Cigarette drops. Cigarette hits tarmac. The tarmac is black and the sparks are red.

Boys lean over.

GENTLEMEN past

251

up past light through windows

FIRST FLOOR white on red

wide out left to right space

shelves   tables

people

light

tiles wood   green carpet green red

GIVE THE GIFT OF INSPIRATION

men two twenties shirts white tills black counters

FICTION

colours books red green blue

covers   paintings   photographs   titles

BLACK INTEREST

light shines in windows wide

ANTHOLOGIES

CLASSICS

spectacles girl twenties blouse white looking CRIME

turn

SCIENCE FICTION AND FANTASY

to stairs

He sways. It is dark. It is hot.

It is the street. The street is dark. The street is long. The street is empty.

He walks the street.

The wall is to the right. The wall is high. The bricks are red.

The street is to the left. The street lights are lit. The flats are on the other side.

He walks down the street. It is dark. The street lights are yellow. The yellow is on the tarmac. The tarmac is black.

He walks down the street. The phone box is red. The yellow is on the red. The red is on the other side. He crosses.

There are no cars and there are no people.

He pulls the handle. The handle is metal. The door opens. He steps in.

There is the smell of the pee. He leans against the side.

The car drives closer. The car drives closer. The car drives past. He sways.

He looks at the phone.

The box is silver. The buttons are blue. The handset is black. The letters are the instructions.

The fingers go into the pocket. The fingers take the coins. The fingers take the coins out of the pocket. The coins drop.

The coins drop onto the floor.

The floor is concrete.

He sways. He bends. The coins shine. The phone box light shines on the coins and the street light shines on the coins. The fingers stretch. The coins are yellow. He staggers. He stops.

The left hand touches the glass in the side of the phone box. He bends. The fingers stretch.

The tips of the fingers touch the coins. The tips of the fingers pull the coins together. The fingers lift the coins.

The fingers pass the coins to the left hand.

He looks. There are two more coins.

He bends. He sways. The tips of the fingers stretch out. The tips of the fingers touch the coins. The tips of the fingers pull the coins together. He lifts the coins.

He stands. He sways. There is the smell of the pee. There is the yellow of the light. There is the black of the handset.

He lifts the handset. He holds the handset to the ear. He listens. There is the tone.

The head holds the handset between the head and the shoulder. The left hand passes the coins to the right hand.

He listens.

The right hand lifts up. The right hand opens. The eyes look at the coins. The thumb pushes the coin to the fingertips. The eyes look at the slot. The fingers push the coin into the slot.

The left hand takes the handset. He holds the handset to the ear. He listens. There is the tone.

He looks at the numbers. The numbers are on the buttons. The buttons are blue.

The right hand goes into the pocket. The right hand opens. The coins go into the pocket.

The ear listens. The tongue licks the lips. The eyes look at the numbers.

There is the smell of the pee. There is the sound of the tone. There is yellow light.

He looks at the numbers. The numbers are worn. The numbers are on the blue.

He looks at the numbers. He presses the numbers.

He stands. He sways. He waits. He listens.

There is the sound of the connection.

There is the light on the street.

The phone at the other end starts to ring.

He listens.
The phone at the other end rings.
He listens to the phone at the other end ring.
He listens.
The phone rings.
He listens.
He puts down the phone.

stairs flights three wide

                windows   sunlight

        LADIES

   open out far left right   space widens

           tiles floor shining black white

           JUICE BAR

men girls twenties aprons talk

        YOUR FREE CATALOGUE

sit   black seat   back to juice bar   cooler

  face stairs   sweat wipe forehead   jacket lap

  women two thirties hair neat short walk to CHILDREN'S

black stand   books facing out

BESTSELLERS

ENGLISH LANGUAGE

FOREIGN LANGUAGE

LINGUISTICS

light   people   books

look   stand   cross tiles   to stairs

The fridge is white.
The fridge is tall.
The doors are two.
The door at the top of the fridge is one third of the length
of the fridge.
The door at the bottom of the fridge is two thirds the length
of the fridge.
The door at the top of the fridge is the freezer.
The door at the bottom of the fridge is the fridge.

LINGUISTICS

wide steps   three flights   white stone

windows   sunlight

LADIES

opens out right left   wide

GAMES   SPORT   TRANSPORT

THIRD FLOOR

map white on black

PHILOSOPHY

woman fifties looking shelves

walks to till   perfume   skirt   long black

RELIGION

LITERARY CRITICISM

MIND BODY AND SPIRIT

couple twenties   COOKERY

girl twenties sits edge chair pulls hair behind ear

looking book blue hardback   photos

CRAFTS

turn

to cream stairs

flights

steps

sunlight from   windows

LADIES

widens out left right   open

FOURTH FLOOR

till queues   PLEASE PAY HERE

SOCIOLOGY

INTERNET STATIONS

people at computers

ACCOUNTANCY

GENDER STUDIES

BUSINESS

PSYCHOLOGY

turn   sweat   to stairs

She is next. She takes two steps. She stops. She looks at the machine.

She opens the bag. She takes out the purse. She opens the purse. She takes out the card. She looks at the machine. She puts the card into the slot.

The card slides in.

She looks at the screen. The sun is white. The sun is white on the screen. She leans forward. The hand shades the screen. She looks.

The letters are on the screen. The screen is black. The letters are green.

She looks at the screen. She looks at the buttons. She presses the buttons. She presses five buttons.

The machine beeps.

She looks at the screen. She leans. She shades. She looks.

She presses one button.

The machine beeps.

She looks. She leans. She shades. She looks.

She presses one button.

The machine beeps.

The hair is long. The sun heats the hair.

There is the whirring.

The people walk up and down the street.

The machine beeps. The machine beeps. The card is out.

The card is out half way. She looks at the card. She takes the card.

Notes slide out. She looks at the notes. The machine beeps. The notes are out half way. She takes the notes.

She folds the notes as she is looking at the screen. She looks at the machine.

She puts the notes in the purse. She puts the card in the purse.

She looks at the machine. The receipt is out half way. She takes the receipt.

She turns. She turns into the sun. She steps away.

She looks at the receipt. She reads the receipt.

The man steps to the machine.

She folds the receipt. She puts the receipt in the purse. She stops.

She stands. She stands in the sun. She closes the purse. She opens the bag. She puts the purse in the bag. She closes the bag.

She looks up. She looks along the street.

up past   GENTLEMEN

past   sunlight   windows

                   cream steps

                   opening out

FIFTH FLOOR

ART A-Z

tills ring bells

                     sunlight

people   looking

MONOGRAPHS

girl thirties hair long black skirt jacket white turns pages

looks up   looks   looks down

FASHION AND PHOTOGRAPHY

girl desk top tight white hair short dyed red talks phone

FILM, TELEVISION AND MUSIC

wide windows   sun   sky

FIFTH FLOOR BAR

POETRY

boy teenage   jeans shirt black   sits chair black magazine

DRAMA

There is the sky. The sky is blue.
There is the plane. The plane is silver.
The plane is in the sky.
The plane moves. The plane moves on the sky. The plane
moves.

There is the sun. The sun reflects on the plane. The plane is high. The plane is on the blue.

There is the line. The line is white. The line is behind the plane.

There are the men. The men are on the bench.

There is the street.

The men look at the street.

There is the dog. The dog is on the pavement. The dog lies.

There is the lead. The lead ties to the bench.

The tongue is pink. The tongue is out. The tongue is wet.

The dog pants.

The eyes of the dog open. The eyes of the dog look at the street. The dog pants. The eyes close.

The men look at the street. The men look at the people. The people are on the street.

There are the cars. The cars are on the street. The men look at the cars.

The men do not speak. The men look at the street.

One man smokes a cigarette. The dog pants.

The eyes of the dog open. The eyes of the dog look at the street.

There is the plane. The plane is silver.

There is the sky. The sky is blue.

There is the line. The line is white.

sunlight

people looking

DRAMA

to stairs   cream   wide   light

LADIES

262

windows   flights three up   in sun

      doors two   shut   dark

                  turn   turn in light

down   stairs   sun

                                        LADIES

                        FIFTH FLOOR

wide   down

            teenage girl boy coming up

                                    down

                              GENTLEMEN

        FOURTH FLOOR

                        INTERNET STATIONS

      sweating   wide   in sun

        three women foreign fifties talking

                              stairs

        LADIES

                                        THIRD FLOOR

              turn

                          sun   on steel

LADIES

                      JUICE BAR

        turn into sun

              man forties suit shelves looking paperback

                    down

                                              LADIES

                          FIRST FLOOR

        wooden tiles pale

                              wide   space

sun

GENTLEMEN

down

left

The jacket is on the grass. The sun is on the grass. The can is on the grass. He sits on the grass. The coke is in the can.

He looks at the park. He looks at the people. He looks at the trees. He opens the packet.

The sun is on the grass. The sun is on the trees. The sun is on the buildings behind the trees. The sun is on the glass of the windows of the buildings behind the trees.

He lights the cigarette.

The leaves are on the trees. There is the heat. There is the heat of the sun. The sun is white.

There is the sound of the traffic in the distance. The coke is in the can. He smokes. The left hand holds the guitar in his lap.

The smoke is a line up. He sits on the grass. He smokes. He looks at the path. He looks at the people on the path.

He places the guitar on the grass. He lifts the can. He sips.

He looks at the grass. The leaves are on the trees. The sun is on the trees. The grass is green.

He places the can on the grass. He lifts the cigarette to the lips. He smokes.

He smokes it. He flicks it. He flicks it out towards the path.

The path is black. There is the sound of the traffic in the distance.

The leaves are on the trees. He sips. He places it down.

The sun is on the grass. The sun is on the trees.

left

three steps   up

wide   floor shining   glass shining

black tables   shelves   books

woman suit at till   paper white speaks man twenties desk

TOP 20

left

through tables   cross tiles

up steps   glass shining

light outside

cars traffic people movement distorted through glass

glass   push

out   revolving

into   light   heat

There is the case. There is the CD. The CD is on top of the case.

The CD is a circle. The hole is in the circle. The hole is in the centre of the circle. The hole is a circle.

There are three sections. There are three sections and there are two colours.

There are three sections on the CD and there are two colours on the CD.

There is the section across the middle. The section across the middle is the biggest section of the three sections. The section across the middle is the size of the two other sections put together.

The colour of the section across the middle is white.

There is the section across the top. There is the section across the bottom. The section across the top is the same size as the section across the bottom and the section across the bottom is the same size as the section across the top.

The section across the top is yellow.

The section across the bottom is yellow.

The section across the top is the same colour as the section across the bottom and the section across the bottom is the same colour as the section across the top.

There is the dust. The dust is on the CD.

There are the letters. The letters are on the CD.

The letters on the section across the middle of the CD are above the hole. The letters on the section across the middle above the hole in the CD are cursive. The letters on the section across the middle above the hole are cursive and in two lines.

There are the symbols. There are three symbols. The symbols are on the CD.

The symbols are on the section across the middle of the CD. There is the symbol underneath the hole. There is the symbol to the left of the hole. There is the symbol to the right of the hole.

There are three symbols.

There are the letters. The letters are on the CD.

There are letters around the edge of the CD. The letters are words and the words are a sentence. The letters are words and are a sentence and are around three quarters of the edge of the CD. The letters are a sentence.

There is the CD. There is the case.
The dust is on the CD.
The CD is on the case.

into light noise white   blaze   heat

blue cars red car red bus

BECAUSE LIFE'S TOO SHORT black on white

left man shirt blue white check sleeves roll up

baseball cap green looks window

PHARMACY

sky blue high

stone edge paving juts up

red lights   pedestrian crossing distance

sun length street   sweat   white

woman forties   tan shorts smoking

man twenties top black blue stripes sunglasses

girl blonde long eye shadow green   looks map looks up

queue white van red bus black taxis cars in heat

brightness

BUS LANE

arrow white on red painted on road

orange lights

flag banners red opposite outside wave ART

fat woman legs

clock over pavement   roman numerals   no hands

sports car yellow accelerates side street

girl twenties breasts big t-shirt watching traffic as crosses

girls four teenage wait lights

black taxi indicates in

blue sky heat

AVAILABLE FOR PRIVATE FUNCTIONS

in chalk white on black against wall

gold lamps

blue   white heat

car white   van white limousine black   red bus

lights distance red

scaffolding covered green plastic

box cardboard small white beside

bag plastic black beside

black railings

sun overhead straight down

sun overhead straight down

black flared trousers flowers around hem teenage girl

holds book looks out cafe window

                    bike chained railings

                CAFE

        green t-shirt

    spectacles girl twenties   high heels turns to

        white t-shirt man   blue jeans

CAPPUCINO

            queue at lights

                            left

                TAKE AWAY

        through open glass doors into cool

    The cat is on the table. The girl is on the chair.
    The hair of the cat is orange. The hair of the girl is blonde.
    The girl looks at the cat. The cat has the eyes that are closed.
The girl looks at the cat.
    The sun comes in. The sun is white. The sun is on the table.
    The sun is on the cat. The sun is hot. The cat heats. The sun
heats the cat. The cat heats in the sun. The cat is warm in the
sun. The cat sleeps in the sun.
    The chair is at the table. The girl is on the chair. The girl
looks at the cat. The cat is on the table.

The girl looks at the cat. The pencil is in the hand and the paper is on the table.

The paper is white. The pencil is red. The lead is black.

The girl looks at the cat. The girl looks out of the window. The girl looks at the cat. The girl looks at the paper.

The paper is white. The girl leans. The pencil touches the paper. The pencil marks. The marks are on the paper. The marks are black and the paper is white.

The girl looks out of the window. The sky is blue. The girl looks at the cat. The eyes are closed. The girl looks at the paper. The fingers move. The fingers move the pencil. The lead stays. The fingers move the pencil on paper. The fingers move pencil over the paper and the black is on.

The eyes open. The eyes look at the girl. The fingers mark. The eyes look at the eyes of the girl. The eyes of the girl look at the paper.

The sun is white. There is the sound of the pencil as it marks. The eyes close.

The eyes of the girl look from the paper. The eyes of the girl look at the cat. The eyes of the girl look at the orange of the cat. The eyes of the girl look at the sun on the orange of the cat.

The girl looks out of the window. The sun is in the window. The girl looks at the paper. The pencil is between the fingers. The fingers mark black on paper white.

The cat is in the sun. The eyes open. The eyes look at the girl.

The fingers stop. The girl looks up. The girl looks at the cat.

The eyes of the cat look at the eyes of the girl. The eyes of the girl look at the eyes of the cat.

out of sun street   through glass doors open

   shade

                              walls green red yellow blue

   glass counter queue   black tills

272

  cooler

        sweat

                        sandwiches under glass

beard fifties   black coffee green cup

                        floor wooden pale

                people sitting tables wooden

    mirrors reflect green red blue yellow

        long hair girl teenage boys two teenage long hair pay

            for   sandwiches cans fruit juice

    rucksacks small   leave   talking   sweat

        girl twenties blue shirt black trousers counter asks

                        blue eyes

    There are people. There are people in the park. There are
people in the corner of the park.
    There are people. There are people walking. There are peo-

ple walking along the path. There are people walking along the pavements. There are people walking over the grass.

There are people. There are people walking into the park. There are people walking through the park. There are people walking to the corner of the park.

The sun is on park. The sun is on the people. The sun is on the corner of the park.

There are men. There are women. There are children. There are men and there are women and there are children in the corner of the park.

The sun is on them. The sun is on them.

There are people. There are people standing. There are people standing in groups. There are people standing alone.

There are people. There are people sitting. There are people sitting on benches. There are people sitting on grass.

The sun is on them in the corner of the park.

There are people. There are people with the placards. There are people holding the placards. There are people holding out placards to people.

There are people. There are people with the papers. There are people holding the papers. There are people selling the papers to people.

There are banners. There are people opening banners. Banners open. There are people lifting up banners and there are banners opening. The banners lift. There are people holding them.

People look placards. People read placards.

People buy papers. People read papers.

People look banners. People read banners.

There is the girl. The girl runs. The girl runs through the trees. The girl runs in sun over grass.

There is the man. The man calls. The man calls the girl.

The girl stops. The girl stops running. The girl turns. The girl looks. The girl looks back. The girl looks back at the man.

There is the woman. The woman walks the path. The path is black and walks to the banner. The banner is up. The woman speaks to them. They give the woman the leaflets. The woman takes the leaflets.

The woman speaks. They speak. The woman nods. The woman turns. The woman walks.

There is the man. The man stands. The man stands alone.

The placard leans. The placard is against him. The beard is grey. The man looks.

The glasses are round. The woman walks. The woman hands to the man. The man speaks. The man smiles. The woman walks. The man reads.

There are people. There are people in a group. There is the group of people. The group is under the banner. The group stand. The group look the sheets. The group start to sing. The sun is on singing.

The eyes look. The eyes look through the glasses. The eyes look through the glasses at the singing. The glasses are round. The beard is grey. The fingers scratch the beard. The eyes look down. The eyes read.

There is a woman. The jeans are blue. The woman walks through. The woman shouts. The woman shouts the people. They look at her. The woman points.

There are people. They lift the banners. They pick up the placards. They hold the papers against the chests. They put the leaflets in the pockets.

There are the groups. The groups walk. The groups walk the path. The groups walk the path in sun. The groups walk the path to road in sun.

They talk. They look down the path. There is the sun. The sun is on them and white. There are the policemen and there are the policewomen. There are the policemen in the sun and there are the policewomen in the sun. The policemen stand in lines. The policewomen stand in lines. The policemen stand along the pavement. The policewomen stand in lines along the pavement. The policemen and the policewomen stand in lines and talk. The sun is on them.

The street fills. The people fill one side of the street.

The sun is high. The sun is higher. The sun is hotter.

People sweat.

The girl is in people. The girl pulls it up. The girl pulls up the jumper. The jumper is blue. The girl pulls up the jumper over the head. The t-shirt is white. The breasts are small. The breasts are in the t-shirt. The breasts are pushed against the t-shirt. The hands are in the jumper over the head in the sun. The breasts are small. The policewoman looks at the breasts. The girl blinks in sun. The girl ties round the waist.

The ball is yellow. They are three. They walk the path. There is the girl in front. The girl in front taps the ball. The ball is yellow. The ball taps into the air. The air is sun. The ball taps into the sun. The racquet taps the ball into the sun.

There are the girls behind are two. The girls behind walk behind the girl in front. The girls behind follow behind the girl in front. In the distance traffic sound. The girls behind two talk and they carry racquets. One of the two is tall. One of the two is the same height as the girl in front.

The sun is on them.

They talk. They look banners. They look placards. They look people.

The people start. They start the walking. They walk out. They walk out into the road. The walking is started.

There is the group of people that is singing. They are singing walking. There is the man blowing the whistle. He is blowing walking. There is the girl shouting into the megaphone. She is shouting walking. There is the group of people shouting back at her. They are shouting walking in the sun.

The sun is on them.

They walk the road. They walk the road in the sun. They walk the road in sun towards the bridge.

Behind there is the van. The van is white. The van is behind them.

The sun is on the van.

There is the van. There is the sunlight. The sunlight is white.

They pick up the cones. The van is white. They roll the tape.

The doors are open. They sweat. They put the cones in the back.

girl eyes blue shirt blue trousers black takes order

brown tray glass counter

sun traffic outside to left street

saucer red on tray

276

                                        plate green on tray

                sandwich plastic wrapped plate

                                        girl shaved head at till

        napkin red tray

        chocolate wrapped green on saucer red

                shaved girl sweat temple

        shirt blue trousers black stirs mug yellow

                machine metal trickles liquid brown

                takes jug stainless big steel   pours froth milk

                        powder chocolate shake

                                girl blue eyes   change receipt

        shaved girl looks up   lifts mug yellow to saucer red

        teaspoon long stainless steel saucer

                The light turns on.

The light turns off.

The light turns on.

The light turns off.

The light turns on. The light turns off and on. The light turns off.

The fingers lift the seat. The fingers unbutton the button. The light turns on. The fingers pull down the zip.

The light turns off. The fingers reach in. The fingers take the penis. The light turns on and the light turns off. The fingers take out the penis.

The fingers hold the penis. The fingertips hold the penis. The light turns on. The eyes look. The light turns off. The fingers point the penis.

He waits.

The light turns on. The fingers point the penis. The fingers point the penis at the bowl.

He pees. The pee comes out of the penis. The pee hits the side of the bowl. The penis pees the side of the bowl.

The light turns off. The pee comes out of the penis. He pees the side of the bowl. The light turns on and the light turns off.

The fingers move the penis. The fingers move the penis to the right. The pee comes out of the penis. The pee falls into the water in the bowl. There is the sound of the pee falling into the water in the bowl.

The light turns on. He pees. The pee is yellow. The light turns off.

The pee comes out of the penis. The light turns on. The light turns off. The light turns on. The light turns off. The pee comes out. There is the sound of the pee falling into the water in the bowl.

The light turns on. He points the penis. The penis is in the fingers. The pee comes out of the penis. The pee falls into the bowl. There is the sound of the pee falling into the water in the bowl.

The pee is the arc. The arc is into the bowl. The arc is from the penis into the water. The pee is the arc into the bowl. The light turns off.

The pee slows. The arc lowers. The sound of the pee falling into the water in the bowl changes. The pee arcs in.

The light turns on. The pee slows. The pee slows slower. The light turns off. He stands still. The drops come out. The drops come out of the penis.

The drops come out. The drops fall into the bowl. The drops are pee. The drops fall out of the penis into the bowl. Two drops fall onto the edge of the bowl.

The fingers shake the penis. The light turns on. The drops fall into the bowl. The drops fall on the edge of the bowl. The light turns off. The drops fall on the floor.

The light turns on. The fingers put the penis back. The fingers pull up the zip. The light turns on and the fingers button the button. The light turns off. The button is above the zip.

It is the dark. The fingers reach. He looks. The fingers feel. The fingers pull.

The water falls into the bowl. There is the sound of the water falling into the bowl.

He turns. He turns to the sink. It is the dark. The hand reaches out. The fingers feel. The fingers reach out for the tap.

The light turns on. The fingers take the tap. The fingers turn the tap. The water comes out.

The light turns off. The water is cold. The water falls on the hands.

The light turns on. He looks. The finger pulls it up. The soap is liquid. The soap comes out. The light turns off. The soap is in the hand. The hands rub the soap. The hands rub the soap in the hands. The hands are under the water. The hands rub. He rubs the hands. It is the dark. The bubbles are down the plughole. The water is cold. He rubs. The light turns on.

The fingers take the tap. The water comes out of the tap. The water drips off the hands. The fingers turn the tap. The water drips off the hands into the sink. The fingers turn off the tap. The light turns off.

He waits. The water drips off the hands into the sink. The water drips off the tap into the sink. He holds the hands up. He holds the hands up over the sink. The water drips.

The light turns on. The box is plastic. The box is on the wall. The box is on the wall above and to the right of the sink. There is the opening.

He moves. The light turns off. The hand moves. The fingers reach. The fingers are at the opening. The opening is empty.

It is the dark. The hands are wet. The fingers go into the box. The box is empty.

He stops. The light turns on. He looks. The box is empty.

The light turns off.

The hands wipe on the trousers.
The light is off.
The hands wipe the trousers.
The light buzzes.
The light turns on. The light turns off.
He turns. The light flicks. The light turns on. He walks to the door.
The light turns off. The right hand unlocks the door. The left hand pushes down the handle. The left hand pushes the door.
The door opens. The light is bright. The light cracks in.
The right hand reaches up to the light switch.
The light turns on.
He turns the light off.

brown tray   mug yellow   napkin red

green chocolate   red saucer

sandwich plastic   green plate

                  past glass to wooden stairs

                                                    down

        cooler

                                        glass   music

floor tiles stone brown

                              walls green orange

tables round wooden pale

chairs pale wood

corner   jacket back chair   sit

coffee sandwich off tray

tray to empty seat

green chocolate   unwrap

sweet   thick

wet melt

coffee   stir   powder chocolate froth

sip   coffee chocolate thick milk

froth chocolate smudge in mug

tear plastic   green yellow out   bread brown

edges green lettuce   cheese yellow

pickle sweet

thick taste

chew

table plastic tangle

bite taste

chew

drums

trousers crumbs   pickle taste sweet

second half   pickle finger   lick

bite

taste thick

pickle sweet   cheese

swallow

red napkin   wipe   crumple green plate

lick lip

coffee sip   chocolate thick coffee milk

jacket   packet green foil yellow   packet green

packet green white sheet

tobacco brown to white sheet

roll

tuck in

roll

lick

stick

lighter   flame   red

suck in

suck

red tip burn   suck in

ash

flick ashtray

smoke

smoke

The van is white. There are two lanes.
The car is green. The car is behind. The car is red. The car is
in front.
The white is dirty. Letters are marked in the dirt.
Sun shines on mirrors and glass.
The motorbike overtakes. The police car overtakes.

suck in

flick

orange wall   cool   music

out   relight

suck in

coffee thick   chocolate   milk hot

girls teenage three centre table sandwiches fruit juices

looks away   talking

     to right woman back thirties

    top black trousers black   legs cross

    shoulder hair brown   curls smoke

suck in

    opposite corner

    man girl twenties

    shirts blue trousers black

   read sheets white   write   talk   calculator

flick

coffee

    bobbed black hair girl   down stairs

   shirt blue trousers black   cloth

table   tidies onto tray   wipes

          PRIVATE green on black corner door

TOILETS green on black corner door   woman waiting

          suck in

                    out

green bowl table   sachets pink red blue

                         flick ashtray

                              sip

The sunlight is in the room.
The windows are open.
The blinds are open.
The desks are six.
The computers are six.
The people are four. The man is one. The women are three.
The four sit at the desks. The four look at the screens. The
four type.
The door opens. The woman is one. The woman walks in.
The flowers are in the hands.
The hair is red. The flowers are pink and the flowers are
white. The flowers are seventeen. The red is dye. The cello-
phane is around them.
The four look up. The four look at the woman. The four
look at the flowers. The four smile.
The woman walks to the desk. The four look at the flowers.
Two of the three speak. One of the three speaks.

The woman speaks. The woman smiles.

The woman puts the flowers on the desk.

Two of the three stand. Two of the three walk to the desk. Two of the three look at the flowers. Two of the three speak.

The woman speaks. The woman smiles.

They speak. They talk. They laugh.

One of the two speaks. The woman speaks. The one of the two nods and speaks. The woman lifts the flowers. The one of the two and the woman walk to the door. The one of the two and the woman talk.

The one of the two opens the door. The woman walks out. The one of the two walks out.

It is hot.

The three sit at the desks.

The blinds do not move.

The three look at the screens.

breathe out

flick ash ashtray red

coffee last   smudged foam chocolate sides

wipe mouth

suck in   out

stub red tip red ashtray

stand

crumbs trousers   wipe

jacket   back of chair   on

                            green yellow foil packet pocket

                               lighter pocket

green packet papers pocket

           wipe hands trousers

                                   sweat

look table   nothing

       look up   girl looking looks away

      across

                         green walls

                          orange wall

stairs wood   pale   up   glass

up

         tills   queue   girls

left

doors open

light   bright   glass   open

out

white   street   noise   sun

The rooms are two. There is the kitchen. There is the living room.
The lamps are on.

There is the smoke. The smoke is in the air. The smoke is in
the air in the living room. The smoke is in the air in the kitchen.

The lamps are on. The lamps are on in the living room. The
people in the living room are eleven. The men in the living
room are six. The women in the living room are five.

The lamp is on. The lamp is on in the kitchen. There are six
people in the kitchen. The smoke is in the air. The women are
four and the men are two.

There is the dog, The dog is under the table.

The smoke is in the living room. The men and the women
are in the living room and they are in groups.

They sit on chairs. They sit on the sofa. They sit on the floor.

The smoke is in the air and the people talk. It is hot and they
drink drinks. The people talk to each other. They talk and they
smoke. The people talk and the people talk and the people
drink. The people drink the punch. The people drink the beer.
The people drink the wine.

The lamps are on.

The smoke is in the room and the music is in the room. The
dark is outside and it is hot.

The music plays. The CD player is plastic. Three tap feet.
One taps thighs.

The plastic is black.

The music is on. The chair is beside the CD player. The CD cases are on the floor. The man is in the chair. The shirt is blue. The man looks at the case. The right foot taps.

The girl is on the floor. The hair is long and the hair is red. The girl sits. The cigarette is in the right hand. The bottle is in the left hand. The eyes are closed. The beer is in the bottle.

There is the woman on the sofa. The hair is short and the hair is blonde and the lamps are on. The woman stands. The smoke is in the air. The woman walks to the door. The woman walks out of the living room. The woman turns right. The woman walks into the kitchen.

The six look up at the woman. The air is smoke. There is the smell of the smoke. The woman speaks.

There are seven in the kitchen. The women in the kitchen are five. There are two men. The dog is under the table.

The lamp is on. The fridge is white. The woman opens. The bottles are in. The woman takes out. The door closes.

The beer is in it. The bottle opener is on the table. The woman walks to the table. The woman lifts the bottle opener. The woman opens the bottle.

It is hot. The bottle opener is on the table. The bottle top is on the table. She swallows.

Seven are in kitchen. One dog is there. The dog is under the table in the kitchen. Three women sit at the table. One man sits at the table. One woman stands at the table. One woman leans back against the sink. One man stands.

The man standing and the woman leaning talk. The women sitting at the table and the man sitting at the table and the woman standing at the table talk. The smoke is in the air.

The bowls are on the table. The dog is under the table.

The bowls are three. The dog is under the table. The lamp is on.

The bowls are plastic. The bowls are big. The plastic is pink.

The vodka is in the jelly. The jelly is in one bowl.

The vodka is in the punch. The wine is in the punch. The fruit is in the punch. The punch is in two bowls.

The jelly is red. The bottles are on the table. The bowls with punch are half-full. The bowl with jelly is full. The lamp is on.

The bottles are on the table. The bottles are seventeen. The jelly melts. Eleven bottles are empty. Three bottles are not open.

One of three bottles is full of red wine. Two of three bottles are full of white wine.

One bottle is half-empty. White wine is in it.

Two bottles are almost empty. Vodka is in one bottle. Beer is in one bottle.

The men talk and the women talk. The men smoke and the women smoke. The men drink and the women drink.

The lamp is on. The dog is small. The hair is black. The tongue is pink. The jelly melts. The tongue licks. The eyes are blue. The hair is long. The hair is brown. The skirt is blue. The legs are bare. The sandals are brown. The sandals are on the floor. The feet are bare. The feet are under the table. The dog is on the floor. The dog is under the table. The dog looks at the feet. The tongue licks the feet.

She stands. The carton is in the fridge. The dog looks up. She walks to the fridge. The carton is in the fridge. She opens the fridge.

The carton is in the fridge. She takes the carton.

She closes the fridge. The carton is in the hand.

She walks to the table.

She lifts the scissors. She folds up the corner. She folds the corner up. The scissors cut. The scissors cut the corner. The scissors cut the corner off. She puts the corner on the table and she puts the scissors on the table.

The juice pours. The juice pours out. The juice pours in. The juice pours out into the bowl. The juice pours out into the bowl on the table.

The bottle is green. The woman puts the carton on the table. The dog is under the table. The carton is empty. The woman lifts the bottle.

The corkscrew is on the table. The woman takes the corkscrew.

The foil is on the bottle. The woman takes the foil off the bottle with the corkscrew.

The cork is in the bottle. Her eyes are blue.

The woman holds out the bottle to the man. The woman speaks. The woman holds out the corkscrew to the man.

The man opens it. He puts the corkscrew and the cork on the table. The man holds out the bottle to the woman.

The woman speaks. The wine pours. The wine pours out. The wine pours in. The wine pours out into the bowl. The wine pours out into the bowl on the table. The wine pours out into the wine and into the fruit and into the vodka and into the juice in the bowl on the table.

The woman puts the bottle on the table. The bottle is empty. The bottle is green. The woman sits.

The man is standing. The woman is leaning. The woman is leaning back. The man standing and the woman leaning are talking. They talk. The dark is outside. There is the smoke. The hand of the man lifts the mouth of the bottle to the lips. The hand of the woman lifts the tip of the cigarette to the lips.

The lamp is lit.

     sun heat on cars buses pavement people

horns

                        blaze

long skirt black   blouse red brown   arms folded breasts

boy short hair close   tracksuit blue white trainers into shop

         hand in hand girl blonde jeans

  man hair black short shorts blue older   t-shirts

            lights red

       buildings tall down length in sun

     queuing traffic waits

noise traffic　　　bus red to stop at lights by railings

people reflections in windows　　　colours

woman thirties　　top blue white　　　　jeans blue

hair brown swing length

with man grey black jeans shirt red

sunglasses both

to crossing　　　　　　　wait red man

LOOK LEFT

white car accelerates lights

red car accelerates lights

sun

buildings white tall

shining

buses three red line

green man   cross

sun on face   blaze

hoarding   building site

ENLIGHTENMENT DAY

suit man grey hair

girl ponytail hair long down neck bare ear white lobe

t-shirt   sunglasses

blue van dust

blinded   squint

sweating

horns

child   eyes

van tied metal ladder rack top

scaffolding

The trolley is full. He pushes it.

He pushes it. The warehouse is big. He pushes it across the warehouse. The lights are on. The roof is high.

He pushes it. He pushes it along. He pushes it across the warehouse. He pushes to the front of the warehouse. He pushes it between. He pushes it between the barriers at the front of the warehouse.

The trolleys are on the right. The trolleys on the right are full. The trolleys are on the left. The trolleys on the left are empty. The windows are in the roof. The roof is high. The kiosk is between the trolleys on the left and the trolleys on the right.

He pushes it. The trolley is full. He pushes the trolley to the right. The trolleys on the right are full. He pushes the trolley to the right. He pushes the trolley up against the trolleys. He leaves the trolley.

The roof is high. He turns and he walks to the kiosk. The kiosk is in the centre. The kiosk that is in the centre is between the trolleys that are on the left and the trolleys that are on the right.

He walks to the kiosk. He walks to the kiosk and he takes it out. He takes the sheet out and walks. He takes the sheet out of the pocket.

He stops walking. He stands in front of the kiosk. He looks at the sheet.

The sheet is crumpled. The sheet is folded. He unfolds the sheet. He looks at the sheet. He puts the sheet on the worktop at the front of the kiosk.

The pens are three. The sheet is one. There are three pens on the worktop of the kiosk. There is one sheet on the worktop of the kiosk.

He picks up the pen. He writes on the sheet. He puts down the pen.

He looks up. He looks into the kiosk. He hands the sheet into the kiosk.

The man in the kiosk takes the sheet. The man in the kiosk looks at the sheet. The man in the kiosk writes on the sheet.

The man in the kiosk looks to the left. The man in the

kiosk lifts a sheet. The man in the kiosk hands the sheet out of the kiosk.

He takes the sheet. He looks at the sheet. He walks to the left. He looks at the sheet. He walks to the left of the kiosk. He looks at the trolleys. The trolleys are empty. The dark is outside the windows. He takes the trolley. He pulls the trolley back. He turns the trolley. The wheels are black. He pushes. He pushes it. He pushes it forward. He pushes the trolley forward between barriers.

He pushes the trolley. He pushes the trolley along. He pushes the trolley across. He pushes the trolley across the warehouse. The light is not outside. The right hand pushes the trolley. The windows are high. The lights are on. The left hand holds the sheet. He pushes the trolley. The warehouse is big. He looks at the sheet as he pushes the trolley.

He pushes the trolley across the warehouse. He looks at the sheet.

There are shelves. The warehouse is big. The shelves are in the warehouse. The signs hang down. The signs hang down from the roof. The roof is high. The signs hang down over the aisles. The numbers are on the signs.

The cartons are on the shelves. The crates are on the shelves. The boxes are on the shelves.

He looks at the sheet. He looks at the signs. He looks at the sheet. He looks at the numbers. He pushes the trolley down the aisle.

He looks at the sheet. He looks at the shelves. He looks at the sheet. He looks at the words. He looks at the shelves. He looks at the boxes. He stops.

The boxes are on the shelves. The boxes are cardboard. The cardboard is brown.

He folds the sheet. He puts the sheet in the pocket.

He lifts the box off. He puts the box on. He lifts the box off. He puts the box on. He lifts the box off. He puts the box on.

The boxes on the trolley are three.

He takes out the sheet. He unfolds the sheet. He looks at the sheet.

He looks at the sheet and he takes out the pen. He leans the sheet on the box. He makes the mark. He puts the pen in the pocket.

He takes the sheet. He looks. He pushes the trolley. He

pushes the trolley to the next aisle. He looks at the sheet. He looks at the numbers.

He lifts the crates off.

He puts the crates on.

He marks it.

He pushes to the next aisle.

He pushes it to the next aisle. The dark is outside. He looks at the sheet. He looks at the numbers.

He lifts the carton off.

He puts the carton on.

He marks.

He pushes the trolley.

He pushes the trolley to the aisles.

He pushes the trolley down the aisles.

He loads.

He marks.

He pushes.

He loads.

There are the marks on the sheet. There is the man in front of him. The ticks on the sheet are eight. He looks at the sheet. He looks at the man. The man speaks. He speaks. The man speaks. He speaks. The cartons are on the trolley. The man punches his face. The crates are on the trolley. He looks at the man. The boxes are on the trolley.

The roof is high. The man smiles. The man speaks. The man looks at him. The man smiles. The man speaks. He looks at the man.

The man smiles. The man speaks. The man turns. The man walks down the aisle.

He looks at the back of the man. The lights are on. The lights are high. He looks at the trolley. He looks at the sheet. He looks at the trolley.

The back of the hand wipes the mouth. The eyes look the back of the hand.

He puts the sheet on the carton. He takes the pen out of the pocket. He marks the mark on the sheet.

The marks on the sheet are nine.

He pushes the trolley. He pushes the trolley down the aisle. He pushes the trolley to the freezer room.

It is cold. There is the sound of the machinery. There are the aisles between the shelves. There are the boxes on the shelves.

There are the cartons on the shelves. There are the crates on the shelves. It is cold.

He pushes the trolley down the aisle. He lifts the boxes. He puts the boxes on. He marks.

It is cold. He walks. He pushes. He stacks. He stacks the trolley. He looks at the sheet. He marks the sheet. He looks at the trolley. He looks at the boxes on the trolley. He looks at the sheet. He looks at the crates on the trolley. He looks at the sheet. He looks at the cartons on the trolley. He looks at the sheet.

He folds the sheet. He puts the sheet in the pocket. He puts the pen in the pocket.

He turns. He pulls. He pulls the trolley. He pulls the trolley behind him. He pulls the trolley behind him out of the freezer room.

It is hot. The trolley is stacked.

He turns the trolley. He pushes the trolley. The trolley is heavy. He pushes the trolley across the warehouse. He looks at the watch. He looks at the numbers.

He pushes. He pushes the trolley across the warehouse to the front of the warehouse. He pushes the trolley across the warehouse and between the barriers. He pushes to the right. He pushes the trolley against trolleys.

The back of the hand wipes the forehead.

He walks to the kiosk. He takes out the sheet. He places the sheet on the worktop.

He takes the pen.

sun on scaffolding

bright heat

bus red double-decker

curly hair man fat squint

blue rucksack woman hair three clips silver flash sun

shade under arcade   hung with lamps

shop windows of clothes

SALE   SALE   SALE white on red

girl back   shoulder length blonde   top blue pale

trousers green tight buttocks   bare ankles trainers white

strap black of bag diagonal across back right shoulder to

hip left curve

out from shade into sun   blaze white

man twenties push asleep child pram dummy

bus brown white at stop

stall fruits orange green red

paving stone cracks

stall   magazines women smile photographs

road traffic right   left

to railings black   through

out to   wide grass   paths stretch in sun down

path brown wide   people   grass green

green trees

trees green grass   people chairs face sun

pigeons grey black strut pick   blaze

trees   green   sun   heat   bright

railings black

green tree leaves

grass   green

right   brown path

people sit grass

traffic noise from road behind

                                    squinting sun

                            right onto grass

green

    The cellophane is transparent. The sheaves are on the cellophane. The sheaves are red. The bread is brown. The bread is on the shelf.

                    green   blue

high blue   pale   heat sun

        jacket off   check   sit grass   jacket to side

    blaze high   far blue

                                                                    heat

            white line crossing blue

            sun blaze heat

                                        blue above green

                                    white line on blue

people sitting grass   deckchairs   walking paths

blue edged green

green edges waving green leaves

green on black on brown against blue

rustle high pale blue

breeze moving leaves

white line trail slow

sun on green   thick heat

foil   paper   tobacco

roll

sun in leaves

white line   green mass moving light green in sun blaze

smoke   white light

white yellow   dark green   dark shadow

                              leaves sway

                  white line

She sits on the floor. She sits in the tunnel.

The floor is concrete. The roof is concrete. The walls are concrete.

The posters advertise the films. The posters advertise the clothes. The posters advertise the shows.

The posters are colours.

She sits in the tunnel. The walls are the concrete. The posters are on the walls. The legs curl underneath. She sits on the concrete.

The child beside plays with the doll. The child beside plays with the doll on the concrete.

The footsteps come down. The footsteps come down the tunnel. She looks up. She looks up the tunnel. She looks at the footsteps.

The cardigan of the child is pink. The eyes of the doll are blue. The eyes of the child are brown. The buttons of the cardigan are white. The doll is naked. The hair of the child is black. The hair of the doll is blonde. The buttons of the cardigan are undone.

The footsteps come. The people come. The people come down the tunnel. The people come round the corner down the tunnel.

She looks up. She looks up along. She looks up at the footsteps. She looks up at the people. She holds out the hand.

She looks at the man. The man looks. The man puts the hand in the pocket. The hand puts the coin in the hand. She nods. The man walks past. The hand puts the coin in the lap. The coins are in the lap. The coins are in the lap of the dress.

She looks up. She looks up along. She looks in the direction. The women walk. The women talk. She holds out the hand. The women walk. The women walk past. The women talk.

The posters are information. She holds out the hand. The

floor is concrete. The concrete is grey. She holds out the hand. She looks at the people. The people walk past.

The woman stops. The handbag opens. The purse opens. The woman hands the coins.

The walls are concrete. The roof is concrete. The concrete is painted. The paint is white. The dirt is on the paint. The white is faded. The paint peels.

She holds out the hand. The child plays with the doll. The people walk. The people stop. The people hand coins. The people pass. The people hand no coins. There are people.

The roar starts.

The roar is nearer.

The people hear the roar.

She holds out the hand. The child plays with the doll.

The people hear the roar.

She holds out the hand. The roar is in the tunnel. The doll is naked. The people walk faster.

green sway   breeze shadow

   green grass tangle   down slope   to

trees green leaves moving waving breeze

blue   cloudless   sun

                              green spikes

      breeze across

         grass green against

   railings black iron curve dark black peel paint

cigarette ends yellow brown white bent ends white

white on green

couples   children

slow line white

silver plane

sweat under arms

cars buses lorries   a siren

flap paper white   sandwich cartons

burger boxes red yellow trapped mesh wire

The stations transmit. The stations transmit the programmes.
The morning is early. The stations transmit.

The stations transmit the programmes across the city.

People wake. People across the city wake. The stations transmit. The televisions turn on. The stations are there.

The stations transmit. The televisions turn on. The stations
transmit the programmes to the televisions across the city.

The televisions turn on. The televisions turn on in the
houses. The televisions turn on in the hospitals. The televisions
turn on in the offices. The televisions turn on in the shops. The
televisions turn on in the schools. The televisions turn on.

The televisions turn on. The colours start. The stations

transmit. The stations transmit the programmes. The programmes are the colours. The colours come out. The colours come out of the televisions.

The colours come into the houses. The colours come into the offices. The colours come into the schools. The colours come into the hospitals. The colours come into the shops.

The colours spill. They spill out.

The televisions are on.

The colours spill out. The colours spill out over the carpets. The colours spill out over the walls. The colours spill out over the faces. The colours spill out.

The televisions are on. The stations transmit. The colours come.

The people look. The people look at the colours. The people look at the colours move.

The people in the beds look at the colours moving. The people standing look at the colours move. The people at the desks look at the colours move. The people in the chairs look at the colours. The people walking past look at the moving colours. The people at the tables look at the colours move. The people on the sofas look at the colours. The colours move.

The colours spill out. The people look at it. The colours move. There are the people looking at the colours move.

The colours are the films. The colours are the documentaries. The colours are the chat shows. The colours are the advertisements. The colours are the soap operas. The colours are the game shows. The colours are the news.

Colours spill. The people look at them. The people look at the colours coming out.

The stations transmit. The stations transmit the programmes. It is the evening. It is late.

boxes red wire mesh metal bins

paths yellow cream orange brown wide

in sun   split green lawn   to trees   distant distance   road

people cars pass bus light shine window mirror light

birds black against blue   black twist jolt

black movement   on pale blue   down

skim leaves   land tangle grass to

peck strut crumbs

black throats   black white beaks

black curve

black against green   spin into pale

black flap black panic from couple hands hold

her black t-shirt   black yellow skirt   brown hair long

her hand   in   his black jeans

hair short blonde   t-shirt blue

scatter black shapes over blue

panicking

The light flicks. The bus drives out.

He is upstairs. It is the upper deck. He looks out. The sun is on them.

He looks out to the right. He turns the head. He looks out to the front. He looks past the heads. He looks past the heads to the front. He looks out the front.

The hands move. The hands move in the air. The hands move fast.

The hands move. The hands move in front of the face. The hands move fast.

The head ducks.

The head ducks again. He talks quick. The talk is loud. The pitch is high. The hands move fast. He ducks.

He ducks. The coat is brown. He pulls the coat close. The sun is in the windows. The finger points to the right. The pitch is high. The fingers move and flick.

He turns sudden. They look away. He looks at them.

There is the silence. Then there is the singing. He sings to their heads.

The bus stops. Schoolgirls climb the stairs. He looks at the schoolgirls. The talk of the schoolgirls stops. He looks. The schoolgirls walk past. The schoolgirls giggle. He looks at the schoolgirls.

The light flicks. The driver looks in the mirrors. The bus drives out.

The schoolgirls walk to the back. The schoolgirls walk to the back seat. The schoolgirls sit. The schoolgirls look. The schoolgirls whisper. The schoolgirls giggle.

He looks out. The hands move. He points. He talks.

The skirts are blue. He turns sudden. He looks at the schoolgirls. The schoolgirls look away.

The schoolgirls giggle.

He looks out the front. He talks. The schoolgirl whispers to the schoolgirl. He frowns.

The schoolgirls giggle.

He points. He talks quick.

The sun is on the bus. The sun is on the windows of the bus.

The skirts are blue. The jackets are blue. The tights are black. The blouses are white.

He pulls the coat around him.

The bus moves down the road. The sun is in the windows. There is the queue to the lights.

He turns. He looks ahead. He looks over the heads. He looks through the window. He talks to the heads. He listens.

The light is green. The bus moves. The sun is on it.

The people are on the pavements. The people walk.

He sings. He points. The schoolgirls look.

He turns.

The bus slows. The bell rings. The light is red. He jumps up. He talks. He sings. The bus stops.

The rail is metal. He holds it. He walks.

He looks at the schoolgirls. The schoolgirls look.

He walks down the stairs.

girl on grass   head rucksack back

looks book   white pages

black letters on   white pages

leans back lies back   knees up   jeans blue

fingers in pages

leaves hiss trees

reads t-shirt tight blue bunched up

birds strut black curves on green

second girl sits

blue jeans   notebook blue knees

noting   writing   ink on white pages

faded blue knees   eyes behind glasses

looking up   down   page white notebook

t-shirt white   cardigan pink

green leaves above   sun   blue

black birds

looks up notebook at

crowds   wide path brown

walking   talking   looking

couples talking walking

bare arms legs on path brown wide

under sun blaze

birds movement

walking   talking

beards breasts   legs   black   shoes   hair   short hair long

trainers buttocks eyes

eyes flick grass   birds flicked

brown frames   wooden deckchairs

It is brown. The top is brown. The drawers are brown.
The folders are in the first drawer. The folders are in the second drawer. The paper is in the third drawer.
The file is on the top. The pens are on the top. The vase is
on the top. The mug is on the top. The pad of paper is on the
top. The watch is on the top. The box is on the top. The box is
cardboard. The tissues are in the cardboard. The vase is empty.

frames brown wooden   deckchairs   stripes wide green white

flapping canvas

noise heat   cars buses lorries   behind

talking   shouts   screams

311

children chase   scream   run

children hold   wave flags

bright

                                        parent shout

                            grey mesh bins

sweating

                    wire paper

white sun

            black birds peck green

girl looks up   looks down

building tall distant above trees tall

points to blue sky

                                        aerials

thin black lines

blue with black lines

grey concrete

windows white reflect sun light black in shadow

birds black

she looks again   down to book

sky sky sun blaze heat light

white sun

plane slow   solid silver white

slow move high right to left in blue above

grey tower white windows

trees green grass

children screams

black bird beaked curve

chasing

spikes green grass under green

looks back to words page book

He is asleep. The head is slumped. The cardigan is green. The eyes are closed.

The shoes are blue.

She pushes it in. There are two people in.

The shelves are along the sides. The shelves are along the back. The shelves are down the middle.

The signs are above the shelves. The cards are in the shelves.

There are the sections for the relatives. There are the sections for the occasions. There are the sections for the ages.

She looks at the signs. She pushes the pram. She looks at the shelves.

She stops. She looks. She looks at the cards.

The hand reaches. The hand takes. She takes it out. She looks at it. She looks at the front. The hand puts it back.

She looks. She takes. She looks. She opens.

She looks. She looks the words. She closes. She puts back.

The assistant wears jeans. The jeans are blue. The blue is pale. The assistant picks the nail.

There is the air-conditioning.

She takes it. She looks at it. She opens it. She reads it. She smiles.

Cellophane wraps the card and the envelope. The mucus is yellow.

She looks at back of it. She looks at the shelves. She looks at the wall.

There is the list. The list is the list of codes. There is the list of codes. There is the list of prices beside the list of codes.

She looks at back of it. She looks at the code.

She looks at the wall. She looks at the list. She looks at the code. She looks at the price.

She turns the pram. She pushes it. She pushes to the till. The assistant looks.

She hands it. The assistant looks it. There is beep. The assistant puts it in the bag. The bag is paper.

She pays. She takes the change. The receipt is under the change. She opens the purse. She puts the change in the purse. She puts the receipt on the counter. She puts the purse in the rucksack.

She takes the bag. The bag is paper. The card is in the bag. The card is in the cellophane in the bag.

She puts the bag in the rucksack. The rucksack is green. The rucksack hangs over the handles of the pram.

The head is slumped. The eyes are closed.

The mucus is under the left nostril. The mucus is yellow.

jeans   looks back to book   grass matted spikes

                                          sun blaze heat

                              girls getting up

                      hands brushing jeans   in sun

        green lawn   birds   cigarette ends

        path light brown wide

black twigs through railings peeling paint

                              tree trunks   shadow

        sun on bins wire mesh black filled spilling

paper in   breeze

plane slow across

white line

distant car flash under trees   grey black black road

shine silver in light sun

white light on windows glass chrome

red bus after   dark windows sway

advertisement colours bright   face smile size side of bus

sun

sun over wide pale orange brown yellow path

white pebbles embedded

stand up brush trousers   jacket

turn

up hill slope

brow   broken three paths   left right centre

                                                              down

                                                   cigarette ends

                        into tunnel dark under road

                        black on white NO SMOKING

                                            cigarette ends yellow brown

                steps tiled

            down tunnel mouth   dark   O open

cool   dirt   dark   faint   light   faint light

                        LADIES   GENTLEMEN

                                                              white

It is hot. It is dark.

They push the door. The lights are on. They walk up the stairs.

The first is big. The beard is black. The jacket is black. The jeans are blue. The jacket is leather. He pushes the glasses back. The hair is long.

The second is thin. The hair is short. The jeans are black. The t-shirt is black.

They walk up the stairs. The sound is in the corridor. They walk to the sound. They walk down the corridor to the sound.

There is the sound of the music. There is the sound of the voices. There is the sound of the laughter.

The corridor is dark. They walk down. They walk to the sound. They walk to the light.

The door is open. The light comes out. The light comes out of the doorway into the corridor. The music comes out of the doorway into the corridor.

They step in. They step into the sound. They step into the light.

They look.

There are twenty-three people. There is the music. There is the light. The glasses are on the table. The wine is in the glasses. The people talk. The people laugh. There is the music.

There are no curtains. There is no carpet.

They stand in the room. They look.

The girls are two. The girls are in front of them. The girls look at the room.

The first smiles. The jeans are blue. The hair is long. The top is red. The hair curls. She smiles. The hair is blonde.

The second is thin. The hair is black. She looks at the room. The dress is blue. The flowers on the dress are red. The flowers on the dress are red. The hair is down the back.

The man with the glasses speaks to the girl with the top. The girl with the curls speaks to the man with the jacket. The man with the jeans that are blue takes the arm of the girl with the jeans that are blue. The girl with the hair that is blonde and the man with the hair that is long walk across the room and talk.

The windows are open. There is the music.

The man looks at the girl. The girl looks at the man. The man speaks. The girl speaks.

The man and the girl walk across the room. The man and the girl walk to the table. The man and the girl stop at the table.

The man speaks. The man looks. The girl speaks. The girl nods.

The wine is in the glasses. The glasses are on the table.

The man lifts the glass off the table. The wine in the glass is white.

The man gives the glass to the girl. The girl takes the glass from the man.

The man lifts the glass off the table. The wine in the glass is white.

The girl sips the wine. The man looks at the room.

The man looks at the girl. The man speaks. The man points. The girl looks. The girl nods.

The man and the girl walk across the room. The man and the girl walk to the wall. The man and the girl turn their backs to the wall. The man and the girl sit on the floor. The man and the girl sit on the floor with their backs to the wall.

The girl sips the wine. The man sips the wine.

The girl looks at the room. The man looks at the room.

The man turns. The man speaks.

The girl turns. The girl nods. The girl speaks.

      light faint

GENTLEMEN   LADIES   on white black

corridor   open   floor white tiles   sinks white

    doors black cubicles in mirrors big over sinks white

                    taps steel dull

                    smell bleach

jeans blue in mirror combing hair

      turns   looks   walks out

cross floor white   bleach smell

mirrored door back black   swing

turn   turn to door   back black

                                                swing back

                bolt metal shines small   lock

look   hang jacket lock metal

        black seat plastic   ceramic white

            look   dry

                                        button

                    zip

sit

            cubicle black

graffiti blue pens wall scrawls   knifed replies scraped in

                                    read

            painted black metal holds paper white

wipe

wipe

stand

trousers up   zip   button

behind   pull chain   sudden noise water falling

jacket   bolt small metal slides back to

mirrored walls over taps steel dull

to sink   jacket shoulder

press   spill tap water hands

soap   bubbles in sink white   rinse

turn

walk to dryer   button   press silver

air whirr   hot noise

dry   rub   rub hands   trousers wipe

321

over floor tiles past mirrors

corner round out

to tunnel dark

roof curves lit faint lines

lit faint lines long light

sweating

dirt

posters colours walls dirt

steps up to voices faces

men women girls

out into cavern bright circle

movement men women walk talk girls cry out

walls maps lines colours

The smoke is in the room.

The curtains are open. The windows are shut.

There is heat.

The hifi is black. The lights are red. The letters are white.

There is the music. The music plays. The music comes from the hifi. The music comes from the radio on the hifi.

The light is outside. The outside is dusk. The birds outside sing.

The singing of birds is silent. The windows are shut. There is the music.

The birds sing in dusk.

He lies on the bed. He lies on the left side. He wears the jeans. The cigarette is in the right hand. The right arm is stretched out.

The chair is beside the bed. The ashtray is on the chair. The right arm stretches.

The cigarette is above the ashtray. The thumb flicks the filter. The birds sing. The ash falls. The ash falls onto the chair.

He looks. He sits. The music is there. The fingers tap the cigarette against the rim of the ashtray. The fingers tap the cigarette against the rim of the ashtray.

He leans the cigarette in the ashtray.

He stands and the music stops. He turns from the chair. He looks at the hifi.

He listens. There is the talk. He listens to the talk.

He turns to the chair. The birds sing dusk. He lifts the ashtray. He puts the ashtray on the floor beside the chair. The chair is beside the bed. It is dusk.

The ash is on the chair. The music starts.

He turns. He listens. He walks to the hifi.

The hifi is black. The letters are white. The letters are on the buttons. He presses buttons. The buttons start it. The cassette is in. The hifi starts to record the music from the radio onto the tape inside the cassette in the tape-recorder.

The lights are red.

He looks at it. He listens to it. He turns. He walks to the chair.

The ash is on the chair.

He kneels.

The left hand is out. The left hand is flat. The left hand is at the edge of the chair.

The right hand is on the chair. The right hand moves. The edge of the right hand moves the ash across the chair over the edge of chair into the left hand.

He brushes the ash off the chair into the left hand.

The ash is in the left hand. The ash is grey.

The left hand is over the ashtray.

The left hand turns.

The tape records.

The ash falls into the ashtray.

The hand wipes the jeans and he blows the chair.

The hands rub together. The hands rub the jeans.

He sits. He sits on the floor. He sits on the floor with the back against the bed.

The music plays. The tape records.

He listens.

The dusk birds sing.

The hand stretches. The hand pulls the ashtray closer. The fingers lift the cigarette.

                                        cry out girls

                 wall maps lines colours

                                    queue

blue t-shirt tight against catch bra strap ridges on back

          neck blonde hair long   jeans light blue faded

          brown eyes look away

                                        queue shuffles

noise   people talking walking   machines

                    blonde brown eyes girl to machine

next

          metal bars shine   thin slot

slip card pink   slit thins pop up   pick up

silver bars push

              heat   noise   sweating

    through

      heat   dust   dim light

    tiles   curve cavern   signs

              men suits   women trousers

                          girl in a dress

          queue to slotted steps brown

        fall   one   one

black rail plastic moving

    dress tightens to one side hip out swing cocked

other side ascending   up out of tunnels

    men eyes children wide shaved boys girls curves women

down wooden slots steps   heat

        train noise distant

    slope out

walls postered   colours

    white blue   black green   yellow red red

lips faces   words   stickers white

        torn

    ANARCHY   black letters on white

    down

    down

PLEASE STAND ON

steps off   step off

click heels black

                                        hair toss

THE RIGHT

to tunnel   cream walls   lit white

                postered colours dirt

The advertisement is white. The bus turns right. The lines on
the street are yellow. The letters are the name of the company
on the side of the bus. The letters are blue on the side of the
bus. The letters are the name of the company and blue above
the door on the side of the bus.

The sun is on it. The decks are two. The windows are around
the top deck. The windows are around the bottom deck. The
people are behind the windows. The advertisement is between
the windows. The advertisement is between the windows on the
top deck and the windows on the bottom deck. The advertisement is white.

The advertisement is white. The letters are black. The letters
are on the advertisement. The photograph is on the advertisement. The photograph is colours.

The bus is along the street. The lines are yellow. It is red.

                                        THE RIGHT

poster colours   people   clothes   noise

colours around boards   coloured

lines names colours

people into other tunnels   signs above lines colours

dim light   dust smell

tunnel curve   out   out to

long length platform stretch   train noise   roar

train   rushing   rushing   to stop

doors open   people out   people at doors crowding

PLEASE MIND THE GAP

people at edges train and platform

people from platform into train

doors slide   jolt

train jerks   out

tunnel rumble

         platform empties

feet and chatter

   heat   sweat

    dust smell

men briefcases   women suits black   girl fat

   blue seat

     poster red black words

 face photograph smiles across tracks

 woman sixties

hat knitted green

    sits   reads pastel magazine

 further along blue seats

boy teenage short hair green top   and

girl teenage long hair red jeans   in arms

kissing laughing   till girl lays head boy's chest

smiling

empty platform   red light sign next train

people from tunnels

sweat under arms

jacket lap

people along platform walking

rumble distant   louder

dust on black dirt tracks shakes

platform filling in heat

push flesh clothes along length

colours grey black   heat sweat

people behind yellow line looking   looking up tunnel

looking at sign

boy girl stand   hands hold   wait

heads turn to   coming roar

flash dirt white   dirt red

speeds   scream in

driver through thick dust window flash   cab dark

wind rush

slows

brakes

slowly to end   stops

doors slide

PLEASE   MIND   THE   GAP

crowd colours   heat   sweat

  hair   colours   necks   feet   train

            she holds his hand

                  platform clumps people doors

    PLEASE LET

colours people clothes out

        THE

        sweat armpits

    white shirtsleeves rolled up

                            PASSENGERS

            crowding out

                      crowd at edges doors

                      OFF THE TRAIN

        colours grey black

It is hot and the windows are open. The fans are three and blow the air and the office is big. The sound of the traffic comes from outside the windows and it is hot.

There are two piles and the piles are of paper. There are two piles of paper on the desk. There are two piles of paper on the desk and the two piles of paper on the desk are to the left of the computer.

She takes the sheet. She takes the top sheet. She takes the top sheet of the pile of paper on the right.

She turns the sheet over.

She places the sheet. She places the sheet down. She places the sheet face down on the pile of paper on the left.

She looks at the next sheet. She looks at the next sheet on top of the pile of paper on the right.

She looks at the screen. She saves the record. She opens a new record. The new record is blank.

She looks at the sheet. She looks at the letters on the sheet. She looks at the numbers on the sheet. She looks at the keyboard. She types.

She looks at the sheet. She looks at the letters on the sheet. She looks at the numbers on the sheet. She looks at the keyboard. She types.

She looks at the screen. She moves the mouse. She clicks the mouse.

She looks at the sheet. She looks at the keyboard. She looks at the screen. She looks at the keyboard. She types.

She looks at the screen. She looks at the sheet. She looks at the screen. She looks at the sheet.

She lifts the sheet. She turns the sheet over. She places the sheet down.

She looks at the sheet. She looks at the screen. She saves the record. She opens the record. The record is blank.

There is the sound of the fans. There is the sound of the traffic outside. The sun is on the leaves of the tree outside the window.

She looks at the sheet. She looks at the letters on the sheet. She looks at the numbers on the sheet. She looks at the screen.

She looks at the keyboard. She looks at the sheet. She looks at the keyboard. She types. She types the letters. She types the numbers. She types the letters and numbers on the sheet into the record on the screen. The sun is outside. The eyes move from the keyboard to the screen to the sheet to the keyboard to the screen to the keyboard to the screen. She types. The fingers move. The fingers move on the keyboard. The fingers press the keys. The letters are on the keys. The numbers are on the keys. The keys are beige. The letters are black. She types.

She looks at the screen. She saves the record. She looks at the sheet. She lifts the sheet. She turns the sheet. She places the sheet.

She looks at the sheet. She looks at the screen. She opens a new record. The record is blank. She looks at the sheet. She looks at the screen. The hand moves the mouse. The fingers click the mouse. She looks at the sheet. She looks at the keyboard. She looks at the screen. She looks at the sheet. She looks at the keyboard. She types.

The man speaks.

She types.

The man speaks again.

She looks up. The room is bright. She blinks.

She smiles. The man smiles. The man speaks. She smiles. She nods.

The man walks across the room. She looks at the man walk across the room.

She looks at the screen.

light dim dirt   noise   people

into carriage   sweat

handrails blue   extinguisher red

left to end   grey seat

doors sliding closed

dust sweat smell   people look

train jerk   start

floor grey

speeding up   lights flash

into dark tunnel   rattling heat

grey floor specks white

slows

girls two argue down carriage

dust   heat

speeds up

chewing woman fifties looks magazine

rush out tunnel to white light

The lights are colours. The lights are on. The lights are off.
The music is there. The music fills.

The smoke is there. The smoke curls. The lights light the smoke. The lights turn off. The lights turn on.

The lights flash. The music is loud. The voices are loud.

The chairs are there. The tables are there. The chairs are around the tables. The chairs are around the tables and the chairs and the tables are around the dance floor.

They are on the chairs. They are on the dance floor. They sit on the chairs. They dance on the dance floor.

They smoke. They drink. They talk. They dance.

The people on the chairs look at the people on the dance floor. The people on the dance floor look at the people on the dance floor.

On the balcony over the dance floor people lean over.

They are at the table. They sit on the chairs at the table. They sit on the chairs at the table and they look at the people dancing on the dance floor.

One bends forward. The others bend forward. The one shouts. The one points. The others look. The others smile.

She stands beside them. She drinks from the glass. She looks. She sips. There is a gap. She looks at him.

She sips. She looks at him. He looks at the people dancing.

There is the heat. The dancers dance. The dancers sweat.

The cigarette is in the right hand and the bottle is in the left hand.

She sips. She looks.

She bends. She bends over the table. The others lean in. She shouts. They listen. She looks at him. She moves the glass in the direction. They look up. They look. They look at him.

She stands. She looks at him. They look at him.

There is the flashing of the lights. There is the music. There is the smoke.

He drops the cigarette end. He stands on the cigarette end.

She sips. The ice cubes are in the drink. The drink is in the glass. The ice cubes are melting. She puts the glass on the table.

The people move. The people move in time. The people move in time to the music. The people on the dance floor move in time to the music. The people on the chairs tap the feet. The fingers on the glasses tap.

The lights flash. There is the heat. There are the ice cubes melting in the glasses. There is the music. There is the smoke.

The lights flash. The lights flash on the bodies on the dance floor. The lights flash on the faces at the tables. The lights flash on her face. She taps the shoulder.

He turns. The lights flash on his face.

She smiles. He sees the colours flash on her face. The smoke curls. The music fills the room. He sees the face. He smiles. The bottle is in the hand.

He smiles. The mouth opens. She leans forward. He puts the arms round her. They hug.

They hug. They move apart. They smile.

The lights flash. The smoke rises from the cigarettes. They watch across the dance floor.

She leans forward. He leans forward. She puts the mouth close to the ear. She speaks.

He listens. He laughs. They move back. She smiles.

There is the heat. He leans forward. The bottle is in the left hand. She leans forward. He puts the mouth close to the ear. They watch across. He speaks.

They move back.

She smiles. She nods.

He smiles.

The song ends. The song starts.

The smoke is in the air. People lean over the balcony. The dancers sweat.

She hears the song. She smiles. She leans forward. He leans forward. She puts the mouth close to the ear. She speaks.

She takes the hand in the hand.

She steps onto the dance floor. She looks at him. The hand pulls the hand. She turns.

He puts the bottle on the table. She turns. She smiles. She waits.

They walk on.

They watch.

There is a space. She pulls the hand to the space. She turns.

They stand in the space. They face each other.

He smiles. She smiles.

The lights flash on. The lights flash off.

She starts to dance.

out   into light rushing

                                        slows   slow

        to stop

                                        empty platform

        doors open hiss

                        no one out   no one in

PLEASE STAND CLEAR OF THE CLOSING DOORS

sweat wipe off forehead

                                heat   jacket lap

        doors hiss shut

                        jerk start   slow speed

                                rock into dark

        black white checked trousers woman forties

        handbag black on seat

                        voice details exits next station

rocking

       faces face windows   reflected

rush into light

The cars are behind the buses. The buses are at the lights. The taxi is at the lights. The lights are red. The people cross.

The people walk to the pavement. The people turn left. The people turn right. The people walk. They walk the pavement. They walk along the pavement.

The sun is on them. The sun is on the pavement.

There are the people walking the pavement. There is the sun and there are the t-shirts. There are the people walking behind the people. There are the people walking. There are the people standing looking. There are the people walking past the people. There are the people standing talking. There are the people standing looking in the windows of the shops in the sun.

The people are on the pavements. The people stop. The people walk past. The people step into the street to walk around. The people look into the shops. The people walk into the shops. The people stand at the bus stops. The sun is on them.

He sits on the pavement. He looks at the feet. He looks at the legs.

The coat is long. The coat is green. He holds the can. The back is against the wall.

The people walk. There are the trousers and there are the skirts. There are the boots and there are the trainers.

He sips. He sips the sip. He looks up. The sky is blue. There is the brightness.

The people walk. The legs move the pavement. The feet touch the pavement, then push away. The sun is bright. The chewing gum is on the pavement. The pavement is grey. The chewing gum is stuck to the pavement. The chewing gum is patches. The patches are white and grey. The white and the grey are round. The white and the grey are flat. The feet walk on the patches. The pavement is grey. The feet walk on the pavement.

He sits.

The hand moves the can to the other hand. The fingers pull down the zip. The fingers take out the penis. He waits. He breathes.

The pee comes out of the penis. He bends over it.

The girl is walking. The girl is looking. The penis is white and the pee is yellow. The yellow comes out of the white. The girl looks at the yellow come out of the white. The yellow comes out over the trousers. The yellow comes out over the coat. The girl looks. The girl looks away.

     rushing in light   rocking

       slower

to stop   faces facing

                    squeak   hiss of doors

people off

  people on

                  dirt floor

         doors beep   hiss shut

           sweating

waits

waits

empty platform

sound magazine page turn

sound train slowing distance

hiss brakes   jolt   slow into dark of tunnel

advertisements   colours   faces

smiles   smiling down

track rattle   sways

NO ADMITTANCE on door

further along   woman two children ice creams

heat

The floors are fifteen. The sun is on it.
The windows are two hundred and forty. The sun is on the
windows.
The zigzag cuts it. The zigzag is white.
The zigzag zigzags between the windows.

The blue is above the zigzag. The blue is pale.
The blue is below the zigzag. The blue is dark.
The sun is on it. The light is on the windows.
Sky is blue.

                             eating ice creams   melting

flash into white light station

     speeding   speeding   slows

                                               slows

                                 stops

doors hiss

                         heat

        man off

                                   man on

              dust smell

heat   empty platform

doors hiss

pause   windows dirt reflect faces

engine winds speed into tunnel

forward rattling   rocking

ice creams held with tips of fingers

woman wipes hands tissue white

rush   rush into light

The top is cotton. The cotton is white.

The skirt is cotton. The cotton is blue.

The straps are white. The straps are cotton. The straps are thin.

The skirt is long. The skirt is blue. The skirt is thin. The skirt is loose.

The cotton is thin.

The bra is lycra and the bra is nylon and the bra is cotton. It is white. The straps are thin.

The cotton is white. The knickers are cotton. The flower is small. The flower is pink.

The sandals are red.

The bag is red.

The towel is yellow.

The hands take off the sandal that is on the foot that is right. The hands put the sandal to the right of the towel that is yellow on the grass that is green.

The hands take off the sandal that is on the foot that is left. The sandal is red. The hands put the sandal that is red on the grass that is green to the right of the towel that is yellow to the left of the sandal that is red.

The sunglasses are on. The sunglasses are black.

The bag is red. The bottle is in the bag. The bottle is plastic. The plastic is orange. The letters are white. The top is black.

The hands open the bag. The hand goes into the bag. The hand takes out the bottle.

The top of the bottle is black.

The hands rub the cream onto the legs.

The cream is rubbed.

The cream is squeezed. The straps are white. The fingers pull the strap of the bra and the strap of the top on the left shoulder down. The shoulder is bare. The hand that is right rubs the cream on the shoulder that is left.

The straps are white. The fingers pull the strap of the bra and the strap of the top on the right shoulder down. The cream is cream. The hand rubs it on the shoulder.

The strap of the bra on the left shoulder rides up. The fingers pull the strap of the bra on the left shoulder down.

The cream is cream. The cream squeezes out of the orange. The cream squeezes out of the black. The cream squeezes on to the pink.

The cups are white. The edges of the cups are above the neck of the top. The breasts are in the cups.

The hands rub the cream on to the top of the chest. The fingers pull the cups. The hands rub the cream on to the top of the chest.

The hands rub the cream on to the front of the neck. The hands rub the cream on to the back of the neck. The hands rub the cream on to the backs of the shoulders.

The cream squeezes out. The hands rub it. The hands rub the cream on the legs. The fingers pull the hem. The hands rub the cream on the thighs.

The hands wipe on the towel.

The top is black. The top is clicked shut. The bottle is orange and the hand puts the bottle in the bag. The bag is red.

The top half of the body leans back. The head moves to the side to look. The hand pulls the edge of the towel. The top half of the body leans back. The top half of the body lies back on the towel. The body lies on the towel.

The thighs close. The head lifts. The eyes look. The fingers pull the hem up. The eyes look. The eyes are in the sunglasses. The head lies back.

The hands move to the shoulders.

The fingers pull down the straps of the top.

The fingers pull down the straps of the bra.

The fingers touch the edge of the top and the fingers touch the edges of the cups of the bra.

The fingers pull up the edges of the cups of the bra. The cups cup the breasts in cups.

The fingers touch the edge of the top and the fingers touch the edges of the cups of the bra.

The hands move to the towel. The hands lie on the towel.

There is the smell of coconut.

    rushing into light

slowing   slower

              slow   to stop

  girls two teenage off   down platform talking

walking teenage

                    colours posters

    beep doors   close hiss

           trickle wet right arm under

      speed   into tunnel

lights flick

             rattle

                                                        hiss brakes

                    heat

                                                rocking   speeding

            slow   slower   slower

                            slow stop in tunnel

    heat   sweating

                                                dust

            dirt thick walls tunnel pipes black

                                        lights flick off

                    wait   on

            hiss brakes

                            slow forward

    rocking

                                        to speed

                                                    faster

slow   into light

    man twenties   biting nail jacket white seat further along

                        CHANGE HERE

    There is the van. The people are six.
    There are the people in the van. The people are six. The six
people are in the van. The six people are in the back of the van.
    The men are four. The women are two. Two of the four
people in the back of the van who are men talk to each other.
One of the two people in the back of the van who are women
reads the newspaper.
    The windows are around the van. The window is on the
front of the van. The windows are on the sides of the van. The
windows are on the back of the van.
    The letters are on the van. The letters are on the front of the
van. The letters are on the sides of the van. The letters are on
the back of the van.
    The man is on the pavement. The man leans. The man leans
back against the side of the van. The man smokes. The man
looks up along the pavement. The man squints. The sun falls
down the street.
    People walk along the pavement. People walk past the van.
    Cars drive along the street. Cars drive past the van.
    It is the morning and it is hot.
    A man walks. The man walks along. The man walks along
the pavement. The man walks along the pavement up to the
van. The man walking along the pavement nods at the man leaning against the side of the van. The man leaning against the side
of the van speaks. The man walking smiles. The man walking
speaks.

                            347

He walks past. He walks past the man leaning against the side of the van.

He walks round. He walks round the van. He walks round to the back of the van.

The heat is on him. The heat is on the metal of the van and the heat is on the windows of the van.

There is the handle. He pulls the handle. He pulls the handle down. The door opens.

He bends. He climbs. He climbs into the van and he closes the door behind him.

The man leaning against the side of the van looks along the pavement. The man leaning against the side of the van sucks the smoke from the cigarette into his mouth. The man leaning against the side of the van sucks the smoke from the cigarette into his lungs. The man leaning against the side of the van breathes out. The man leaning against the side of the van looks along the pavement.

He stands. He looks along the pavement.

He turns. He walks across the pavement. He walks to the door. The door is open. The door of the office is open onto the pavement.

He looks in. It is darker in.

He speaks. He speaks to the man in the office. He holds the cigarette cupped down away. He speaks. The man in the office speaks. He nods.

He turns. As he turns he lifts the cigarette to his mouth and then sucks the smoke out of the cigarette. He turns into the sun. He drops the cigarette onto the pavement. He stands on the cigarette.

The sun is on the pavement. The sun is on the man. The sun is on the van.

He walks across the pavement. He looks up along the pavement at the people walking. He walks across the pavement to the door of the van.

He opens the door. The door is white. The letters on the door are black. He gets in.

He sits behind the wheel. He looks at the keys. The key is in the lock. He turns the key. The engine starts.

He looks at the street. He looks at the cars. He looks at the pavement. He looks at the people.

The sky is blue. There are no clouds. There are trees in the distance down the street.

He turns. He looks at the office.

The people in the back of the van wait. They turn. They look out of the window. They look at the office.

He turns on the radio. The music starts. He looks at the street. He looks at the people. He looks at the cars.

The man walks out of the office. The tie is blue. The suit is grey. The folder is in the left hand. The clipboard is in the left hand.

The sky is blue. The light is white.

He steps into the sun.

He blinks. He looks up the pavement. He crosses. He crosses the pavement to the van. He walks round. He steps onto the street. He walks round the van. He walks round the front of the van. He looks at the cars.

The driver turns off the radio. The music stops.

There are people in the back of the van. There are seven people in the back of the van. The seven people in the back of the van look at the man in the suit. The seven people in the back of the van look through the window in the front of the van at the man in the suit. The driver looks at the man in the suit.

The man in the suit waits. He looks down the street. He looks at the cars.

He waits.

He steps out. He turns. He opens the door. He gets in. He closes the door.

The man in the suit sits. The man in the suit puts the folder on the dashboard. The man in the suit puts the clipboard on the dashboard. The man in the suit wipes the hand on the trousers. The man in the suit reaches up behind and pulls and clicks the seatbelt in.

He turns to the driver. He looks at the driver. He turns further. He looks at the people. He speaks. He smiles. He turns to the driver. He speaks.

The driver nods. The driver looks in the mirror.

CHANGE HERE   sweating

no one off

349

dirt on windows

heat

posters colours walls

hiss close

forward slow

dark tunnel

rattling

windows reflect people seats carriage

short hair girl twenties reads ZANZIBAR

trousers pale green   t-shirt white

sudden out rocking

into daylight sudden brightness

blue sky

trees   shrubs

            people looking up out windows

                                    rattling corner

other direction train passes   faster faces eyes wide

            sun

sudden into tunnel dark

        jolt   curving

        out into station of   pillars

                                    sunlight

There is the sound of the voices of the crowd. There is the sound of the voice of the commentator. There is the sound of the interference.

He walks into the hall. The cupboard is under the stairs. He takes out the ironing board.

The door of the cupboard under the stairs is fastened with a bolt small and steel.

The stripes are white and the stripes are blue. The cover on the ironing board is stripes. He carries into the living room. The legs are blue and he pulls them.

It is nil–nil.

He walks into the kitchen. The iron is on the shelf. He takes the iron. He takes the iron to the sink. The centre of the tap is blue. He turns the tap and water falls. The water thins. He thins the water. He holds the iron. The water thins into the opening. The opening is on the front of the iron.

The tap is turned. The water stops.

He sweats. He walks into the living room. There is the sound of the voice of the commentator.

He puts the iron on its end. The curtains are open. He puts the iron on its end on the ironing board. The sun is in the street and on the cars. He puts the iron on its end on the stripes.

He plugs it. He turns it. The light reds.

The bag is on the floor. The bag is beside the sofa. It is nil–nil. The shirts are in the bag. He takes them out. He puts them on the sofa.

The light is on. He takes the shirt. It is nil–nil. The collar opens onto the board. There is the throw in. The collar is white. He irons it.

He turns it over. He irons it.

The shirt is white.

He spreads the right front. He spreads the right front out. He spreads the right front out on the board. He irons it.

There is the sound of the chanting of the crowd. There is the sound of the hissing of the iron. There is the heat. There is the tackle.

The left front spreads out. He irons. There is the free kick. There is the sun on cars outside.

The back is spread out onto the board. The stripes blue show through the white. The iron irons. The iron makes patches of wet dark on the white. There is the cross. There is the voice of the commentator.

He irons the patches. The wet dries. The shirt is white.

It is nil–nil.

He spreads out the right sleeve. He irons the right sleeve. He turns over the right sleeve. He spreads out the right sleeve. He irons the right sleeve. He sweats.

He irons. There is the injury. The stretcher is brought on. He is naked to the waist. There is the booking.

He irons the left sleeve. The shirt is ironed. He looks at the sofa. He looks. He places the shirt on the sofa.

The car passes in sun on street.

It is nil–nil. He walks up the stairs. He walks into the bedroom. He opens the wardrobe.

In the living room there is the sound of the voice of the

commentator and the sound of the interference and the sound of the chanting of the crowd and the sound of the iron hissing.

He drops them onto the sofa. He lifts the ironed shirt. He lifts one hanger. He hangs the shirt on the hanger. There is sweat on him. He buttons the second button. He hangs the hook of the hanger on the handle of the door.

The player is waved back on. He lifts the shirt. He opens the collar.

It is nil–nil. He spreads the collar out onto the stripes. The collar is white. There is the goal kick. He irons.

The tree is outside. The sun is on the tree outside.

The leaves of the tree are yellow where the sun is on them.

The leaves of the tree are green where the sun is not on them.

metal pillars painted dull red hold bars concrete cream

tangle metal glass roof support

slow through station in sunlight

out   backs of houses

washing

sweat

sun on windows

colours graffiti walls

sun a triangle on the seat

white t-shirt nipples

into tunnel   sudden

rattling

into platform

slow   slower

stop

doors

MIND THE GAP PLEASE WHEN LEAVING THIS TRAIN

The doors slide open and the people walk in.

There is light. The light falls white through the roof. The light shines on the steel. The light shines on the glass.

There is the air-conditioning. It is cooler.

There are lights and there are colours. The lights shine on the colours. The colours reflect the lights.

The red is bright. The green is bright. The black is bright. The blue is bright.

There is the noise of voices. There is the noise of movement.

They walk in. Through the sliding doors they walk in. They walk over the floor that shines. They walk past the glass that shines.

They walk. They look in the windows. They look at the colours. They look at the signs.

They walk across the floor that shines. They walk to the lifts. They walk to the escalators. They walk to the stairs.

There are three floors. The lifts connect the floors. The escalators connect the floors. The stairs connect the floors.

They stand on the escalators and they look up at the backs of the people above them. They stand in the lifts and they press the buttons. They walk the stairs and the handrails are steel.

There are shops. There are the shops that sell the mobile phones. There are the shops that sell the CDs. There are the shops that sell the books. There are the shops that sell the perfumes. There are the shops that sell the electrical goods. There are the department stores. There are the cafes. There are the chemists. There are the shops that sell the underwear for women, the shops that sell the suits for men, the shops that sell the toys for children.

There are the people. There are the people walking past the shops. There are the people looking into the shops. There are the people in the shops.

There is the fountain. There are the seats around the fountain.

There are the rides. There are the children on the rides. The mothers and the fathers stand looking at the children on the rides.

There is the noise.

There is the light.

MIND THE GAP PLEASE WHEN LEAVING THIS TRAIN

girls up stairway to exit

wait

wait

doors hissing

forwards   into tunnel dark

sweating

sprawls blue jeans girl twenties seat brown jacket asleep

out   sunlight   sky

roofs   tiles   sun shines

speed through station   train opposite platform

speed through second station platforms empty

train past opposite direction   faces

above park   green   sun   men t-shirts blue cricket

building tall   dark glass

slows   judder   judders

cables colours string frame side track

light

boarded up

curve right slow   sunlight   heat

slow   slow   to stop   platform

            stand

to doors

                    NO SMOKING

        posters in brown frames

MIND THE GAP PLEASE WHEN LEAVING THIS TRAIN

            colours

                            movement

white

                            doors hiss open

    The girl is in the room. The girl is alone. The girl sits. There
is silence. The lights are dim.
    The door opens. The woman comes in. The man comes in.
    The man looks at the girl. The woman looks at the girl. The
girl looks at the painting.
    The man and the woman walk across the floor. There is the
sound of the feet walking across the floor. The man and the
woman look at the paintings. The man and the woman walk
across the floor. The man and the woman look at the paintings.

The man and the woman look at the girl.

The man and the woman walk to the door. The man opens the door. The woman walks out. The man walks out. The door closes.

doors hiss

over gap step

white concrete white sun heat blaze

long hair woman thirties

cross-legged concrete platform

sitting reading   looks up

looks down

heat   bright   white

train opposite platform   faces

doors beep hiss behind

doors beep hiss in front   faces

walk platform white

train behind out   train in front out

walk platform   concrete step   sit sweat

further along platform sign   lights   destinations lines

sun on concrete grey concrete white

sweating

woman turns pages

backs of houses   shrubs   windows in sun

rails

train   speed through   rattling

faces

speeds away   into distance   rattling   sun

sun on heat   blue sky

no clouds

platform edges yellow lines

people seats   waiting   newspapers

white paint   MIND THE GAP   grey concrete

heat

waiting

It is hot. The women are two. The pages are twenty two.

The woman with the hair that is short eats the salad. The woman with the hair that is short drinks the coke.

The woman with the hair that is long eats the sandwich. The woman with the hair that is long drinks the water.

The woman with the hair that is short speaks to the woman with the hair that is long as they eat. The woman with the hair that is long speaks to the woman with the hair that is short as they eat.

The coke is in the bottle. The bottle is plastic. The water is in the bottle. The bottle is plastic. The salad is in the container. The container is plastic. The sandwich is in the container. The container is plastic.

The bottle is empty. The bottle is empty. The container is empty. The container is empty.

They put the bottle and the bottle and the container and the container in the bin under the desk.

They stand. The woman with the hair that is short lifts the pages. The pages are twenty two.

They walk down the stairs. They speak to each other as they walk down the stairs. They walk into the room.

The machine is in the corner. The woman with the hair that is long lifts the lid. There is the glass and there is the light under the glass.

The woman with the hair that is short places the pages on the table. The woman with the hair that is short takes the top page off the top. The woman with the hair that is short gives the page to the woman with the hair that is long. The woman with the hair that is long places the page face down on the glass. The woman with the hair that is long puts down the lid. The woman with the hair that is long puts in the card.

The woman with the hair that is short speaks. The woman with the hair that is long nods.

The woman with the hair that is long presses the 1. The woman with the hair that is long pushes the button that is green.

There is the sound of the machine. There are no windows. The light comes out of the edges. There is the heat. The page comes out on the tray.

The woman with the hair that is short takes the page. The woman with the hair that is short looks at the page. The woman with the hair that is short speaks. The woman with the hair that is short puts the page back in the tray.

The woman with the hair that is long nods. The woman with the hair that is long presses the 2. The woman with the hair that is long presses the 9. The woman with the hair that is long presses the button that is green.

There is the sound of the machine. There is the light at the edges. There is the heat. There are the pages coming out.

The women talk. The women talk and the pages come out. The women talk and sweat.

There is the change in the sound of the machine. The women look at the machine. The page comes out.

The woman with the hair that is short lifts the pages. The pages are thirty. The woman with the hair that is long lifts the lid. There is the light. The woman with the hair that is short squares the pages. The woman with the hair that is long lifts the page. The woman with the hair that is short taps the edges of the pages on the table. The woman with the hair that is long places the page face down on the floor. The woman with the hair that is short places the pages face up on the table.

The woman with the hair that is short takes the page off the top. The woman with the hair that is short hands the page to the woman with the hair that is long. The woman with the hair that is long turns the page over. The woman with the hair that is long places the page face down. The woman with the hair that is long closes the lid. The woman with the hair that is long presses the 3. The woman with the hair that is long presses the 0. The woman with the hair that is long presses the button that is green.

The noise starts. The light starts. The pages start.

The women talk. The women laugh.

There is the change in the sound. The page comes out. She lifts them. She lifts the page. She squares the pages. She places the page face down on the page face down on the floor. She taps the edges of the pages against the table. She lifts the page. She places the pages face up on the table. She places the page down.

The woman with the hair that is long closes the lid. The woman with the hair that is long presses the 3. The woman with the hair that is long presses the 0. The woman with the hair that is long presses the button that is green.

The pages come out.

They talk. There is the noise of the machine. The woman with the hair that is short speaks. The woman with the hair that is long nods. The woman with the hair that is short nods. The woman with the hair that is short walks out of the room.

There is the sound of the machine. There is the light from the machine. There is the smell from the machine.

There is the heat.

There is the sweat in her armpits.

She lifts pages. She stacks. She taps. She presses buttons. The pages come out.

She looks at the nails of the fingers of the left hand. The fingers are closed together. The nails are pink.

She wipes the nails on the fingers of the left hand against the front of the dress. She looks at the nail on the smallest finger of the left hand. She lifts the nail on the smallest finger of the left hand to the mouth.

The pages come out of the machine.

The machine runs out of paper after the twenty-sixth copy of the twelfth page.

The packets are stacked on the floor. She tears the packet open. She pulls out the bin.

There is no paper in the bin. She fans the paper. She places the paper in the bin.

She tears the packets. She fans. She places the paper in the bin.

She fills the bin.

She closes the bin.

She looks at the machine.

The machine makes a noise.

The pages come out.

She lifts them. She taps them. She places them.

She presses buttons. Pages come out. There is the heat. There is the smell.

The woman with the short hair walks into the room. The woman with the short hair carries the cup. The woman with the short hair speaks to the woman with the long hair. The woman with the short hair gives the cup to the woman with the long hair as the woman with the long hair speaks to the woman with the short hair.

The woman with the short hair speaks. The woman with the long hair speaks. The woman with the short hair speaks. The woman with the long hair sips. The woman with the long hair nods.

The pages come out. The women speak. There is the sound and there is the light and there is the smell. There is the heat.

The sound changes. The sound stops. The light stops.

The women speak. The woman with the short hair stacks the pages. The woman with the long hair sips the coffee. The women speak. The woman with the long hair places the cup on the table. The woman with the short hair places the pages face up on the table. The woman with the long hair lifts the lid. The woman with the long hair lifts the page. The woman with the long hair closes the lid. The woman with the long hair places the page face down on the twenty one pages face down on the floor.

The woman with the long hair lifts the cup.

The woman with the long hair drinks.

The women speak.

There is the heat. There are the women talking. There is the cup of coffee in the hand.

There are twenty two stacks of thirty pages each face up on the table. There is one stack of twenty two pages face down on the floor.

white on grey   MIND THE GAP

sweating

footbridge metal white over tracks

train   slow   rattling in   to stop

doors   people out   people in

doors hiss close

pause   then out

train   sound rattling   into distant

blue sky   white light

traffic in distant

sun on concrete

silence

traffic hum

bench metal   man turns page newspaper

people down steps to platform in sun

walk along looking signs

red lights   times   destinations

white light

white light falling

people wait

train pulls in furthest platform

faces looking out   people out people in

woman thirties out puts down suitcase lifts handle

drags wheels along concrete

sweating

concrete grey

train pulls out   blue red white   dirt

train drivers over footbridge white

sun on metal

mobile phone ringing down platform

sudden man guitar singing bench opposite platform

people look   look away   look again

waiting

listen

stand   left   heat   walk platform in light

phones   green notices

machine chocolate   instructions

cartoon character   blue red green smile

red lights   INSERT COINS

pocket   push coins slot   amount displayed

more coins   metal falling in metal

MAKE YOUR SELECTION

look   press numbers keypad

                              guitar singing behind

                    train slow

            INSERT COINS red light

    look   buttons   press buttons

    INSERT COINS

            look   button RETURN COINS

                                      sun back head

train pulls in

            people stand   lift bags suitcases

            INSERT COINS red lights

                                  door open hissing

            turn

                        people off train

The comics and the CDs are on the table. He takes the comics and the CDs.

He places the comics and the CDs on the floor. The comics and the CDs are beside the bed. The comics and the CDs are in the pile on the floor beside the bed.

The comics and the CDs are on the floor.

The television is on the chair.

He walks to the chair. The chair is brown. He lifts the television. The television is black.

He walks to the table. He carries the television to the table. The table is brown. He places the television on the table. The television is black.

He walks to the chair. He kneels on the chair.

The box is cardboard. The cardboard is brown. The box is behind the chair.

The plastic is black. The console is plastic. The plastic is on the cardboard. The cardboard is brown. The plastic is the console. The console is on the box. He lifts the console. The plastic is black. The cardboard is the box.

He balances off the chair. He stands. He walks to the table.

The table is wood. He places the console on the wood. The console is beside the television.

He walks to the chair. The wood is the chair. He kneels on the floor.

The leads are black. The controller is black. The controller is on the leads. The controller is under the chair. The leads are under the chair.

He pulls the leads and he pulls the controller. The controller is on the leads. He stands. He walks to the desk.

The console is on the table. The television is on the table. The console is beside the television. He puts the leads and the controller on the table. The leads are black.

He leans. He lifts the plug. He lifts the plug of the television. He drops the plug behind the table. The plug is white.

He stands. He lifts the plug. He lifts the plug of the console. He pulls the plug. The leads pull. The leads are ravelled. The lead of the plug is tangled with the leads of the console.

He unravels. He unravels the leads. The leads are black. He finds the end of the plug lead. He plugs the end into the console. The plug is black. He leans. He drops the plug. He stands.

He kneels. The block is white. The block is on the floor. The block is on the floor under the table. The plug is white. The plug is on the floor beside the block under the table. The plug is black. The plug is on the floor beside the block under the table.

He pushes the plug into the block. He pushes the plug into the block.

He crawls back.

It is dark outside.

He takes the lead. He connects the lead to the console. He leans. He connects the lead to the television. He stands.

He takes the lead. He connects the lead to the controller. He connects the lead to the console.

He looks at the television. The button is on the television. The button is black. He pushes the button. The television turns on. There is grey.

The flap is on the television. The flap is black. He lifts it. The buttons are under the flap. The buttons are small. The button is under the flap. He presses this button. The channel changes. There is grey. He presses the button. The channel changes. There is grey.

He looks at the console. The console is off. He looks at the button. The button is on the console. He presses the button. The light on the console comes on. The light is red. There is the whirring.

The button is under the flap. He looks at the television. He presses the button. The channel changes. It is grey. He presses the button. The channel changes. It is grey. He presses the button. The channel changes. It is colours.

He looks at the television. The colours spill out. It loads.

He walks down the stairs.

The woman is in the kitchen. The woman is mixing in the bowl.

The man and the girl are in the living room. The man and the girl are looking at the television.

He speaks to the woman. The woman looks up. The woman speaks. The woman points to the fridge.

He opens the fridge. There are the cans. He takes one can. The can is cold.

The bedroom is up the stairs.

He puts the can on the table. The table is under the television. The chair faces the television.

He sits. It is loaded.

He looks.

He lifts the can. It is cold. There is the ring. He pulls. There is the click and then there is the hiss.

He sips.

He looks.

PRESS PLAY TO START

MIND THE GAP

crowd off

others waiting edges doors

sun heat on concrete white concrete grey

people up steps to exit

sunlight on windows

sweating

people up step onto train

step over gap into

blue handrails

NO SMOKING

to seat   jacket lap   heat

                    doors hiss   slide shut

        heat

The drawing pins are two. The colour is gold. The card is on the board. The drawing pins pin the card to the board. The board is brown. The board is on the wall. The wall is blue.

The card is a photograph. The photograph is of writing. The writing is written in pen.

The numbers are two. The numbers are beside each other. The numbers are beside each other in the top right hand corner. The first number is 21. The second number is 1. The second number is circled.

The lines are twelve. The words that are crossed out are seven. The title is at the top. The title is underlined.

                        seat   sweating

            doors hiss shutting   jolt in light

        jolts

                    pulls

into speed out   from platform

        cables   orange yellow blue red green

                in dirt along track edge in sun

371

man yawning opposite plastic bag white

black on white WHISTLE beside track

slows

             in sun

white flowers on track edge bushes green

blues sky

backs of houses

             sweat

sign dirt 53.8

        slow to platform

colours   signs posters   people

  The light is in the centre. The light is lit. The light is orange. The light goes out.

  The light is at the top. The light is red. The light turns on. The cars stop.

  The man is red. The man turns off. The man is green. The man turns on. She crosses.

There are many people and heat. The people are on the pavement. The heat is on the pavement. The people walk the pavement. She stands to the side. The man pushes the pram past. The man nods. She walks. She walks along. She walks along the pavement. She walks to the shop. She walks to the door. She walks into the shop.

The clothes are on the left. The food is on the right. There are the shelves. She walks to the right. She walks the aisle. She walks to the cabinets.

The shop is cool.

The people are in front of the cabinets. The sandwiches are in the cabinets. The people look into the cabinets. The lights in the sides and the tops of the cabinets shine on the sandwiches in the cabinets. It is cool. The sandwiches are in the plastic. The people look at the sandwiches.

She looks into the cabinet. She looks at the sandwiches. The sandwiches are in the plastic. The plastic is clear. The labels are on the plastic. The letters are on the labels.

The meat is in the sandwiches. The cheese is in the sandwiches. The fish is in the sandwiches.

The people stand at the cabinet. The people look at the sandwiches. She takes the sandwich. She looks at the label. The letters make the words. She reads the words.

She walks round to the next aisle.

The basket is in the cabinet. The apples are in the basket. The apples are red. She looks.

The apples are red. She takes it. It is cold. She looks at it. It is red. She looks at the skin. The label is small.

She walks along. There is the sound of voices. There is the sound of movement. There is the sound of tills.

There is the street outside. The street is outside the windows.

She walks down. The cans are in the cabinet. The bottles are in the cabinet. The cartons are in the cabinet.

There are the different colours. There are the different flavours.

The carton is plastic. The plastic is clear. The liquid is orange. The label is on it. The label is the name of it. She takes it.

She looks up. She holds the sandwich and she holds the carton and she holds the apple. She looks across the shop. She looks at the tills.

colours   signs   lights

hiss open

                    station signs red blue white

        NO SMOKING red on white

                    WAY OUT black on yellow

    heat   light   sweating

                                    hiss shut

                        jolt   forward

    into darkness tunnel   rocking

girl teenage   trainers white dirt looking window behind her

            jeans frayed hems blue   cardigan black

        t shirt white   blue bag canvas

                slow into platform

staircase blue metal

He bites the chocolate. She sucks the ice-pop.
The sun is into the street.
They laugh. They walk the street.
The houses are on the left. The houses are on the right.
There is the heat. The sun is on the cars. The chocolate is soft. The ice-pop is melting.
The jeans are black. The t-shirt is white. The dress is green.
She speaks. She smiles. He laughs.
The right hand holds the chocolate.
She speaks again. He laughs.
She speaks. She smiles.
He speaks. She speaks. They look at each other. He laughs. She smiles.
She speaks. She points. She points at the shoe.
He looks. He stops.
She stops. He speaks.
He hands her the chocolate.
He kneels. She looks.
He ties the lace.
He stands. She hands him the chocolate.
They walk.
He bites the chocolate. She sucks the ice-pop.
The sun is bright. The sun falls into the street as they walk.
She smiles.
She speaks.
He laughs.
The dress is green.
The chewing gum is on the pavement.
The pavement is white.
The light is white.

blue metal staircase over bridge

tracks   platforms   sun

pull out rattling

girl trainers lies head back   in sun   eyes close

              dust

                                    thick heat

laughing down carriage shouting teenagers

woman plastic bags rustle   stands

                          light through window

                 into platform   sudden stop

doors open jerk

The left hand holds the packet. The right hand opens the packet. The cigarettes are three.

The left hand holds the packet. The left forefinger holds the lid of the packet open. The finger and thumb of the right hand take the cigarette. The finger and thumb of the right hand put the cigarette between the lips.

The left forefinger closes the lid. The left hand puts the packet into the bag. The left hand holds the bag open. The right hand goes into the bag.

The right hand takes out the lighter. The end of the cigarette is between the lips. The left hand cups around the lighter and the end of the cigarette.

The right thumb flicks the lighter. The lighter does not light.

The right thumb flicks the lighter. The lighter lights.

The right hand holds the lighter to the end of the cigarette. The left hand cups around the lighter and the end of the cigarette.

The mouth sucks. The mouth sucks in. The mouth sucks in air. The mouth sucks in air through the cigarette.

The paper lights. The tobacco lights.

The paper burns. The tobacco burns.

The left hand opens the bag. The right hand puts the lighter into the bag.

The right hand takes the cigarette. The right hand takes the cigarette away from the lips.

The smoke breathes out.

       doors open jerk

                              man off

 woman plastic bags off

     engine hum   platform empty

                     still heat

   wait   sun on glass

        waiting

 slide shut   brakes hiss

heat   start

out of sun into tunnel darkness rocking

then out   sudden into white

bridge high   rail tracks   blue sky   white sun

vibrating   speed   speed

height above city   cloudless

houses   below   warehouses roads cars

factories signs   traffic queue

building tall red and blue windows painted on

bridge   canal

factories   red brick

slow   over street slow   rocking slow

traffic queue street

slow in   slow   to platform stop

The wall is behind. The eyes are brown. It lies on the floor. The hair is white and the hair is brown. The radiator is on the wall. The knots are in the wood. The ears are up. The metal is painted cream. The tongue is pink. The tag is round and the tag is blue. The radiator is the metal. The eyes are brown. The skirting board is wood. The floor is blue. The teeth are small. Paint has dripped on the blue. The paint is orange. The dots are on the muzzle. The dots are black. The floor is varnished.

slow to platform stop

     up

          other people up

               to doors

      hissing open

out to sun white   grey concrete

           walls red brick

movement   people walking   walking

       crowd to steps

    out of sun into shade

still hot   pee smell

        people   shoulders

                left down steps crowd

                        paint yellow walls

left again   down second flight

grey concrete   cracked glass window

                down

                        tiles cream dirt warping

        can red silver by wall on ground

        crowding down   follow

                        shuffle movement

        to passage along

                to opening out   gates glass metal

queue people

wait

shuffle

look to right outside barriers doors outsun on street

pink card slit

pops up   take   push bar steel

pink card pocket jacket over arm

through to grey concrete

queue people at ticket office

right

wide opening

out

into white light heat noise bright traffic street

sun blaze   white

The cap is green. The apron is green. The hair is inside the cap.

There is the sound of the machines. There are the shouts. There is dim light.

She stands in front of the machine. The machine is in front of her. The machine is metal. The metal shines.

She presses the button. There is the sound of the start of the machine.

The metal shines. There is the metal. There is the flat metal. There are the sides at the edges of the flat metal. The sides at the edges of the flat metal are metal. The flat metal slopes at the end. The slope slopes to the funnel. The funnel is metal. The metal shines.

The cartons are cardboard. The cardboard is grey. The cartons are stacked.

There are the cartons. There are the cartons stacked. There are the cartons on the cartons. There are the cartons stacked on the floor. There are the cartons stacked on the floor beside the machine. The cartons are many.

The cartons are grey. The cardboard is the cartons. The cardboard is grey.

The eggs are in the cartons. The cartons hold the eggs. The eggs are many.

There is the heat. She sweats under the green. The sun is outside.

She stands in front of the machine and she stands to the right of the cartons.

She lifts the top carton.

She lifts the top carton with both hands.

She lifts the carton above the metal.

The metal shines.

She tips.

The eggs fall. The eggs fall out. The eggs fall out onto the metal. The metal shines and the eggs crack. The eggs break. The eggs slide the metal. The eggs and the eggshells slide down the metal. The eggs slide into the funnel. The eggs slide into the machine. There is the change in the sound of the machine.

The carton is empty. There is the stack of cartons to the right of the machine. She sweats. There is the stack of cartons to the right of her. The cartons are empty. She places the carton empty on the stack of cartons empty to the right of the machine.

She turns to the left. There is the stack of cartons. There is the stack of cartons to the left of the machine. The eggs are in the cartons. She lifts the carton. She lifts the carton with both hands.

The hands move the carton. The carton is above the metal. The metal shines. She tips.

There is the heat.

The eggs fall. The eggs fall out. There is the smell of the eggs. The eggs fall onto metal. The shells crack. The shells break. The eggs slide out. Eggs and shells slide. The eggs and shells slide on metal. The metal shines. The eggs and the shells slide on the metal into the funnel. The funnel is into the machine. The shells are into the machine. The eggs are into the machine. The pipes are at the bottom. The pipes go across the floor. The metal shines. There is the sound of the machine.

She lifts. She moves. She tips.

She lifts. She moves. She tips.

The egg does not fall out. The egg is stuck to the cardboard. The cardboard is the carton. There is the sound of the machine. The hand hits the top of the carton. The egg falls.

She places the carton on the right.

She lifts the carton on the left.

She moves it.

She tips it.

The eggs fall out.

The eggs that do not break are three. The eggs that do not break catch against each other at the mouth of the tunnel.

She turns the carton. She pushes the eggs with the corner of the carton. The eggs crack. The eggs fall in.

She places the carton on the stack. She turns. She lifts the carton off the stack. She turns. She tips. The eggs fall out.

The eggs crack. The shells break. The eggs slide.

She turns to the right. She places the carton. She turns to the left. She lifts the carton. She turns to the centre. She tips the carton.

The eggs fall out. The shells break. The shells crack. The eggs flow out.

The eggs crack. The egg cracks. The chick is green. The chick is in it. The chick is dead. The chick sticks to the shell. The chick and shell slide into funnel.

She looks at the chick and the egg. The chick and the egg

slide into funnel. She looks at the chick and the egg slide in. The metal shines. There is the heat. There is the sound of the machine.

She places the carton. She turns. She lifts the carton. She turns. She tips the carton.

The eggs fall out.

She places. She turns. She lifts. She turns. She tips. She looks. She uses the corner.

She places the carton on the stack.

She sweats. There is the heat. There is the sound of the machine. There is the smell of the eggs.

She turns. She lifts. She turns. She tips. She turns. She places. She turns.

                        out into sun   blaze

pavement sun

                                        traffic waiting street

      people waiting standing looking

                        people walking left right sun

right   shop   neon MOBILE PHONES red in window

                  cream pavement cracks in sun

         NO PARKING white on blue

     right corner

CONFECTIONERS   TOBACCONISTS STATIONERS

right again   shadow railway bridge

cooler darker   white droppings pavement

car white through green light

cooing

grey cream pavement

and out   into sun

It is the bus stop. It is the queue. The cars are in the street.
They stand.
The sun is on the people. The sun is on the cars. The sun is
on the street.
It stops. Two men get out. The shirts are white. The sleeves
are short.
The queue sweats. The men sweat. The sleeves are short.
The sun is on the street.
They walk to the back.
He opens the door. The dog is big. He clips the lead to the
collar. The dog jumps street.
The car is in the street. The sun is on the street. The sun is
on cars. The traffic queues behind the car. There is the sound of
cars. There is the sound people. There is the sunlight along
street.
It is the shop and the man runs. The man runs into street.
The jacket is red.
He runs into street. Cars brake. He runs between the cars.
There is the sound of the horns.

The dog strains. They see him. He sees them. The queues watch. The dog barks. They shout. He sees dog. He runs. They run.

He turns. He runs. The cars move. His face is sweat. The people at the stop look. He runs.

The men run. The dog runs. The railing is to his waist. The light is white. He leans. He leans forward. He leans over. He swings his leg. The foot scrambles. The sun is bright along the street. He is half over. The hand catches the red. The hand pulls.

The people in the cars look. The people at the stop look.

They pull him back. They pull him into street. The queues watch. There are dark patches on the white shirts under the arms. The dog barks. The dog strains. The man pulls the dog back.

He speaks. He is speaking. His hands move. The sun is on the sweat on his face. They put their hands in his pockets. The queues are watching. The jacket is red.

The bus pulls in.

sunblaze

white droppings

building blue red tall in distance

cars colours sound in sun both directions

sun on face

on right entrance bus garage   big   dark

buses inside

concrete cracked brown

across street bushes green trees in heat

railings steel grey

sun

building tall blue red   windows painted on down length

cones plastic white yellow

sun on cars

arrows white on blue

right   over cracks pavement

right   stop at crossing   red man   cars blur buzz

sweat

The clock is on the table. The clock is plastic. The plastic is black. The face is white.

The clock ticks.

The hands are three. The two hands are black. The one hand is red.

The hand that is black and long points to the fifty nine. The hand that is black and short points to just before the seven.

The clock ticks.

The red hand points to the seven.

The curtains are closed.

There is ticking.

The hand moves. The hand that is long and that is black moves. The hand that is black and that is long moves and it points to the sixty.

The hand moves. The hand that is black and it is short moves. The hand moves and it is short and it is black and moves and points to the seven

The hand does not move. The hand that is red does not move. The hand that is red and that points to the seven does not move. The hand that is black and that points to the seven and that is short covers the hand that points to the seven and that is red.

The alarm rings.

The alarm rings in the room.

The alarm rings.

The alarm rings in the room.

The alarm rings.

The duvet moves. The duvet moves and the hand comes out. The duvet moves and the hand comes out and the hand moves across. The duvet moves and the hand comes out and the hand moves across and the alarm rings. The duvet moves and the hand that is red points to the seven and the hand comes out and the hand moves across and the alarm rings and the fingers are touching the table. It is hot and it rings and the table is beside and the hand is moving on the table and it rings and it touches the clock and it rings. The alarm rings. The plastic is black. The arm is out of the duvet and the fingers move over the plastic and the ringing. And the hand feels the clock and the plastic and the alarm rings and the hand touches the switch and the fingers touch the switch and the ringing stops the ringing.

The clock ticks. The hand moves under the duvet. The duvet rustles. There is ticking.

The clock ticks.

The clock ticks.

The clock ticks in the room.

It is hot in the room.

The clock ticks in the room.

The hand moves. The clock ticks. The hand that is long and that is black moves and it points to the one.

The clock ticks.

The clock ticks.

There is the ticking in the room.

The clock ticks.

The door opens.

The woman walks into the room. The handle of the door is the metal. The handle of the mug is the ceramic. The handle of the mug is in the hand of the woman and the tea is in the mug and the door is painted white. The clock ticks. The handle of the mug is white and the mug is white. It is ceramic. The woman turns on the light. The paint on the door is white. The light is white. The light is in the room.

The light is in the room. The handle is in the hand of the woman. The curtains are thick. The letters are on the mug. The light comes from the bulb. There is the heat. The tea is in the mug. The sunlight is in the gap in the curtains. The letters are blue. The curtains are brown. The milk is in the tea. The clock ticks. The sugar has dissolved. The light is in the room.

The woman walks to the bed. The table is beside the bed. The woman puts the mug on the table. The woman puts the mug beside the clock on the table. The clock ticks. The woman puts the mug beside the clock on the table beside the bed and the woman speaks.

The woman speaks.

The clock ticks.

The woman speaks.

The woman speaks.

He mumbles. The duvet moves. The eyes move. The eyes open.

The eyes flood with light. The light floods the eyes. The light is white. The eyes close. He turns in the bed.

The woman turns. The woman walks to the door. The clock ticks. The light is on. There is the sound of the music on the radio in the kitchen down the stairs. The light is in this room. The woman walks out of the room.

The clock ticks.

The clock ticks.

The clock ticks.

The hand points to three.

The clock ticks.

The clock ticks.

The clock ticks.

The tea cools.

The hand points to four.

There is the sound of the birds and the traffic outside. There is the sound of the radio in the kitchen.

The woman walks into the room. The woman stands. The woman looks at the bed. The heat and the light are in the room. The woman walks to the bed. The woman bends. The woman puts the hand on the duvet. The woman puts the hand on the duvet on the bed.

She shakes. She shakes him. She speaks.

The eyes open. The light whites into the eyes. The eyes blink.

He looks. He looks at her. She speaks. She points.

He nods. He looks round.

The light is in the room. There is the heat. There is the sound of the music on the radio downstairs in the kitchen.

He nods. He looks round. He licks the lips.

She looks at him. He stretches. The tongue licks the lips. She speaks. He stretches. He stretches in the bed. He sits up.

He sits up. She speaks. He nods. He speaks. She speaks. He nods. The woman turns. The woman walks out of the room.

He yawns.

The hands come out. The hands come out from under the duvet. The hands rub the face.

He looks.

The light is white. The light is in the room. The light is from the bulb. The light is white. The bulb hangs. The light comes from the bulb out into the room. The light fills the room. The light comes from the bulb that hangs from the centre of the ceiling and the white fills the room.

He leans back. He looks round.

The light is in the room.

He scratches the head.

There is the sound of the music on the radio in the kitchen.

He turns. The hand takes the handle. The hand lifts the mug. He sips.

red man   sun white

cars blue white   red   lanes three

     black on yellow OFFICE SUITES AVAILABLE

across road on wall

      paint peeling blue

   black beard waits centre island

        blue jeans   shirt white blue

              cars stop   wait

               man green

cross to island   black beard past

  red man opposite   cars pass   van blue

               sun

There are the books. The books are on the shelves.
There is the dust. The dust is on the shelves.

            sun on street

red man

cars blue green

no clouds

blue

tree hangs down leaves

trickle sweat

cars slow to stop

man green   cross

white light

OFFICE SUITES AVAILABLE

railings bent grey dirt

past tree hanging leaves   heat

police car at lights white striped red

torn poster paper on lamppost

THE PLEASURE BOAT gold on blue dark

glitter gold in sun

papers cardboard cans on pavement from plastic black

The trees are green. There is the sun. There is the breeze. The breeze moves the tops of the trees. The blue is the sky. It is the afternoon.

The sun is in the garden. The grass is green. The green is pale. She places the towel on the grass.

The towel is green. The towel is old. The towel is green on the grass. The trousers are old. She kneels on the towel.

She bends forward.

The handle is red. The prongs are black.

The soil is dry. The brown is pale.

The soil is on the prongs.

The shade is in the corner. The bird flies.

The heat is in the garden.

The bird lands on the wall. The dog is in the corner. In the corner is the shade.

The bird looks at the garden.

The dog is in the corner under the trees. The head of the bird flicks. The dog looks at the bird. The tongue is pink. The tongue is out.

She bends over the flowerbed.

The dog lies the head on the paws.

The bird flies.

white sun   PLEASURE BOAT

red flowers green boxes   blue above windows dirt

brown benches wood

three men pints football shirts looking

spilled rubbish pavement past

heat   sun on face

sun on blue building tall   tower into blue

windows painted on

traffic noise   three lanes   cars   vans

OPEN TO PLAY

up bridge hump   canal right   brick red blackened

green wall

barge canal red painted sides

girls two ahead

TRUE?   FALSE?   on billboard opposite

sweating

They stand. They stand in the line. They look.

It is the morning. The door is locked. The cars drive into the car park. The sun is on the cars. They look at the cars.

They stand on the ramp. The ramp is the concrete. The sun is on the ramp. The ramp leads to the door. They stand at the railings. The railings are the metal. They look down. Below there is the path and then there is the grass and then there are the trees.

They look at the cars. They look at the car park. They look at the people get out of the cars. They look at the people lock the cars. They look at the people walk across the car park.

The sun is on them. It is morning. There is the sound of the cars. There is the sound of the birds.

The birds are in the trees. The people walk below. The people walk down the path. They lean over the railings and they look at the people walk down the path below.

The people walk down the path. The people turn left. There is a door. The people walk through the door.

They wait on the ramp. They wait. The door is locked. They lean over the railings. The cars drive into the car park. They look at the people and the cars. The people walk down the path.

There is the sound of bells in the distance.

TRUE?

girls two walking sun

blue jeans   shoes black

t-shirt red STOU in black on back

hair long brown

skirt long black top white   hair red blonde neck

                    hips sway buttocks under skirt

              strap bag black crosses shoulder left to hip right

                  white tow truck   blurs

        car blue   white car

          heat   sun   black car   black smoke

        bright sun on chewing gum white circles pavement

              girls right down steps to sun on canal water glint

                  trees

                  yellow DO WHAT WORKS on red

    The boxes are in the corridor. The boxes are stacked. The
boxes are six. He walks the corridor.
    The boxes are six. The boxes are stacked. The boxes are
stacked against the wall. There are three stacks. There are two
boxes in each stack.
    There is the label on the top of each box. There is the label
on the side of each box. The blue is the label on the top of each
box. The white is the label on the side of each box. The label on
the top of each box is small. The label on the side of each box
is big. The letters are black. The cardboard is brown.
    He unlocks the door. He opens the door. He walks into the
office.
    The sun is in the windows. The sun is on the floor. The sun
is on the desk.

There is the sound of the traffic on the street outside.

He walks behind the desk. He places the plastic bag on the floor. He takes off the jacket. He hangs the jacket over the back of the chair.

He walks to the window. He opens the window.

He unbuttons the button. He loosens the tie.

The boxes are in the corridor. He rolls the sleeves. The sleeves are white. He rolls the sleeves of the shirt. He rolls the sleeves of the shirt as he walks into the corridor.

He lifts the first. He carries the first into the office. He places the first on the floor in the centre of the office.

He walks into the corridor.

He lifts the second. He carries the second in. He places the second beside the first on the floor in the centre of the office.

He walks to the boxes in the corridor.

He lifts the third. The third is lighter than the second and the third is lighter than the first. He carries the box into the office. He places the third.

He walks into the corridor.

He lifts the fourth. He walks into the office. The fourth is heavier than the third. He places the fourth on the floor beside the first and beside the second and beside the third.

He stands. He sweats.

He lifts the fifth. He carries the fifth into the office. He places the fifth down on top of the first and the fourth.

He walks into the corridor. The sun shines into the corridor through the skylight. The dirt is on the skylight.

There is one box in the corridor. He lifts it. He carries the box into the office. He places the box on the desk.

There is the heat. The hands are wet. The hands wipe the trousers. The arm wipes the forehead.

He walks to the door.

He shuts the door.

He walks to the desk.

He walks behind the desk.

He sits.

The right hand goes into the right pocket of the jacket that hangs over the back of the chair. The hand takes out the packet. The hand takes out the lighter.

The fingers take it out. The fingers place the end in the mouth. The fingers take the lighter. The fingers flick the lighter.

The flame flicks up. The fingers hold the flame to the end. The mouth sucks in.

The mouth sucks in air. The mouth sucks in air through the cigarette. The mouth sucks in the air and the smoke through the cigarette into the lungs. The air sucks in the flame. The tip reds.

He breathes out.

He places the lighter on the desk. He sucks in. He sucks in the smoke. He looks at the boxes.

The drawers are three. The drawers are in the left of the desk. He pulls the top drawer.

He searches.

He looks up. He looks up at the top of the desk. He looks at the ashtray. The ashtray is glass. The glass is clear. The glass is chipped. The ash is in the ashtray. The ends are in the ashtray. The ends are four. He leans the cigarette into the ashtray.

The windows are behind him. The sun is on him. The sun is on the desk. The smoke rises up.

He pushes the first drawer. He pulls the second drawer. The eyes look in. The hand goes in.

He searches.

He takes it out. The handle is black and yellow. The blade is metal.

He lifts the cigarette. He sucks in the smoke and he stands. The smoke breathes out. He leans the cigarette in the ends.

He stands. He leans. He leans over. He leans over the box.

The left hand moves the screwdriver to the right hand.

The tape is brown. The tape is thick. The tape seals the box.

The edges of the two flaps of the lid of the box fit together. The tape tapes the edges together. The tape tapes over the edges. The tape is brown. The cardboard is brown.

The sun is on his back. He sweats.

He places the edge of the blade of the screwdriver on the centre of the tape where it joins the edges of the two flaps of the box together.

white sun

DO WHAT WORKS

left of pavement paving stones cracked white

right of pavement tarmac grey black strips

fence wood grey overhung leaves berries green red

white van indicating into lane

sweat

white AHEAD ONLY arrow on tarmac black

sweat trickle

bus   red bumpers   blue   slow hill

sunshine reflects window

view far down street to far red lights in sun

right under grey back road sign

right into paved over area

heat sun face   heat

weeds green round trunks black thin

                            trees green leaves

                                 paper white blowing

     cans

                                   cigarette ends

beyond   cars queue to petrol station

         trees behind railings   sun

       tall of building blue   into blue sky

        bench metal black under trees

               noise of traffic

The floors are two.

There is the ground floor. The door is in the middle of the ground floor.

There are twenty-five windows.

There are six windows to the left of the door.

There are six windows to the right of the door.

There is the first floor. The window is in the middle of the first floor.

There are six windows to the left of the window.

There are six windows to the right of the window.

The window is above the door. The flagpole is above the

window. The flagpole stretches out from the wall. The flagpole stretches out over the pavement.

This sky is blue.

The door is black. The sign is on the door. The sign is white. The sign is blank.

The flagpole is metal. The paint is grey. The paint peels. The metal rusts.

metal black bench

one sheet metal holes curves over four legs black

slabs of grey red paving stones

right past bench

line four trees trunks

plastic mesh green holds poles thin wooden

black grille weeds

queue cars left to petrol station

sun on car windows

building tall blue right light blue dark blue fifteen stories

windows edged red   into blue cloudless

                                past trees

                        past building

                sun on face

        ENTRANCE in distance

                cars around edges of building

It is the night. There is no sound.

She sits on the chair. The chair is blue. The bottle is on the table beside the chair. The glass is on the table beside the chair.

It is the night.

The humming starts. The humming stops.

She speaks.

The humming starts.

The left hand lifts the bottle. The right hand unscrews the cap. The right hand puts the cap on the arm of the chair. The left hand lifts the bottle to the lips. The lips open. The liquid slides out. The liquid slides between the lips. The liquid slides into the mouth. The liquid is gold. She swallows.

The right hand takes the bottle. The left hand lifts the glass. The right hand tips the bottle. The liquid slides. The liquid slides out of the bottle and the liquid slides into the glass. The liquid is gold.

The left hand places the glass on the table. The right hand moves the bottle to the left hand. The right hand lifts the cap. The right hand screws the cap on the bottle. The left hand places the bottle on the table beside the glass. The right hand touches the glass. The right hand lifts the glass.

She sips.

She sips.

The humming starts.

The humming stops.

She sips.

She sips.

The humming starts.

The knees draw up. The head rests on the knees. The left arm is around the legs. The head rests on its side on the knees. The right hand holds the glass.

The eyes close.

The humming stops.

The eyes open.

She sits up.

She sips.

She sips.

She stands.

She walks to the chest of drawers. The right hand places the glass on top of the chest of drawers. The right hand opens the drawer at the top of the chest of drawers.

The letters are in the left of the drawer. The book is on top of the letters in the left of the drawer.

The right hand lifts the book.

The right hand and the left hand slide the drawer shut. The right hand passes the book to the left hand. The right hand lifts the glass.

She walks to the chair. She sits on the chair.

The book is a paperback. There is the photograph on the front. She looks at the photograph.

She sips.

The hand places the book on the table. The hand places the glass on the table. The hand lifts the bottle. The hand unscrews the cap. The hand lifts the glass. The liquid slides. She sips.

The hand places the bottle on the table. The hand places the glass on the table. The hand lifts the cap. The hand lifts the bottle. The hand screws the cap on the bottle. The hand puts the bottle on the table. The hand lifts the glass. She sips.

The feet draw up. The feet tuck under. The hand puts the glass on the table.

The right hand takes the book.

The eyes look at the book. The eyes look at the front.

The hands turn the book. The eyes look at the back.

The hands turn the book.

The fingers open the book.

The fingers turn the pages.

through cars parked blue white red

grey stone heat

brown slabs concrete

sun

lampposts thin black   into blue   over car park

manhole covers four round black

blue pale car   back flat tyre left

heat   sweating

football white on pavement by black railings

sweat   wipe forehead shirt sleeve

through black railing gate

left right metal handrails silver in sun

narrow grid silver metal under feet

stripes black white cross tarmac

The women are on the grass. The sun is on them. One woman is alone. She lies face down. Two women lie face up beside each other. Another woman lies face up. A woman sits beside her. She drinks from the bottle. She wears the sunglasses. She looks round.

The sun is on them.

The men walk to the bench. The men carry the bags. The men are three. The men sit on the bench. The men wear the suits.

The bags are plastic. One bag is white. He opens the bag. He takes out the sandwich. He takes out the bottle.

The bags are plastic. Two bags are blue. They open the bags. They take out the cartons. The cartons are yellow. The food is in the cartons. They take out the forks. The forks are plastic and the plastic is white. The cans are cold.

The men look at the women. The women look at the men.

They eat.

Two men walk to the bench. The men wear the suits. The men carry the bags. The bags are plastic.

The three men move up. One man sits on the bench. The other man places the bag on the grass. He takes off the jacket. He looks at the grass. He places the jacket on the grass. He sits on the grass. He faces the bench.

They open the bags. They look at the women. The women look. They take out the sandwiches. They take out the cans.

The men eat. The men drink. The men look at the women. The men talk.

The pigeon flies onto the path. The eyes move in the head. It walks around the men.

They are a man and a boy and a dog and they walk down the path. The man holds one end of the lead. The other end of the lead is attached to the collar. The collar is around the neck of the dog. The tongue of the dog is pink. The lead is brown. The dog sniffs at the grass. The collar is red. The man pulls the lead. The dog follows. The dog is black.

The sun is on the women.

The flowers are in the bed. The bed is a circle. The bed is in the centre of the grass.

The woman sits up. She lifts the bottle to the lips. She looks at the flowers. She looks at the men. She looks at the flowers. The flowers are red and the flowers are blue and the flowers are yellow. The sunlight is on the flowers. The sunlight is on the women. The sunlight is on the men.

The woman looks through the sunglasses. The woman looks at the men. The water is warm. The woman looks at the back of the shirt of the man sitting on the grass. The shirt is white. The white is darker under the arms.

She lies back.

They finish the eating. They drink from the cans. The cans are cold. They talk. The man who sits on the grass lights the cigarette.

The park is white. The park is white with light.

The squirrel runs out. The squirrel runs from the shade. The squirrel runs onto the grass. The squirrel runs into the sunlight.

The squirrel stops.

The squirrel looks round. The squirrel looks at the men. The squirrel looks at the women.

The men look at the squirrel. Two women look at the squirrel. The squirrel twitches. The squirrel runs.

The men watch the squirrel. The squirrel stops. The women watch the squirrel. Two women walk down the path. The squirrel runs. The blouse of one woman hangs out of the skirt at the back. The squirrel runs to the base of the tree. The skirt is grey and the blouse is white. The squirrel runs up the tree.

The woman looks. The man who sits stands. The hand brushes the back of the trousers. He bends. He takes the sandwich wrapper. He takes the can. He takes the bag. He places the can and the wrapper in the bag.

The woman lying on her own sits up. She looks round. She looks at the watch.

The men on the bench stand. They place the cans and the cartons and the bottle and the wrappers and the forks in the bags.

The woman stands. The hand brushes the back of the skirt.

He lifts the jacket. The hand brushes the jacket. The hand hangs the jacket over the shoulder.

She lifts the bottle. She unscrews the lid. She drinks.

They walk towards the arch. The bin is beside the arch.

She screws the lid. She places the bottle in the bag. She
places the towel in the bag.
    They put the bags into the bin.
    She places the cardigan in the bag.
    They walk through the arch.
    The pigeon lands beside the bench.

  sunlight

     stripes black white

  to paving stones brown   to supermarket

    blue plastic mesh around bottom tree trunks

      sun white

       cars parked either side heat

  people   trolleys   plastic bags white

    children laughing across   run

     cars past slow

    signs yellow paint on tarmac black

woman long dress red shopping back car glances

                    red posters   advertisements

        cashpoint queues two

    past trolleys rows silver

                handles red pushed into handles red

            man bald fifties glasses rattles tin yellow

                        into shade

    in shade magazines in stands near door   car magazines

        behind stands dog tied   lies facing glass doors

            shop movement inside colours   ears flick

    colours confusion blurs   movement through glass

                    blur   heat

The shelves are against the walls. The labels are on the shelves.
The books are on the shelves. The labels are on the books.
    The tables are three.
    There is no sound.
    The man sits at the first table. The man sits back in the chair.
The man holds the newspaper. The man sits and the man reads.
    The girl sits at the second table. The books are two. The
books are open. The books are on the table.

She reads. The tip of the finger moves under the line.

She stops the reading. She turns. She looks at the second book. She reads.

She bends forward. She writes.

The counter is beside the door. The counter is long. The counter is chest height.

The man sits behind. The man looks at the monitor below the counter.

The dress is blue. The eyes look at the shelf. The dress is long. The eyes look at the books on the shelf. The eyes look at the spines. The shoes are black. The eyes look at the words. The stockings are black. The eyes move to the end of the shelf. The hair falls. The eyes move to the shelf below.

There is no sound.

The eyes move over the spines. The eyes move over the words. The spines are colours. The eyes reach the end. The eyes move down.

She turns. She bends at the waist. The fingers lift the hair behind the ear and the eyes move.

The eyes stop. She leans. She looks. She kneels.

She takes the book. The carpet is red. She looks at the front. She looks at the words. She turns it. She looks at the words.

She pushes the book back into the shelf. She pushes the book between books.

She kneels up on the carpet. She looks at the next spine. She looks at the next spine. She takes the book.

The book is in the hands. The eyes are on the book. She sweats under the arms. The letters are black. She reads the words.

She opens.

The first page is white. The fingers turn the page. The eyes look. The fingers turn the page. The eyes look at the words.

There is no sound.

The fingers turn the pages. The carpet is red. There is rustle of the newspaper. The eyes look at the sentence.

She closes the book. She pushes the book back into the shelf.

through glass doors revolving

light

colours   people   movement

queue cigarette desk right

left counter woman under DRY CLEANING

over aisle blue letters

FRESH FRUIT AND VEGETABLES   on white

red orange green

shoppers crowd

trolleys baskets

children

apples red   oranges   yellow peppers   red   green   cucumbers

bananas yellow curves

down aisle beans spaghetti tins

through people trolleys

to back

people looking talking

FRESH FISH AND MEAT

She turns the engine off.

She takes off the seatbelt. He takes off the seatbelt.

She winds the window up. He winds the window up.

The child is singing.

She speaks. He nods.

They get out of the car. The sun is white on the road. The sun is white on the driveway.

He pushes down the button. She slams the door. He slams the door. She locks the door.

The sun is down on them.

He takes the keys out of the pocket. She puts the keys in the pocket. He unlocks the front door. She walks round the car.

He lifts the letters. He looks at them. There are three. He steps in. He puts them on the table. He turns.

She unclips the harness on the seat. She lifts the child. The child puts the arms round the neck.

The child looks at the street. The street is white. The boy rides the bicycle past. The child looks at the boy ride the bicycle past.

She lifts the bear. She pushes down the button. She slams the door.

He speaks. She looks. He points at the front door. She nods.

As he walks to the boot she carries the child to the front door. As she puts the child on the floor in the hall he opens the boot. As he lifts the bag from the boot she lifts the letters from the table.

The child walks into the living room. The child walks to the toys beside the wall.

She opens the letters.

He carries the bags into the kitchen. He puts the bags on the table.

She reads.

411

The child plays and talks.

He walks out to the car. She puts the letters on the table.

The bags are plastic and he carries them in. He carries them in and he puts them on the table in the kitchen. The back of the hand wipes the forehead.

The child turns. The child stands. The child looks up. The child looks up at the shelves on the bookcase.

She takes off the jacket. She sweats under the arms.

He walks into the hall. He sweats under the arms.

She hangs the jacket on the coat stand.

He puts the arms around her. He kisses the cheek. She smiles. The child looks. The child speaks.

They turn. He lets his arms fall. They look at the child.

The child is smiling. They smile at the child.

The child looks at her. The child speaks. The child points back into the living room.

She smiles. She nods. She speaks. She steps forward. She lifts the child.

He steps into sun. There are three left. He lifts them. He slams the boot.

She and the child look at the DVDs on the shelf. She points to one of the DVDs. She looks at the child. She speaks.

The child nods then speaks.

She speaks. She points.

The child speaks.

She speaks. She points.

The child nods. The child speaks. The child claps the hands.

He puts the bags on the table. He walks into the hall. The jacket is on the coat stand. He searches the pockets. He takes out the keys.

She stands the child on the floor. She kneels. She reaches to the wall. She turns the plugs on.

The child claps the hands.

He locks the boot. He walks back into the hall. He closes the door. He locks the door. The keys hang from the lock.

The child claps. The child turns. The child walks to the bean-bag. The child sits.

He unpacks. He unpacks into the fridge. He unpacks into the cupboards.

She presses the buttons. She puts in the DVD. She looks at the controller.

The DVD starts.

The child looks.

She sits on the sofa beside the beanbag. She pulls the hair of the child away from the eyes and behind the ears. She speaks. The child nods.

He packs the bags into one bag. He opens the door beneath the stairs. He puts the bag of bags into the bag of bags.

She reaches down. She pulls the strap off the right heel. She pulls the strap off the left heel. She pulls off the shoes.

The child looks at the colours moving.

The windows are open.

She smoothes the hair of the child. She lifts the shoes. She walks into the hall.

He turns on the tap. The water falls into the kettle.

She walks up. She stands behind him. She puts her arms around him.

meat red   wet shine behind glass

FRESH POULTRY

past FRUIT JUICE

MILK

carton blue lift

man jumper colours   notepad writing   glasses black

cold in aisle

past trolleys   shoppers looking shelves

DELICATESSAN

girls blue uniforms behind counters right

colder

margarines cabinet stack left   bright light

LOW FAT

FRESH READY MEALS

bread smell hot

There is the queue. She looks up the street. There are no spaces.
The queue moves. The sun is white. The sunglasses are black.
The car is parked. The car indicates out.
The sun is along the street.
The car in front stops. She stops.
The parked car drives out.
The car in front indicates in. She waits. The car in front
drives forward. The car in front stops. The car in front reverses.
The car in front reverses into the space.
She drives on. She passes the parking car. She stops at the
end of the queue. She waits.
The sun is on them. The sun is on the cars. The sun is on the
people.
The queue moves.
The window is down. She looks at the clock.
The people walk the pavement. The people look the win-
dows shops.
The queue moves.
The side street is left ahead.

She flicks. The light flicks. There is the ticking.
She waits.
The queue moves.
She accelerates. She turns left. She drives the street. The spaces are none.
She turns left. She drives the street. The spaces are none.
She turns left. She drives the street. The spaces are none.
She stops at the end of the street. There is the queue. She indicates left. She waits.
The sky is blue. It is noon. The sky is blue.
The car stops. The driver waves.
She drives out. As she drives out she waves. She lefts.
She joins the queue.

BAKERY

loaves brown   cellophane   stacked stands

  corner queue

girl's hair long   t-shirt white tight nipples   lifts loaf

    bread smell

                                    into aisle

BREAD

packaging green red blue plastic paper

    different loaves   different colours

reading label man   twenties   long shorts   t-shirt blue

            sliced   prices

waxed paper blue   red   white   sliced white   lift

           down

to side aisle

                   trolleys two block aisle

  move to side

   woman thirties tanned pushes trolley past smiling

CLOTHS AND POLISHES

SOAP POWDER

sweat sticking

The sunlight shines into the room. The sunlight shines onto the dust. The dust is on the television. The dust is on the video recorder. The sunlight shines on the plastic. The plastic is black.

The door opens. The girls are two. The girls walk into the room.

The girl holds the box. The jeans are blue. The t-shirt is yellow. She walks to the corner.

The girls speak. The other girl sits on the sofa. The jeans are blue. The t-shirt is white.

The television is in the corner. The dust is on it. The video recorder is under the television. She reaches behind. She presses. The panel on the video recorder lights. She presses. The light on the front of the television lights red.

The girls speak. The girl kneels on the floor. The girl presses the button on the front of the video recorder. The girl presses the second button on the front of the video recorder. There is the sound of the video coming out.

She takes the video out of the video recorder. She places the video on the floor.

She opens the box. The sun is on the side of her face. She takes the video out of the box. She puts the box on the floor. She places the video. She pushes. There is the sound of the video going in.

She stands. She bends. She picks up the video on the floor. There is the box on top of the television. She takes the box. She opens the box. She puts the video in the box. She closes the box. She puts the box on top of the television.

The sun is on the side of her face.

The controller is on top of the television. She takes the controller.

She looks at the controller. The plastic is black.

She presses the button.

The channel appears.

There are the colours. The colours come into the room. The sound comes into the room.

She looks at the controller. She presses the button. The colours stop. The sound stops. There are words.

She turns. She walks to the sofa. She sits.

They watch the screen.

They speak.

They watch the screen.

The colours move. The music is in the room. The girl in the t-shirt that is white kicks off the sandals that are pink. She puts the feet under her.

They look at it. There are the colours moving and there is the music.

The girl in the t-shirt that is white looks at the girl in the t-shirt that is yellow.

417

The girl in the t-shirt that is white speaks.

The girl in the t-shirt that is yellow looks at the girl in the t-shirt that is white.

The girl in the t-shirt that is yellow speaks.

The girl in the t-shirt that is yellow looks at the controller black plastic.

The girl in the t-shirt that is yellow looks at the colours moving.

She stands. She walks to the window. The window at the top is open.

She closes the window.

She looks at the street. There are the cars. There is the sun on the cars.

She pulls the first curtain. She pulls the second curtain.

The room is dimmed.

The girl in the t-shirt that is yellow walks to the sofa.

The girl in the t-shirt that is yellow sits on the sofa.

SOAP POWDER

BISCUITS

floor dull tiles   lights bright on people trolleys shelves

child crying trolley seat   wet cheeks   stares

JELLIES AND CUSTARDS

left   BREAKFAST CEREALS

down aisle looking

different colours   different makes

                                        lift box

        to end

                        out

                                tills   queues

                        BASKETS ONLY

            fifties bald patch man

                        woman forties blue skirt

basket   OVEN CHIPS ECONOMY   blue chocolate

    voices   tills ring   movement   shining

            bell   bright light

                        queue moves forward

    The lights are on. The lights turn off. The lights are off. The
lights turn on.
    The people look up. The people look at the lights. The peo-
ple look down.
    There is the heat.
    The train slows. The train stops.
    The people look up.

There is the woman with the hair that is short. The woman with the hair that is short speaks. The woman with the hair that is short looks at the watch that is on the wrist that is left.

There is the heat. There is the smell of the dust. There is the smell of the sweat. There are the people.

There is the man in the suit. The man in the suit looks at the woman with the hair that is short. The man in the suit looks back at the newspaper that is between the hands.

The boys are two. The boys sit. The two boys that are beside each other look up the carriage. The legs swing. They do not speak.

The train is in the tunnel. The dirt is on the tunnel walls. The dirt is black.

The train does not move.

There is the teenager who is the boy and there is the teenager who is the girl.

The teenager who is the boy lies back in the seat that is blue. The teenager who is the boy leans the side of the head against the partition that is glass. The eyes are closed and the legs are wide. The photograph is on the t-shirt.

The teenager who is the girl takes off the jacket that is denim. She folds it. Her t-shirt is white. She looks down the carriage. She looks up the carriage. She looks across the carriage.

The teenager who is the girl looks at the teenager who is the boy. The teenager who is the girl looks at the face of the teenager who is the boy. His eyes are closed. She looks at his jeans.

The woman in the trousers that are black turns the page of the book.

The man with the bag that is plastic looks at the floor.

queue forward

noise people tills

woman   metal basket on top pile metal baskets

oven chips belt   chocolate belt

NEXT CUSTOMER PLEASE belt

put bread   milk   cereal   belt

blue teenage uniform boy   hair short

beep items scan   down counter slide

man fat at end fills bag plastic white red letters

ALL TILL-TRAINED MEMBERS OF STAFF

The map is on top. The magazines are on top. The books are on top. The books are twenty-five.

The map is bent. The books are on top of each other. Two crumple the map. Magazines are on top. The map is torn.

Twenty-nine books are on the first shelf. Three covers are hard. Twenty-six books are paperbacks.

The spines are colours. There are three white. There are eleven black. There is green. There is gold.

The spine is purple.

Twenty-eight books are on the second shelf. One is horizontal on six. Twenty-seven are vertical.

Twenty-two books are on the third. Two are in a case The spine of one of the two has half a photograph. The spine of the other has the second half of the photograph.

There is the packet of sweets. The packet of sweets is on the fourth shelf. The box of tablets is beside the nail-clippers. The knife is on the fourth shelf. There is the fork. The knife is clean. There is the tablespoon. There is the teaspoon. On the fourth shelf there is the tissue. The dish is on the shelf. On the fourth shelf there are three receipts. The tissue is crumpled. The lottery ticket is folded. There are eight coins.

Seventeen books are on the shelf which is the fifth shelf. There is the magazine. Four are paperbacks. There are thirteen hardbacks.

Sun is on it. It is black.

heat

fat man back trouser pocket

two cards to teenage boy blue

boy slots cards till

next till girl long hair white t-shirt nipples

on till sign blue WELCOME YOUR CUSTOMER on black

man buttons press   waits looking

boy hands   man takes cards

takes bags   walks

sign NEXT CUSTOMER PLEASE behind milk bread cereal

woman forties   oven chips   chocolate belt

sweat

There is the noise of the machine. The clothes are inside. She sips. The clothes spin. The noise is in the room. It is the final spin.

The noise is high.

The noise drops.

The spinning slows.

The noise deepens. The noise lessens.

The machine is white. The window is the circle and the circle is glass. The clothes slow tumble.

There is the click. The noise stops. The spinning stops.

She looks at it. She stands. The mug is on the table.

She pulls it. The handle pulls towards her. The sky is outside. She pulls the clothes.

The clothes tangle in the ball. The door is open and the sun is on the floor. The clothes are on the table. The mug is on the table. She pulls the clothes apart.

The sheet is white. The sky is blue.

She takes the corners. She opens the arms. She folds. The white is wet.

The sheet is white. The sky is blue.

She walks into the yard. The lines are plastic. They are blue. The concrete is dry. It is white. The sheet is white.

The sheet is wet. She holds it above the line. She drops the corners behind. She drops the corners in front in sun. The line is blue. She pulls it out and along the line. It is wet.

It is white. The sun is white.

She walks in. The container is plastic. The plastic is white. She walks out.

The pegs are blue. The lines are blue. The sky is blue.

She pegs. It is white. The pegs are the plastic. The plastic is blue. The white is wet.

She pegs it out.

She places the container on the concrete.

The concrete is white. The sheet is white and clean.

She walks in. The clothes are wet and tangle. She pulls them out. There is the blouse. The pillowcases are two.

The duvet cover is white. It is wet. There is the lace. She pats it. There it is. It is hard. She opens it. She reaches in. It is wet in.

She pulls out the ball. The ball is plastic. The plastic is white.

The sky is blue. It is hot and she walks out. The sun is hot. The concrete is white.

She drops the corners behind. She drops the corners in front wet. It is white. The lines are blue. There is the noise of the birds. It is wet. She bends to the pegs. There is the noise of the traffic in the distance. There is the line white on the blue.

oven chips chocolate   she packs bag looking till

        boy speaks   card   money

    light flash above next till blue uniform girl looking back

                        woman away with plastic bag

to end of till   plastic bag   flap open

        uniform bread scanner   beep

                                sweat back

    bread bag

    passes milk scanner   no beep

            milk scanner   no beep

                    looks label   types number

                    milk bag

              cereal scanner   beep

boy red spots   speaks

          money pocket   hand across

                  cereal bag

                      change   receipt

        change pocket   receipt leave on side

              lift bag   thanks

    left

          past cigarette desk queue

                              turn glass panes

    Cars pass. Cars pass. Cars pass.
    The gate is metal. The gate is tall.
    The cars pass. The buses pass. The taxis pass.
    The policemen stand. The policemen are two. The police-
men stand in front of the gate.
    The cars pass. The cars pass in both directions.
    There is the gate. There is the side street. The gate blocks the
side street.

The policemen stand. The policemen are two. The policemen stand behind the gate.

The drivers are in the cars. The sun is on the cars. The drivers drive.

The sun is on the buses. The passengers are in the taxis. The drivers drive. The passengers are in the buses. The drivers drive. The sun is on the taxis. The passengers look out.

The vans are two. The vans are white. The sun is on the vans and the policemen are in the vans. The policewomen are in the vans. The policemen look out of the windows. The policewomen look out of the windows of the vans.

It is early in the evening. It is hot and it is bright.

People travel.

There are people in cars.

People travel home. People travel home from work. People travel home from work in buses.

There are people in buses.

There are the people in taxis travelling home from work.

The road is across. There is the concrete in the centre. The sun is on it. There are three lanes on each side. The concrete is grey. The traffic drives past in both directions.

The gate is tall. The side street is on one side. The gate blocks the side street. The policemen are behind the gate. The policemen are in front of the gate. The policemen are in the vans. The policewomen are in the vans. The vans are on the concrete.

The sun is white.

There are barriers. The barriers are metal. The barriers are to the waist. The barriers are linked together on the opposite side of the road to the gate.

There are the barriers. There is the road. There is the gate.

The side street is behind the gate. The traffic is in the road. The people are behind the barriers.

The people sweat. The people in the cars sweat. The people in the taxis sweat. The people in the buses sweat. The policemen sweat. The policewomen sweat. The people behind the barriers sweat.

The sun is white.

The people behind the barriers face the gate. The people behind the barriers chant. The people behind the barriers hold the banners. The people behind the barriers shout. The people behind the barriers whistle.

The people in the buses look at the people behind the barriers.
The people in the taxis look at the people behind the barriers.
The people in the cars look at the people behind the barriers.

The policemen wait. The policewomen wait.

The people behind the barriers look at the gate. The people
behind the barriers look at the vans. The people behind the barriers look at the side street.

People travel home from work.

                         out glass   turning

          white heat blaze light

                         man bald   tin rattle yellow

no dog

                                                right

                    sun on cars car park glinting

                         white stripes black stripes

               girl teenage jeans blue pale trainers white

     man   plastic bags boot car from trolley

          blue sky cloudless

                                        sweating

buses red   people queuing with bags plastic white

behind black railings

NOT TO PUSH YOUR TROLLEY BEYOND THIS POINT

over grid silver metal

to grey pavement

circles grey white chewing gum

cigarette ends

blue sky cloudless

heat

people wait

exhaust fumes black from bus   smell   metal heat

blue sky over

It is hot morning. They sit in the front.
There are three. One reads the newspaper. One drives. One
sits in the middle.

There are women pushing prams. There is sun. There is no traffic.

He turns the corner. He drives to the side. He stops.

The engine runs. They speak. He stays in the seat. They get out.

The trees are down the sides. The sunlight is on the trees. The street is white.

The plastic is green. The numbers are on them. The bins are the plastic. The wheels are two. The bins are down the sides of the street. The sun is on them.

They walk. They take the handles. They wheel them to the back. They hook on. The bins lift and the bins tip and the rubbish falls out. The rubbish falls into the back.

The lorry is slow. They walk. They wheel. They hook. They press the button. The bins lift. The bins tip out.

The lorry drives the street. They sweat. They walk to the sides of the street. They walk to the bins. The lorry drives between the trees. The sun is on it.

They take the bins. The bins are green. The lorry is slow. They take the bins back. They sweat. The lorry drives between the bins. They walk the sun in the sun in street.

They stop. The sun is above.

They get into the front.

They are sweating.

There is the smell of the rubbish. There is the smell of the sweat.

They eat the sandwiches. They drink the coffee. They light the cigarettes.

They get out. They walk. The lorry drives down the streets. The heat is in the streets. The metal heats. They drag the bins. There is the dust.

The flats are at the end. He walks down the driveway. He walks through the car park to the back. He wipes the hand on the forehead. The bins are at the back.

The bins are metal. The metal is grey. The grey is stained. The heat is on them. The bins are four. The bins are big. The wheels are on them four each.

He drags. He drags through the car park of the flats. He drags up the driveway. He drags onto the road. He drags to the back. He hooks. He presses the button. It lifts. It tips.

He unhooks. He drags down the driveway. He drags through the car park. He drags to the bins.

The metal is hot. The handles are plastic. The handles are hot.
He drags the next.
He drags it back.
He drags the next.
He drags it back.
He drags the next.
He drags it back.
He sweats. He drags it back and there are two plastic bins
left. The sun is hot. There is the smell. The sun is on his back.
The two are small. The wheels are two. The plastic is green.
He drags. He drags to the lorry. He hooks. He presses.
It lifts. It tips.
He unhooks. He drags. He drags it back.
One is left.

                    right   exhaust fumes

     left   away

      sun white burn face   blind

  cloudless

         squint

            yellow line edge road

   to island middle road

cone plastic yellow white arrows white on blue

      tarmac   buildings   warehouses

green red bushes around car park of factory units

dark windows

cross to pavement

white with sun

car passes red

corner   left

blue garage doors of blue warehouse

shrubs in sun

paving stones crooked cracked

past car pale blue parked   red L on white on bumper

motorbike shining metal parked car park

sun on face

blue cloudless

squinting

long warehouses street stretch to sun

The computers are off.

The monitors are blank. The monitors are black.

The sun is in the windows. The sun is on the desks. The sun is on the computers. The sun is on the monitors. The sun is white. The room is empty.

The computers are fifty-six. The computers are on the desks. The desks are sixty. The rows are six. There are ten desks in each row. Four desks in the last row are empty. There are computers on six desks in the last row. There is a computer on each desk in the first five rows.

The room is empty. There is no sound.

There are the openings in the desks. The openings are in the back right corners of the desks. The openings are round. The openings are small.

The computers are back to back. Leads lead from the backs of the computers to the openings. Leads lead from the backs of the computers through the openings. Leads lead from the openings under the desks to flaps in the floor.

The monitors are black. The sun shines the monitors.

There are books on eight desks. There are sweet wrappers on five desks. There is a crisp bag on one desk. There are bottles on three desks.

The bottles are plastic. The bottles are empty.

There are floppy disks in the floppy drives of two computers. There is a floppy disk on one desk. There is a data stick in the back of one computer. There is a CD in one CD drive.

The room is hot. The room is empty. The room is silent.

The computers turn on.

down warehouse street squinting

plastic yellow bag gutter

sun on street

van green black parked entrance warehouse

                                        sweat armpits

in sun trees bushes green edges warehouse parking

                car passes blue end street

                                    sweat temple trickle

        looking   cross opposite pavement

        poles metal   stripes black white edge pavement

        manhole cover metal black

                post-box red distance

no movement   heat   still

        street

        pallets wooden brown stacked

iron corrugated wall painted cream

left across warehouse parking empty

distance   houses behind trees

slabs concrete wide   rainwater grooves

two men unloading white van

fire alarm yellow on wall up above windows

sun on concrete   brick

right   along path   down steps six

pavement   grey weeds edge

red car passes

house windows across street

The towel is around the head. The towel is around the body.
She walks out of the bathroom. She walks onto the landing.
She walks out of the landing. She walks into the bedroom
    The curtains are closed. The light is on.
    She takes off the towel around the body. She rubs the towel
on the arms. She rubs the towel under the arms. She rubs the
towel on the breasts. She rubs the towel under the breasts. She
rubs the towel on the stomach. She rubs the towel on the neck.

She rubs the towel on the back.

She bends. She rubs the towel on the left thigh. She rubs the towel on the left leg. She rubs the towel between the legs.

She bends. She rubs the towel on the right thigh. She rubs the towel on the right leg. She rubs the towel between the legs.

She sits. She lifts the left foot. She dries it.

She lifts the right foot. She dries.

She leaves the towel on the bed. She stands.

She takes off the towel around the head. She rubs the towel on the hair. She bends. The hair is long. The hair hangs down. She rubs the towel on the hair.

She walks. She opens the drawer. She takes it out. She plugs it in.

She dries the hair. She brushes the hair.

She turns it off.

She unplugs it. She puts it in. She closes the drawer.

She opens the drawer.

The knickers are white. She pulls up the knickers.

The bra is white. She fits the cups around the breasts.

She closes the drawer. She opens the wardrobe.

The dress is blue. She pulls the dress over the head.

The sandals are brown. The toenails are painted red.

She sits.

She looks in the mirror.

The powder is brown.

The liner is black.

The lipstick is pink.

She stands. She closes the wardrobe. She walks to the window. She opens the curtains.

The sun is bright. The sun is morning. The sun comes in. The sun is the street.

She walks to the bed. She lifts the towels. She walks to the window. She hangs the towels over the radiator.

She walks out of the bedroom. She walks onto the landing. She walks down the stairs. She walks into the hall. She walks through the hall. She walks into the kitchen.

She turns on the radio.

There is the sun through the window and there is the music on the radio.

She makes the bowl of cereal. She makes the mug of tea.

She eats the bowl of cereal. She drinks the mug of tea.

The DJ talks. The music plays.

She puts the bowl in the sink. She puts the spoon in the sink. She puts the mug in the sink.

She walks out of the kitchen. She walks into the hall. The handbag is on the floor by the wall.

She looks in the mirror. She presses the lips together. She looks at the clock. She looks in the mirror.

The watch is on the table. She lifts the watch. She puts the watch around the wrist.

There is the sound of the music on the radio in the kitchen.

There are the keys in the door.

There is the sun through the glass in the door.

She lifts the handbag. She walks out of the hall. She walks into the kitchen.

She turns off the radio. The sound of the music stops.

She walks out of the kitchen. She walks into the hall. She walks to the door.

She looks in the mirror.

She turns the key. She takes out the key

She opens the door. There is the brightness. There is the brightness on the street.

She steps out.

She turns. She closes the door.

She puts in the key. She turns the key. She takes out the key.

She turns. As she turns she puts the keys in the handbag.

She looks up.

The sun is the street.

   red blur accelerate past in heat

cross to pavement   houses semi-detached

                hedges green

   left   white car parked   rust

green hedges   walls red brick of   gardens

sun length street

red chimneys brick

van white along street   slows   parks ahead

cars parked blue   white blue   blue   red   along road in line

weeds cracks paving

parked van engine ticks

right   down side street

sweating

blue car parked   back bumper buckle bent scrape black

van blue parked by post-box red

white light

The bodies tangle. They tangle.
The bodies tangle. The bodies tangle.
The bodies are on the beds. The bodies move. The bodies
tangle. The bodies tangle moving limbs. The limbs tangle. They
are tangling. The bodies entangle. They entangle.

The limbs are entangled. The bodies are entangled. They are entangling.

It is the morning. In every part of the city bodies tangle. The bodies are entangling. The limbs entangle. The pieces of the bodies fit into the pieces of the bodies. In every part of the city entangle.

It is the afternoon. In every part they entangle. The bodies entangle. The bodies entangle on the desks. The bodies entangle on the grass. The bodies entangle in the cars. In every part of the city bodies tangle.

It is the evening. The bodies entangle in every part of the city bodies are entangling. The bodies move slow. The bodies move fast. They entangle. In every part entangle.

It is the night. It is the night in every part.

The bodies entangle with the bodies.

The bodies move. The bodies slip.

The bodies entangle.

cross by white van

to tow truck rusting blue white red on corner

sun fall on black tarmac street

quiet

tree-lined   long ahead stretches down

sun shining length on blue car red car red van black car

rubbish bag green side pavement

hedge clipped square neat

sweat sun

children two black silhouettes on white holding hands

in red triangle

SCHOOL black on white

branches spreading upwards to blue cloudless sun

bird moves in twigs

stripe concrete white uneven

by manhole old black round

semi-detached   pebble dashed

windowsills white dirty

left   over tarmac road patchwork shades

past car red driveway

sun on

black circle dish satellite roof

right

gate wooden brown   ten strips

bin green plastic   lid black

                                    up path sweat

windows on ground floor left

                windows on first floor left

        windows on first floor right

door on ground floor right

There is the heat. The bags are plastic. The hands hold the handles.

He walks the street. The street is hot. The sunlight is in the street. He walks though the stalls.

There are the shoppers. The cars queue. The shoppers talk. The shoppers pick up the things. The sellers shout.

He walks through the stalls. There is the heat. There is the hill.

The bags are heavy. The handles cut into the hands. He sweats. The cars pass. He is in the sun. He walks up the hill.

He stops. It is the top. He places the bags pavement. He wipes the face. The face is sweat. The sun is hot on him. The alley is on the left. The sun is hot. He lifts the bags. He sweats. He walks the alley.

The buildings are high. On either side the buildings are high. The buildings are on either side.

The shade is in the alley. He walks the shade in the alley. It is cooler in the alley.

He walks into sun. He walks out of the alley into sun in the car park.

The cars are parked. The cars are red. The cars are blue. The cars are white.

The cars are green.

The cars are yellow.

The cars are black.

The cars shine in the sun.

The cars heat in the sun.

The sun heats the cars. There is the smell of sun heating cars.

He walks through parked cars. He walks across the car park. He walks to the lane.

The lane is short. The lane leads up. The bags hurt the hands. The handles of the bags cut into the hands. The lane leads to the gates.

The gates are open and black. He walks through the gates open and black. The gates are big. He walks through them. He walks into the park.

The sun is in the park. The sun is on the grass. The sun is on the people in the park. The sun is on the trees. The trees are green. There is the line of white on blue.

He stops. The hands put down the bags. The bags are on the path. The bags are white. The letters are on the bags. The letters are black. The tarmac is black. The tarmac is the path.

The hands wipe the shirt. The hands wipe the forehead. The hands are red and sweat. The forehead is sweat. The hands wipe the shirt. The hands rub together.

The sun falls down on the park. The light is white. The hands lift the bags. He walks.

He walks the path. He walks the path through the park. The people are in the park. He looks at the people in the park.

There is the sound of the traffic in the distance. There is the sound of children shouting. There is the bench. The man sits on the bench. The man reads the newspaper.

There is the blanket. The women are two. The women are on the blanket. The faces are down.

He looks at the legs.

441

The path is by the river. The bottle floats in the river. The paper floats in the river. The ducks float in the river.

The handles cut into the hands. He looks at the ducks. There is the sun.

The woman stands. The woman stands in the sun on the bank. The children are two. The child who is girl stands to the right of the woman. The child who is boy stands to the left of the woman. The woman and the children throw the bread to the ducks.

He walks the path. The sun is on him. The sun is on the swimming baths. He walks the path. The path passes the doors. He walks past the doors of the swimming baths. The doors of the swimming baths are open. He looks in the doors of the swimming baths. He walks past the doors of the swimming baths.

The path turns left. He turns left. He walks it. He sweats.

The path goes along the wall of the swimming baths. He walks beside the wall of the swimming baths.

The girl sits on the grass. The top is cotton. The cotton is pink. The girl reads. The sunglasses are on top of the head. The cotton is thin. The cotton is tight. He looks at the girl.

They punch his face. The bags drop. He falls back. He falls back. He falls back against the wall. The punch hits the face.

The wall is white. The head ducks. The arms come up. The head ducks into the arms.

There is the heat. The sun is in the park. The girl looks. The punches hit the arms. The fists punch.

He swings. The wall is behind. He swings out. He misses. The punch hits his face. The second punch hits his face. He falls back. He falls back against the wall.

The sun is on the trees. The girl looks.

He pushes them back. The kick swings. The kick swings at him. The kick hits.

The face wet. The face burns. There is the taste of salt. There is the taste of blood. There is heat. The fist punches the face.

They shout. The arms and the hands cover the face. The fists punch the arms and the fists punch the hands. The kicks swing.

The face is wet. The face burns. They punch the face. He stays up. The wall is behind.

The punch hits the face. The head jerks back. The head hits the wall.

They are crowded. They shout. The girl looks. The sun is on the grass. There is the line on the blue.

They shout. They stand back. He jumps. He jumps forward. He swings the fist left. The punch hits the one swinging to kick.

The face is wet. He runs.

He runs. The sun is on him. The sun is on the grass. He runs on the grass. The sun is white.

The girl looks. The face is wet. There is running.

door wood brown right ground floor

two rows   three glass panes blue green red in top half

letterbox brass   number plate brass gleam sun

jacket   out keys pocket   key bronze in   turn

open to hall shadow   sheet white over radiator

stairs right   carpet pattern red

passageway

sun fills kitchen through window back door

letter on carpet   bend   lift

read

close door behind

dust smell   heat

                down passage

                        first left   door white

key silver long in   left turn   open

room   sunlight through windows dirt

        duvet blue bundle bed   blue shirt

                bag letter bed beside coat hanger

                                jacket chair

light

    windows light sun reflects room in black square television

        plastic bag   to door   out   close behind

            left   lino red kitchen

                        sunlight fills

window   garden roses overgrown

                                  plate white   spoon

knife   saucepan blue   on draining board metal

                        taps stained shine sun

box cereal on microwave cream

       bag plastic to sideboard   milk out

      open fridge   milk shelf beside carton green white

       bag   bread   to shelf in fridge

close fridge door

       bag   cereal   to cupboard

      bag plastic crumple

     cupboard under sink   open

     plastic bag into plastic bag under sink

                    sun blaze window

                                        sweat

        cupboard under sink close

                    sideboard   lead out kettle white

sink   cold tap turn   water sparkle into spout

        pull spout out from water away   tap turn off

        sideboard   kettle plug   switch click

                            to door

There is the gull. There is the lamppost. The gull is on top of
the lamppost. The gull looks at the street.

            out door kitchen

                                    hall dim

                first left

left   turn   door close   slide bolt steel silver

            seat black plastic seat cover fluff pink

446

curtains net white dirty   tiles roses pink

seat lift

unzip

yellow   splashes water   stains edge

last drops

wait

shake

zip

handle down silver push

bowl sudden water splashing

bolt slide silver steel

open   out

hall dim

right into kitchen   sun

left   red lino

kitchen window shine   sunlight heat

to bathroom

stains edges bath sink

open window blows curtain net against

bottles plastic   yellow   white   blue windowsill

bath taps   sponge

tap hot turn sink

water out   shining

white cracked soap

above windows wallpaper roses peel damp

off tap

blue towel on rail

dry

out

to kitchen   filled light

kettle steam to cupboard above

mug white sideboard

kettle clicks   cupboard right

jar red letters glass   top brown unscrew

leave top sideboard

sink

open drawer   no spoons

rack   spoon dry   dull steel   stains   shake

to sideboard

one spoon brown to mug

heat sunlight on back

top brown screw jar glass   to cupboard   close

kettle lift

water out shining to mug on brown turn black

stop pouring

down kettle

fridge open   smell

carton green white door

lift flap up

to side board

milk white   into   mug   black browns

flap down   fridge   carton door   shut door

to sideboard

stir spoon coffee

sink   drop spoon in

sideboard   lift mug   wet circle sideboard

kitchen door

out   hall dim   dust

first right   open   bedroom

close door

dust   to corner by window

sun through glass   dirt

lift jacket   sit armchair orange

mug white cardboard box   under shelf

beside mug blue dry coffee stains

jacket pocket

yellow green foil

The door of the cupboard is white. She opens the door of
the cupboard. She takes out the loaf of bread. The cellophane is

around the bread. She opens the cellophane. She takes out the slices. The slices are two.

The door of the cupboard is open.

She closes the cellophane. She places the bread on the shelf. She closes the door.

The bread is white.

She places one slice into the first slot. She places one slice in the second slot. She presses the lever.

The toaster is green.

The door of the fridge is white. She opens the door of the fridge. She takes out the margarine. She closes the door. The tub is plastic. She places the tub on the side. She takes off the lid. The plastic is white. She places the lid on the side.

The margarine is yellow.

She unplugs the lead. She lifts the kettle. She takes the lid off the kettle. She places the lid on the side.

She walks to the sink. She holds the kettle under the tap. She turns the tap. The water falls into the kettle.

The tap is metal. The water is water.

She turns the tap. She walks to the side. She lifts the lid. She places the kettle on the side. She places the lid on the kettle. She plugs in the lead. She presses the button.

The light is red.

She opens the cupboard. She takes out the plate. She places the plate on the side. She takes out the mug. She places the mug on the side. She closes the cupboard.

The mug is red.

She opens the drawer. She takes out the knife. She places the knife on the plate. She takes out the spoon. She places the spoon on the side. She closes the drawer.

The plate is white.

The bowls are two. The bowls are on the side.

She takes the lid off the bowl. She takes out the teabag. She places the teabag in the mug. She places the lid on the bowl.

There is the sound of the kettle.

She takes the lid off the bowl. She places the lid on the side. She takes the spoon. She places the spoon in the sugar. She places the sugar in the mug. She places the spoon in the sugar. She places the sugar in the mug. She places the spoon in the mug. She lifts the lid. She places the lid on the bowl.

The sugar is white.

She opens the fridge. The door of the fridge is white. She takes out the milk. The milk is in plastic. She closes the door. She places the milk on the side.

The cap is red.

There is the sound of the kettle.

She looks at the toaster. She looks at the wall. She looks at the socket. She walks to the socket. She presses the switch.

unfold flap foil green yellow

heat   dust   quiet

        push sides   opens out

                                out green packet

        out paper white   lay on thigh

pull tangle lump brown   from green foil yellow

                        onto centre paper white

fold green foil yellow to beside white mug blue mug

lie paper tobacco   first two fingers left hand

        hold paper tobacco left thumb

        fingers right hand pull tobacco along white

heat

fold edges paper together

slide rolling edges together

edge under tuck

lick yellow edge shine

stick

pull tobacco string end

end lips

lighter

light end

suck in

suck in

breathe out

lift end lips

                                        suck in

        out

   smoke curl in heat

put cylinder white tip red ashtray glass

                                    mug white

                        hot sip

                                                sip

        mug left hand   right hand lift cigarette

   suck in

                                        out

            suck in

                        out

   sip   hot

                              suck in

                                              out

                    suck in   hold

                              out

white walls white ceiling orange curtains

                              down mug

        cigarette ashtray

                    sunlight on dust in air

lift mug

                        drink   thick warm coffee

            ashtray   cigarette

                        cigarette out

    There is the smell of the metal. There is the smell of the
metal heating. There is the smell of the metal heating in the
sun. There is the smell of the metal of the cars heating in the
sun.
    The plane is in the sky.

The women sweat under the arms. The sweat is wet under the arms.

There are no clouds.

The woman with the hair that is red and long wipes the forehead that is wet with the back of the hand.

The woman with the breasts that are big in the t-shirt is in the car that is green.

The woman in the suit that is blue presses the buttons on the radio that is black.

The woman with the fingernails that are painted purple presses the button to wind the window down further.

There is the sound of the helicopter.

The cars wait.

The sun is bright on the walls of the buildings along the road.

The sun is bright on the metal of the cars.

The sun is bright on the faces of the people in the cars.

The men sweat. The men sweat in the shirts. The armpits sweat. The sweat is in the armpits. The sweat soaks into the shirts.

There is the line of the white across the blue.

The man wearing the tie that is red loosens the tie that is red.

The man in the car that is blue looks in the mirror at the face of the woman who is chewing.

The man humming flicks the ash out of the window.

The man talking on the mobile phone wipes the sweat off the forehead that shines with the back of the hand.

orange curtains

cigarette out   black tip

lighter   light

suck in

out

up   letter off bed   sit

envelope white   stamp orange

black circle postmark

sweating

thumb under flap tear

unfold

one sheet

blue paper   address   no date

words

words

refold

into envelope

envelope on cardboard box beside mugs

suck in

out

flick ash

mug   coffee last

flick ash

suck in

out

smoke curls tip

sunlight through window

suck in

hold

out

fold stub white ashtray glass

in sun

up   to window

                          car passing blue in street

            cars parked sun length of street

      open top middle window small slide handle into place

        sun on cars

                  dust spin in sunlight

curtains heavy orange dust

                                    pull left   close

            pull right closed edge over left

                                          room dark

                  cross   to door

                  light switch

        room fill light

There is the heat.

There are the people on the pavement. The people walk the pavement. The people walk the pavement both directions.

There is the heat. There is the light. There is the sun.

The material is faded. The material is dirty. The material is red and the material is blue. The material is crumpled. The material is on the pavement against the wall.

The man is in the material. The head is shaved. The dog is on the pavement. The dog lies. The man looks at the people. The dog sleeps.

The man looks at the people. The man looks along the pavement. The man sweats. The man sweats in the material. The man looks at the woman in the skirt that is white. The woman in the skirt that is white walks the pavement. The woman in the skirt that is white walks the pavement along. The man looks at the woman in the skirt that is white. The woman in the skirt that is white looks up. The woman in the skirt that is white looks at the man.

The man smiles.

The woman in the skirt that is white looks away.

The light is on the windows and the light is on the mirrors. The cars drive the street. Light reflects. The heat is on the street and on the people. There is the sound of the cars. There are the buildings. There is the sky.

The woman in the skirt that is white looks at the man. The man looks at the woman in the skirt that is white. The man holds up the cup. The woman in the skirt that is white looks away.

The man looks at the woman in the skirt that is white.

The woman in the skirt that is white looks at the man. The woman in the skirt that is white looks at the cup. The woman in the skirt that is white looks at the man. The woman in the skirt that is white stops.

The woman in the skirt that is white opens the handbag that is white.

The woman in the skirt that is white opens the purse that is green.

The woman in the skirt that is white takes out the coin.

The woman in the skirt that is white puts the coin into the cup that is polystyrene that is white that is held by the man in the material.

The dog sleeps.

electric light yellow

door   out

passageway   left

lino red kitchen

cupboard white   rim metal silver

take down glass   smears

cupboard close

to sink

white light through window

tap hot water turn   spills glass

rinse

turn tap   stop

water from glass drops shake   sink

tea-towel red white stains

          .

        dry glass

                   to sink

             cold water tap turn

let run   cold

         into glass splashing

turn tap down   fill glass

  lift

        drink

           swallow

    to water

             fill again

     lift   drink   swallow

rinse glass

leave side   turn off tap

dry hands tea-towel

                                                        out

                        to passageway

                                                right

                                into light

electric

                door   close

                        squared bedspread blue white in mirror

books   CDs   shelves in mirror

            white door silver metal handle in mirror

                                            to chair

                sit

                                        green foil yellow

roll

    The buses are two. The buses are red. The buses wait at the
lights.

roll white

lighter cardboard box ashtray mugs two

light

suck   in

smoke

dust

smoke curls

heat

smoke

cigarette   ashtray

lean

side chair

magazines floor colours   words

lift

cigarette

suck in

advertisements   LITERARY CRITICISM

photographs

photograph black white man suit tie

LITERATURE

magazine over lap

photograph black white

girl twenties   smoking   holding notepad

advertisements

colours

smoke

pages

LETTERS

ART

It is the evening. It is the dark. It is the heat.

The table is beside the bed. The lamp is on the table. The lamp is on.

She looks at the book.

The pillows are behind her. The headboard is behind the pillows.

She looks at the book. She looks at the words. She turns the page.

There is the sound of the page turning. There is the sound of the car passing.

She turns the pages.

The cigarette is half. The cigarette is in the ashtray. The ashtray is on the table. The ashtray is glass. The lighter is on the table. The lighter is red.

She takes the half cigarette. She takes the lighter. She lights the half cigarette.

She smokes. She turns the pages. The fingers flick the ash into the ashtray.

There is the heat. There is the sound of the cars.

She looks at the ashtray. The cigarette is in the fingers. She stubs in the ashtray.

She reads.

The smoke is in the room. The lamp is on. The curtains are closed.

She reads.

There is the sound of the cars.

There is the heat.

The eyes follow the words to the end of the paragraph.

The fingers fold down the corner of the page.

The hands close the book.

She places the book on the table.

The clock is on the table. She looks at the clock. She slides the button forward. The light on the clock turns red.

She half turns. She pulls the pillows. The pillows lie flat. She reaches. She turns off the lamp.

There is the dark. There is the dark in the room. There is the sound of the car passing outside.

She lies in the dark. The dark is black. She closes the eyes.

There is the heat. There is the sound of the cars. There is the dark.

She lies. She listens. She listens to the sound of the cars passing on the street.

She turns. She turns on the side. She turns on the right side.

The fingers of the right hand hold the corner of the pillow.

There is the dark.

Cars pass.

There is the heat. There is the heat in the room. She pulls the covers away.

There is the sound of voices in the distance. There is the sound of voices in the distance and there is the sound of cars passing. She listens.

The voices get clearer.

She listens to the voices. The voices get nearer. The voices are two. There is the voice of the man and there is the voice of the girl. There is the laughing.

She listens. She listens to the voice of the man and she listens to the voice of the girl. There is the dark and there are the voices. The voices are louder. She listens to the words. She listens to the laughter.

The voices are outside the window. She listens.

She turns. She turns on the side. She turns on the left side.

The dark is black. There is the heat. There are the voices outside.

She listens to the voices. The voices move past. The voices move up the street.

There is the sound of the car passing. There is the sound of the voices. There is the sound of the voices fading.

She listens.

smoke

ART

words

words

smoking

smoke curls

fold cigarette ashtray

crush tip

pages

words

magazine   drop bed

dust   smoke in air

up

chest of drawers

top right drawer pull   open

coins round shining pile

lift handful   to front right trouser pocket

shut drawer

to door   open

passageway

right to front door glass top half colours

shine sun   red green blue

left of door phone black on wall

lift phone

humming

display lights DIAL NUMBER

press buttons beeping

humming

clicks

rings

ringing at other end

INSERT COINS in display

ringing

rings

rings

dead

no sound

humming   buzz

female voice   PLEASE HANG UP AND TRY AGAIN

PLEASE HANG UP AND TRY AGAIN

PLEASE HANG UP AND

                                                        hang up

                        phone to ear

                humming

                                        DIAL NUMBER in display

        press buttons

        humming   clicks

                                                        rings

                        ringing

                        rings

                                                        rings

display INSERT COINS

                                rings

                                                        dead

                                472

PLEASE HANG UP AND

He looks at the band.

The guitarist plays the guitar. The bassist plays the bass. The drummer plays the drums. The singer sings.

She looks at the band.

The singer screams. The guitarist jumps. The bassist jumps. The singer rolls on the floor.

He looks at her. He looks at her across the dancefloor.

The hair is blonde. The hair is piled up on the head.

The dress is short. The dress is black. The dress is against the hips.

The people stand around the dancefloor. The people look at the band. The people look at the singer scream. The people look at the guitarist jump. The people look at the bassist jump.

He looks at her. He looks at the hair that is blonde. He looks at the hips that are in the dress.

She looks at the band.

He holds the cigarette in the fingers. He lifts the cigarette to the lips. He smokes. He looks at her.

She holds the neck of the bottle in the fingers. She lifts the bottle to the lips. She drinks. She looks at the band.

The singer jumps. The guitarist jumps. The bassist jumps. The song ends.

He looks at the band. The people clap. He looks at her. She lifts the bottle to the lips.

He looks at her. He walks across the dancefloor.

He stands beside her. She looks at the band. He looks at the band.

The singer wipes the face on the towel. The drumsticks click four times. The song starts and the noise fills the room.

The people look at the band. She looks at the band. He looks at the band. The smoke is in the air.

He looks at her. He leans forward. He speaks.

She looks round. The eyes are blue.

TRY AGAIN

PLEASE

hang up

hall   dust

dim

wallpaper yellow

coins to pocket

right   down passage

left   door open

electric light

bedroom

mirror

shut door

chest drawers   top right

coins   clink on top of others

                                    one spinning

shut drawer

                              chair

foil green yellow   green packet white paper

            tobacco

                                    roll

                                    stick

                                    smoke

smoke

    magazine on blue white duvet

                    FICTION

    photo black white   woman

    child behind glass   window   raindrops

        words

      smoke

         dust

        words

letters   black white

          words

     ART

hands smell   metal

       suck in

     out

It is the midday. It is the heat. The windows are open. The curtains are closed.

There is the sound of the children playing in the street.

The women are three. One woman is standing. Two women are sitting.

The man is in the bed. There is the sound of the breathing of the man in the bed. The women look at the man in the bed.

There is the break between the two curtains. The sunlight

shines through the break. There is the line of sunlight across the foot of the bed.

The woman walks to the bed. The woman looks at the head. The woman places the hand on the head.

The breathing stops. There is a sound. The breathing starts again.

The woman looks at the face. The hand is on the head.

She turns. She walks to the two women sitting.

The women whisper. There is the sound of the whispers.

There is the heat. There is the sound of the breathing. There is the sound of the children outside.

She walks to the door. She opens the door. She looks at the man on the bed.

There are the two women sitting.

There is the one woman standing.

There is the man in the bed.

There is the sound of the breathing.

There is the heat.

There is the line of sunlight across the foot of the bed.

There is the sound of the children playing on the street outside.

words

POETRY

suck in

words

pages

end

magazine drop side chair

                                        suck in

                        room

        cigarette out

                                            stub out

  room   books   light

        up

                                orange curtains

    door   open   out

                            passageway   dim

                                    cross passage

            door

                                into toilet

  unzip

coughing   spit toilet

                                        wait

                            wait

            wait

                nothing

                                        wait

    pee

                        splashing loud

        splashing

                            yellow

slows   stops   drips

                                shake

                        in

                            zip

pull chain   sudden   water noise

              net curtains dirty brown

        out

        right   kitchen   lino red

sun through window bright

              into bathroom

        water   cracked soap   wash hands

    sun through net curtains dirt onto bath

                                        dry

out

              kitchen

                          window

                                    sunlight

              garden green

sky blue

to cupboard

bowl white on sideboard white

to microwave   box cereal

open cardboard   open bag plastic

orange flakes   scratch white bowl

fold bag plastic   close cardboard

to cupboard shelf   close cupboard

fridge

shelf door   carton white green

heat sun on back

milk white into white bowl orange flakes

carton fridge door shelf   close door

sink   drawer   spoon

crunching cold wet

chewing

crunching   cold   wet

swallow

second spoon   chew   milk

third spoon

cold wet   sweet

spoon

swallow

milk bottom bowl

tip bowl edge   spoon along cups milk flake bits

swallow

another   swallow

                              wipe mouth back hand

sink

        tap

                        water spark sun

    rinse bowl spoon   cold   to drain on side

        rinse teaspoon sink   to side

                              hands wipe trousers

                garden through window

        turn   to door   out

                                              passageway

            right   into bedroom

                        close door

        sit bed

                                              room

mirror reflects electric light

                                                              heat

bend   lace left   shoe off   drop by wall

    lace right   shoe off   drop by wall

                                           up

trousers   button   unzip

                                   off right leg

                                       left leg

         throw chair

shirt   buttons white   undo   to chair

              shirt blue on bed to chair

       chair orange   light

                     to door

switch off

dark

in

covers up   round   under

light edges curtain

black room

left side   left hand under head

right hand tuck neck pillow

heat

warmth

close eyes

dark

dry mouth

black

heat

right toes pull sock off left foot   kick

left toes pull sock right foot   kick

feet push socks   bottom   bed

close eyes

black

dry mouth

heat

quiet

heat

covers down

close

black

car distance

  listen

        dark

                            wait

                                black

                        mouth dry

                                    turn

                    right cheek pillow

                close eyes

    dark   heat

                        black

                                waiting

                                    black

    There is the paper. The paper is white. There are the lines.
The lines are grey. There is the margin. The margin is blue.
    He looks at the paper.

He lifts the pen. The pen is black. He unscrews the cap.
He looks at the paper. He looks at the white.
He leans forward.
He looks at the white.
He looks.
He sits back.
He looks at the white.

                                        black

                                black

                slower

        heat

                        horn distance

                covers

                                        warmth

black

                                dry mouth

        dark

                                black

wait

warmth

black

slow

lick

black

warmth

heat

black

black

black

waiting   slow

black

black

heat

                                    listen

wait

              black

                        black

        dry

                                    heat

slow

              black

                              black

              warm

wait

dry

black

dark

black

black

black

wait

black

black

black

black

black

black

black

REALITY STREET titles in print

Poetry series

Kelvin Corcoran: *Lyric Lyric* (1993)
Maggie O'Sullivan: *In the House of the Shaman* (1993)
Allen Fisher: *Dispossession and Cure* (1994)
Fanny Howe: *O'Clock* (1995)
Maggie O'Sullivan (ed.): *Out of Everywhere* (1996)
Cris Cheek/Sianed Jones: *Songs From Navigation* (1997)
Lisa Robertson: *Debbie: An Epic* (1997)
Maurice Scully: *Steps* (1997)
Denise Riley: *Selected Poems* (2000)
Lisa Robertson: *The Weather* (2001)
Robert Sheppard: *The Lores* (2003)
Lawrence Upton *Wire Sculptures* (2003)
Ken Edwards: *eight + six* (2003)
David Miller: *Spiritual Letters (I-II)* (2004)
Redell Olsen: *Secure Portable Space* (2004)
Peter Riley: *Excavations* (2004)
Allen Fisher: *Place* (2005)
Tony Baker: *In Transit* (2005)
Jeff Hilson: *stretchers* (2006)
Maurice Scully: *Sonata* (2006)
Maggie O'Sullivan: *Body of Work* (2006)
Sarah Riggs: *chain of minuscule decisions in the form of a feeling* (2007)
Carol Watts: *Wrack* (2007)
Jeff Hilson (ed.): *The Reality Street Book of Sonnets* (2008)
Peter Jaeger: *Rapid Eye Movement* (2009)
Wendy Mulford: *The Land Between* (2009)
Allan K Horwitz/Ken Edwards (ed.): *Botsotso* (2009)
Bill Griffiths: *Collected Earlier Poems* (2010)
Fanny Howe: *Emergence* (2010)
Jim Goar: *Seoul Bus Poems* (2010)
James Davies: *Plants* (2011)
Carol Watts: *Occasionals* (2011)
Paul Brown: *A Cabin in the Mountains* (2012)
Maggie O'Sullivan: *Waterfalls* (2012)

Narrative series

Ken Edwards: *Futures* (1998, reprinted 2010)
John Hall: *Apricot Pages* (2005)
David Miller: *The Dorothy and Benno Stories* (2005)
Douglas Oliver: *Whisper 'Louise'* (2005)
Ken Edwards: *Nostalgia for Unknown Cities* (2007)
Paul Griffiths: *let me tell you* (2008)
John Gilmore: *Head of a Man* (2011)
Richard Makin: *Dwelling* (2011)
Leopold Haas: *The Raft* (2011)
Johan de Wit: *Gero Nimo* (2011)
David Miller (ed.): *The Alchemist's Mind* (2012)

For updates on titles in print, a listing of out-of-print titles, and to order Reality Street books, please go to www.realitystreet.co.uk. For any other enquiries, email info@realitystreet.co.uk or write to the address on the reverse of the title page.

REALITY STREET depends for its continuing existence on the Reality Street Supporters scheme. For details of how to become a Reality Street Supporter, or to be put on the mailing list for news of forthcoming publications, write to the address on the reverse of the title page, or email **info@realitystreet.co.uk**

Visit our website at: **www.realitystreet.co.uk/supporter-scheme.php**

Reality Street Supporters who have sponsored this book:

Lightning Source UK Ltd.
Milton Keynes UK
UKOW042020040113

204441UK00004B/17/P